YOUNG WILLIAM

Young William

P. J. Harrison

JANUS PUBLISHING COMPANY
London, England

First published in Great Britain 2011
by Janus Publishing Company Ltd,
105–107 Gloucester Place,
London W1U 6BY

www.januspublishing.co.uk

British Library Cataloguing-in-Publication Data
A catalogue record for this book is available from the British Library

ISBN 978-1-85756-717-5

Cover Design: Ultimate Signs

Printed and bound in Great Britain

Contents

Acknowledgements

In no particular order, I would especially like to thank the following three people for helping to provide me with the encouragement and advice I needed which has helped towards the publication of this book:

Angela Goldthorpe:

After reading my early poetry Angela, one of the two lodgers I had at the time, said my work was unusual, gritty and unpolluted. She stated that it was quite original and it would be good to continue writing and expressing myself in this way because she thought I had not been influenced by modern writers.

Edwin Courtenay:

My friend of many years, he was the one who helped provide some early inspiration and it was he who had the insight to suggest that, after seeing a fairy-tale castle in a private tarot reading, I might find myself in a position of writing children's fiction sometime in the near future. Within a week or so I had ideas for seven stories and now I have over 190 ready to feed publishers with. I remember shrugging my shoulders at the time and thinking yeah, yeah, me? A former motor engineer, bakery manager, cleaning contractor, builder and now a writer? However, I have long since eaten my words.

Sir Colin Sampson:

I was lucky enough whilst being a self-employed builder to have been recommended to Sir Colin to carry out many repairs, extensions and improvements to his home. This was at the beginning of my creative writing surge (1997–2001) and with me not being so widely read, I asked him for advice with regards to phrasing. So whilst taking tea with a titled lady and gentleman, I used the opportunity to seek advice from someone much more accomplished than myself. I didn't want to write like other writers had done, but I was looking for insight and comparisons without looking as if I had copied someone else's style. His reply was, 'Dickens – he is the one I think is the most appropriate if you want to look for unusual phrasing. Yes, he is the one you should look up, Paul.'

I did happen to have an old copy of David Copperfield I had found in a box of old books from a jumble sale, so I remember choosing several points at random and opening each page to see how the great master had expressed himself. And here I am now ...

Introduction

On 23 April 1564, William Shakespeare was born at Stratford-upon-Avon and three days later he was christened at Holy Trinity Church. The ancient church is situated alongside the River Avon in the oldest, southern part of the town and is under a constant state of repair and restoration. Donations are received from all over the world to help preserve the building which is steeped in history. Alongside other medieval features, the main porch has a thirteenth-century knocker and in the past fugitives could claim protection for thirty-seven days from within its confines. About the time of William's birth, Henry VIII's reformation was in the distant past in Stratford and the Catholic decorations had been painted over in the church.

The main artery for Stratford was the medieval bridge that was built in the late fifteenth century by Sir Hugh Clopton, a well-known figure from the area. This allowed Stratford to flourish, giving it an open-trade route leading to London and many other towns; a far cry from the rickety old wooden bridge which was often ripped apart by annual floods. Queen Elizabeth I reigned around this time and England was deeply engaged in a profitable piracy war with Spain.

William's father, John Shakespeare, moved from Snitterfield to Stratford, where he established himself as a whittawer, a worker of soft leather. His business flourished and he soon became a leading citizen of the town, later marrying Mary Arden of Wilmcote, who was the youngest of eight daughters. Mary inherited most of her father's estate when she married and tragically her first two babies died at birth. John was one of fourteen Burgesses who rose rapidly through the ranks to chamberlain and finally town bailiff, today's equivalent of a mayor. The plague, or pestilence, resurfaced from time to time and took with it whoever was within jumping distance of the black rat flea. For those who weren't affected by the plague life went on, but most people lived in cramped housing conditions and some even lay level with animals, just a breath away from the pungent stench of putrefaction and faeces.

John Shakespeare owned a shop on Henley Street, which was situated in the northern part of the town. The property opened out onto the street, but to the rear of the property they had a garden for growing vegetables and keeping fowl. From here, they sold goods made from leather, alongside barley, wool and many other items they could barter with, even exchanging goods instead of money changing hands.

The town had a common muck heap for both animal and human waste. Most families kept their own livestock, so the streets would have resembled a sprawling farmyard, with none of the modern conveniences of ordered parking facilities and pavements we are used to today. Workers were paid by the town to keep the streets clean, but their idea of cleanliness meant scraping away the thick filth and leaving the rest to wash away. An accumulation of mud, straw and animal droppings of all kinds littered the streets and tethered horses, carts and livestock were commonplace. Children would play and run errands amongst the filth and were expected to work from an early age to assist the family income.

Priorities were little more than food, warmth and shelter for most. Wages were related to a good harvest and should the crops fail, some families would inevitably starve. Many people ate from wooden trencher boards, the remains being fed to the chickens; the board would then be stacked ready for the next meal. Hygiene and germs were seldom considered and were low down on the list of priorities, along with bathing. With unsprung carts for transport, modern-day niceties such as toothpaste, showers and flush toilets were technologies not even dreamed of. Only the wealthy had the luxury of candles to ease the long winter nights. These were times of long summer working hours and even longer winter nights for everyone.

Rain was welcomed for the life it nourished, not complained about for spoiling a day out, a holiday or a barbecue, and survival meant you had to follow the seasons and store provisions to get you through the winter. From all this William Shakespeare left a life of dirt and grime to shine through as the famous playwright we know of today.

Shakespeare's head for learning laid the foundations for his livelihood and fixed his destiny. He grew up shoulder to shoulder with high infant mortality, long working days and the gritty lifestyle of the period. However, from our padded perspectives of today, past living conditions could easily cause a frown or two. But back then you were born into the lifestyle and knew no different. You would have accepted it as easily as we accept our modern lives today which most of us take for granted.

John, William's father, was tall compared to other men of the time; he always kept a neatly trimmed beard and he had a deep, cutting voice. Mary, his mother, was the opposite; she had a dry, patient voice and would never lose her temper, no matter what the situation. Being the youngest, she had experienced an upbringing with several elder sisters looking after her and the union of two of them from opposite backgrounds made them the perfect match. Mary's wisdom often accompanied John to his many meetings and her ideas would reap rewards. She had learned to read and write and grew to be the silent power behind her successful husband.

The Early Years

'Look at our son, John,' Mary said as she stroked baby William's head. 'He is growing so strong. His eyes study us both as if we were hundreds.'

John squeezed Mary's hand and looked down to the well-padded crib, wobbling to and fro on the wooden floor. 'Yes, he smiles as if he can understand every word or loving thought. I wonder what will he be, my love. Another glover, perhaps, or maybe a wheelwright, or even a merchant dealing in gold.'

'With a grip like this he could be a swordsman or even a juggler of cannon balls,' Mary said as William gripped her fingers tightly, provoking a smile in her.

'He will be warm tonight. We have enough logs to make this room like an oven,' John said happily. 'But look, he has a belly feather in his hand from the down. Perhaps he may end up being a scribe of sorts.'

John was at a gathering of the town aldermen four years later. It was a light-hearted start to the meeting because business seemed to be prospering for most in attendance. At around this time, attention was diverted from William with the arrival of his first brother, Gilbert, who was now 2 years old. The family unit was increasing steadily and Stratford was becoming more prosperous. John had followed a steady line of promotion from constable, affurer, burgess and chamberlain to alderman, all the while continuing with his former job of ale-tasting. Many of the other aldermen wanted to sit near John at the meeting and to be seen in his proximity, including Henry Bull, a farrier; Samuel Topton, a local scholar who was the secretary; Robin Exton, the baker; and Colin Saxford, the brewer.

There were many other aldermen present who were not involved in the early part of the conversation, but they had valid points to make and other matters to discuss later on at the meeting.

'How is young William then, John?' asked Samuel. 'Have you taught him the trade yet? Or bold speeches to follow you to this table?'

'No, not quite,' he replied with a smile. 'He can speak well, though – better than some twice his age – but Gilbert is catching up with him all too quickly.'

'So, perhaps we will see him at this same table in twenty years time,' said Samuel with a smile. 'We would benefit from a younger mind. Or maybe he will even speak better than you, eh, John.'

Henry patted John on the back. 'Yes, we could do with a new town speaker. You should bring him to the meetings dressed in his Sunday best.'

'Enough of your jesting about, my son.' John looked towards the papers in front of the secretary. 'We have work to do. What is it I hear about a lame soldier?'

'Well,' Henry gently shook his head from side to side, 'all he seems capable of is feeding the ducks; apart from telling those gruesome tales of his about Warwick Castle, that is. He came here to live with his sister, but he just seems to hang around folk trying to gain their attention.'

'What stories does he tell the ducks?' asked Samuel looking puzzled. 'Do they stop to listen?'

'No, not ducks,' Henry said quickly, 'children, townsfolk, whoever will listen to his slurred speech from the ale he drinks as he staggers around the streets.'

Samuel frowned. 'Where does he get his ale? No one would be fool enough to give it to him.'

'Oh, it's some of his own brew, I believe,' Henry replied.

'What of his stories then, Henry?' John twisted a compass between his fingers. 'How does the soldier frighten our children with tales of Warwick Castle?'

'Murderer's Gate,' Henry said with a worried look. 'He says, "Look up, children," when they come near him, then he tells them how he used to pour oil and stones down on the attackers beneath. But he speaks as if he were over 300 years old. He must have been there and heard an old tale or two, you know. To impress or frighten must be his aim. The children have begun walking down the middle of the street now to avoid him and his worrying words.'

'That is not the kind of thing I would like my sons to hear while feeding the ducks,' said John, 'so we must find him something to do. He has fought for all of us, really. I think we must try to help him. Although he may have fought for our country, we do not want tales of worry and trouble to be told on our streets for evermore. There must be something we can find him to do.'

'He is, of course, missing a leg,' Robin said tentatively. 'His crutch is plain to see. I believe he was trampled on by a horse during a hunt.'

'And I have heard he is blind in one eye,' said Colin, adding a further twist to the tale.

'Oh, if that be the case, then we must think of something else,' John said, drifting into deep thought. 'Perhaps counting the ducks.'

All the men sitting at the table laughed out loudly, but this invited further humorous comments.

'He would, of course, lose count if he should blink.' Colin winked to those gathered all around, to raise more smiles from the other men at the table.

'I am sure we could find something useful for him to do.' John's eyes wandered to accompany his thoughts. 'Would he be able to stride out and measure fields? This would be more useful to the town than counting ducks and it would keep him fit.'

A few men at the table tittered and then they all laughed out loudly, accompanied by many banging the table with their hands to applaud him.

John realised what he had said. 'No, my mind is elsewhere. If he strode out a field, he would make the seed holes for vegetables with his sticks. Laugh while you can, my friends. You may not see me foul my words as poorly again.' He laughed with them, even though the humour was of his own making.

'It would still be a kind of measure, John,' Robin said, trying to encourage more laughter to follow. 'But then we would need to employ someone to pull his crutch out of the soil every time he went forward a pace.'

When everyone at the table had ceased laughing, John lifted his hand to indicate that he wanted to continue with the business at hand. Then he glanced at the secretary, who was holding a sheet of thick, waxy paper relating to a more serious matter. Most men at the meeting were illiterate, so John's findings had to be taken down by the secretary, who would prompt them with the next item for discussion.

'The ale, John,' the secretary whispered, looking up from the piece of paper. 'A pressing matter.'

John nodded to acknowledge the secretary and inhaled deeply through his nose. 'My next item for discussion is Sampson's Ale.' John smiled slightly as he looked up to recall his experience. 'I am sure you are all aware of the complaints we have before us and our own experience of the same.'

All the men at the table nodded to agree, before paying further attention to what he was about to say.

'Is it so then, John?' Colin asked expectantly, looking at the other aldermen assembled around the table who had also lifted their heads, showing interest and falling silent.

'My opinion is this,' John said seriously, but still half smiling. 'If I had taken in a quantity of Sampson's ale before this meeting, I would have had an excuse for my careless words earlier.'

This brought further smiles from some of the men, though his reference to the injured soldier was still in mind.

'So is it good then, John?' Henry looked at his colleagues to support his genuine surprise. 'His ale is good? The ale that tasted like washing water that we all sampled is as honest as fresh lamb.'

John answered with a firm nod, while looking at the table in order to avoid the many eyes before him. 'Yes, I find it so. I think the sample ales we have been given … well, they may have been thinned down by others. Possibly Riften's, but I will set about tasting theirs next and questioning the opinion of the other complainants. We may have been checking the barrels on hearsay, rather than where the finger pointing towards bad ale had been lifted from.' After John finished speaking, he looked up to his astounded colleges to invite comments about his decision.

'I, er, respect your judgement, John,' Robin said, inviting Henry and Colin to agree with his disclosure. 'But we three have imbibed of the thin ale together, as indeed you have.'

Some nodded to support Robin, but the others let their heads be still. They knew John had great wisdom and more so than most sitting around the table.

'That is my point and purpose for testing,' he said. 'We may all have been given ale from the same watered barrel, but I have checked eleven barrels, all as strong as the cask surrounding them – I can tell water from ale.' John nodded to emphasise his firm stance, but he didn't offer any expression of compromise for the decision.

Others at the table may have tasted thin ale, but it could have been given them to fuel a complaint. No further words to question John's judgement were exchanged between the aldermen. Enough had been said to prove the ale's worth.

'What follows now, John?' asked Colin. 'Have you further checks or suspicions in mind?'

'No, I have none,' he replied. 'But I will say this. They who are responsible for this foolish trick should be wary of my findings. I doubt the scum will come to the surface again, or even rise anywhere near to the top of the offending barrel.'

This brought a lighter note to the ending of the ale debate. If anyone present still had doubts or an interest in the opposition's ales, at least they now knew John's decision was a firm one. The subject quickly changed from ale to bread, just as Robin's wife brought in a taste of the day's freshest to share. With the meeting adjourned for this early break, Thomas Eldman, a friend of John's, came to sit beside him to exchange local gossip. Thomas was a general trader who specialised in barley and he would often move vast quantities all over the county to different brewers.

'What do you think is the cause of the pestilence, John?' Thomas threw a crust out the window, to be fought over by the rats. 'It takes whoever it likes, fit or unfit. Like the bread here, we never know if it will be soft or hard till the day it arrives.'

'Wealth, my friend, but this is between you and me,' he whispered and glanced to check for others who might be listening. 'Most who die are from the not-so-well-off houses. However, it has also taken one or two quite wealthy citizens with it.'

'Wealth!' exclaimed Thomas loudly, inviting attention. Thomas realised he had spoken out too strongly, so he whispered, 'How can wealth put off the pestilence?'

'It is nature, my friend.' John pointed out towards the fields. 'Look at the wildlife and plant life in the forest and hedgerows. When an animal dies or leaves its dung behind, out come the flies and the following stench. You wouldn't keep a rotting carcass in your house, would you?'

'No,' said Thomas, looking quite bewildered. 'But what is your point?'

'My suggestion is this,' he whispered as people started to shuffle their chairs about. 'On a smaller scale, the poor eat more bad meat than the wealthy. They consume meat that is nearer the state of becoming a rotting carcass and putrefaction than we do. With the flies, the filth is able to jump from pile to pile. Lesser or greater, it will jump so. This is why our house is brushed out daily. There are no chickens or droppings in our rooms. Flies live outside with the lice. Do you see now?'

Thomas nodded slightly and then turned to take his place back at the table, stroking his chin in deep thought.

'Perhaps I might suggest this at a later meeting, John,' he said, turning back to whisper. 'It is certainly a mystery to all how it chooses its victims. Would you mind if I should propose such a thing as regular sweeping out?'

John raised his eyebrows and nodded to agree.

John returned to his own chair, wetting his crust of bread with milk as he did so and letting a cat take it from his hand. Thomas was still deep in thought when the meeting recommenced; once more John's wisdom had caused an unsettling frown.

The meeting continued as normal after the break, but John's authority was absolute. There was a hint of humour to his words and he acted from plain common sense, turning the debate by pulling the reins of command either way. John was a successful businessman and he earned great respect from the other men. Some aldermen were there by wealth alone, but they seemed to respect John's position and few would challenge his wisdom for the time being.

Later that day John and Mary sat by the fireside after supper, chatting about the day's events. However, as the conversation progressed, they noticed William teasing the cat with Mary's quill.

'Look,' John pointed with raised eyebrows, 'both are playing with and learning from different ends of the same game. One will never write with one and the other will never jump to door height to catch one in the air.'

'I saw him looking over my shoulder earlier,' she said. 'Have we any spare paper he could write on?'

'No, not paper, my love,' John replied. 'Oh! the cost. But with hands as tiny as his, a butterfly's wings, perhaps ...'

Mary nodded slightly, but as she gave more thought to John's reply, an idea came to her. 'I have the very thing!' She sprang to her feet.

'What is that?' He reached down to pick up her quill. 'Surely not best linen?'

'Honesty seeds,' she answered brightly, making a hasty dash for the kitchen. 'I think they may be just right.'

'Honesty?' He frowned. 'Honesty?'

Mary returned with a bunch of honesty seeds that she had hung up ready for a flower arrangement. Once this type of seed pod had dried out, the flat seeds were sandwiched between a thin layer of the dead plant. She pulled a handful away from the stems, held them up to the candlelight briefly and then handed them to John.

'These may, indeed, be the answer,' John said, looking at the remains of her quill. 'But I think he will need a smaller quill.' With this thought, he found a discarded blackbird feather and proceeded to cut the end to form a nib. He leaned over and dipped the new quill in the ink to try it out and it worked as easily as Mary had suggested.

'William,' John called, holding up the new quill, 'I have something for you, son.'

William stopped what he was doing and ran immediately to his father's side to take the quill and seed pods.

'Here you are, William.' John mimicked the action of a quill with his finger. 'Try making a cross to begin with, then one day you will be able to write like your mother.'

'Thank you, Father.' William carefully took them from his hand. 'Can I help you now, Mother?'

'Yes, but with your own paper seeds.' She looked down and pulled a few more of the seed pods from the stems. 'You can send the new baby a kiss by your own hand now.'

'When will I have a sister, Mother?' he asked.

'Soon, William,' she said, glancing up at John while rubbing her stomach. 'Soon, I hope, but it will be God and good wishes that decide if it is to be a sister or a brother.'

William soon learned to draw a cross on the seed pods and then he sent his mother kiss after kiss until all the seeds were used up. It was a step nearer to writing properly and was a much better alternative to tracing letters on the butter at meal times or marking the bare earth with a stick.

The Christening

The next great occasion in William's life was his sister Joan's christening at Holy Trinity Church. All the family had come from various surrounding villages and had met up at the Shakespeare home on Henley Street. When they had all arrived, they set off to walk through the town towards the church in a neat family group. John had worked his way up from an alderman to town bailiff, so their choice of clothes reflected this. The family was dressed in Sunday best and they walked with heads held high, nodding here and there as they passed people they knew. It was a blustery day and each time the group passed a building, a sudden blast of wind made them each falter with their steps. William was now five and was holding hands with his 3-year-old brother as they jumped between the exposed dry areas of the rough road. As they did this, William began to notice the crowds watching them, so he began to play up and pull Gilbert from side to side more forcibly, becoming more out of step with the ordered family procession the more adventurous he got. His mother wanted to keep him in check, but to avoid being seen giving William a clout in public. She leaned over and grabbed his ear, twisting it hard as she whispered into it.

'Keep in line with the rest of us, William,' she scowled under her breath, 'or I will jump on *your* toes when we get home and there will be no supper for you.'

William did as he was asked, but his attention was soon turned towards where some men from the family group had broken away. A young farmer had got the wheel on his cart stuck in a deep rut in the road and was struggling to free it by whipping his horse and slapping the reins. The men walked across to help him heave it out, whilst the women looked on patiently. The farmer thanked them for their help and was soon on his way, so the men stepped back in line, dusting themselves off and wiping the dirt from their hands. William had been inquisitive from an early age, so he slowed down to ask his mother something about the incident.

'Mother,' he said with an increasing frown upon his face. 'Why did the men not charge the farmer for the help they gave him?'

'Oh, it was just a kindly deed, William, to help him on his way.'

'But Father says we have to charge for all leather, stitches and work, why is this different? The man could have been stuck there all day if it were not for our help.'

'Oh, William, life is not just bitter fish oil or sweet honey. There are places in between where we use good reasoning and perform good deeds. Would you have given the man a coin if he offered to help you from a deep well?'

William nodded his head to agree, but he was already forming new questions in his mind to pursue his point.

'No, Mother, I would not pay him anything, but I would offer to sweep out his backyard in exchange for his help.'

Mary smiled to herself, but nodded for him to continue on his way as she struggled to hold on to her bonnet in the wind. Soon, the bustle of the gusty morning was left outside as they were ushered into the church, where they waited, speaking in hushed whispers for the service to begin. Only the sound of whispered conversations could be heard echoing around the church as the townsfolk shuffled around to find their regular places.

All the relatives huddled around the font, eager to see the preacher's finger mark the fresh cross on Joan's forehead with the water. John and Mary were proud of their third born, who looked well nourished and had strong limbs like her brothers before her. With it being so blustery outside, most people wore hairstyles likened to badly stuffed scarecrows. With infrequent washing, those without hats had to smooth down their greasy hair as best they could. The outline of the congregation looked more like a badly trimmed hedge, with offshoots of hair pointing in all directions. William was at the mischievous age where he ran around exploring his surroundings, but he was being held in check by having his collar tugged at by the nearest adult. He soon settled down with a further glare from his mother and a warning tilt to her head. William knew what was behind that look, so his arms were soon by his side.

The church was packed with townsfolk and all eyes were on the family group, especially with their high-standing position in the community. This was an important day for the Shakespeare family; for everyone in town knew them and most of John's colleagues were also present.

William was glancing between the dark church doors and his relatives, who had their noses pointing towards the font. He'd had a fear of dark shapes since an early age and the church had plenty of them. Suddenly, his attention was snatched from the door, past several heads, to an enviable view of the font and his smiling relatives. An aunt, sensitive to William's lack of height, lifted him for a moment so he could see what was happening. The sound of the water trickling from the preacher's hand was soon lost as the baby's cries echoed around the church, evoking smiles and whispered praise from all those nearby. William's mind wasn't at the developmental stage where he was able to make firm judgement from his comparisons yet as he was still quite young. He took in fleeting pictures of the occasion, though he could fathom no reason for the strange gathering that culminated with his sister crying.

Black doors, strange, eerie shadows, water, crying – why? William puzzled, before relaxing to let his weight overpower his aunt. Her grip weakened enough to allow William's face to slide past her rough clothes and leave him standing on the floor again. After rubbing his sore face, William took another sheepish glance between the onlookers and up to the dark oak doors again. He was still frightened of the doors, so he clung to the nearest arm for safety, hoping it would end soon and he could leave.

Why are we all here? thought William. They say it's for a Christening. The preacher muffles high and low, the crowd pressing together and their smells becoming one. But why? I like being by the river best, skimming stones, catching fish and finding eggs. Oh, how I wish we could go home. Folk walk past, going somewhere and coming from another place. Now most of them find themselves here, listening to the preacher's drone and feeling this cold stone.

After the extended service, the family walked back to Henley Street to eat and celebrate the occasion. William, though, had other ideas along the way. Not quite understanding what the sanctity of a Christening was, he decided to do the same to Gilbert as the preacher had done to Joan. As they passed a water trough, William splashed Gilbert in the face several times to see what would happen. The reaction was similar with Gilbert as it had been with Joan, making him cry instantly, but Mother was just behind him and he felt the back of her hand on his backside. William's tears began to well up as he stepped back to ask her why she'd hit him, his expression portraying hurt and pain.

There were no witnesses this time, so Mary could let him feel her instant dislike without the fear of being watched.

'Why, Mother?' he asked sadly. 'I have merely done to Gilbert the same as the preacher did to baby Joan.'

'An animal trough, William,' she scowled, 'is not a place of worship; it is where the Devil and cattle drink side by side!'

William was still puzzled by the remarks and the speed of his mother's lashing. However, he soon got back into line and kept his eyes forward all the way home. He took his punishment well, but his mind was reaching for answers in an attempt to understand the day's events.

John's business was doing well, so food was spread out on the table to reflect this. William remembered the day more for the pinched cheeks, pats to his head and his mother's wrath, rather than for the fact it was Joan's special day. Whilst watching his relatives make conversation, William noticed several in attendance who clearly hadn't eaten well for a good while or so. The bread and ham they consumed would probably have lasted them another fortnight, or even a month, but today it disappearing so quickly that the prospect of leftovers seemed remote. To disguise their greed, some of them smiled and laughed to distract watching eyes away from their antics. Not William's, though, who found himself watching them even more. At that time William was oblivious to their diversion ploy, but he took a mental note of their actions, because they didn't eat like his family did at the table and they had no manners. He was brought up to always chew and swallow his food and he wasn't accustomed to seeing it being stuffed it into pockets for later like these people did. William had begun to observe his surroundings without questioning or mimicking what he saw, just soaking up the actions of others and storing them for later consideration.

After a short time, William did his usual disappearing act, sneaking upstairs to the room he shared with Gilbert, known as the 'lads' room'. He felt quite out of place that day, so he thought it better to retreat for a short time. If he got the chance, William would spend many hours daydreaming, looking through an open window, gazing across the rooftops and down to the street below.

'Huh!' sighed William, looking down into the street below. What rules I have to bear. But for me it's different. What did Mother say? Oh yes, it's like bitter and sweet or something between, but what rules to the in-betweens have? Splashing Gilbert is wrong, yet splashing Joan is right. Father charges for every stitch, yet the farmer has help for nothing. All the horse dung there will smell the same. There won't be some that smells of pear and another part of bread. It's not fair. What if the horse yonder had three legs one day, then four the next? I think some days he would walk about in circles, then the next he would be straight and proper. I wonder if I could be like this horse, changing to suit each need. Just then William heard his father calling him from below, interrupting his train of thought.

'William, it is time to say goodbye now. Come on down.'

'Yes, Father,' he said quickly. But as he walked across the room, further thoughts came to him.

Yes, Father, he thought. In future, as I walk, I will have four legs to think on now, for not all things are as I had thought. Now I will study things before speaking. No longer will I walk and stumble on life as if I had three legs.

William quickened his pace and vaulted over the short handrail at the top of the steps, then leapt down two at a time.

'Here I am, Father,' he said with a smile. 'I am ready to kiss all, bearded or not.'

Laughter filled the room and Gilbert ran over to stand next to William, not quite knowing what all the fuss was about.

Mary stood with John, watching them saying goodbye to everyone.

'I gave him a good clout earlier,' she said. 'But he acts as if he had just found a gold coin, showing no remorse.'

'Yes, Mary. He is learning, though. I never have to tell him twice, or thrice, for he learns from each knock the first time. I think he will become more than a glover, but there's more rough to come off his ways before his days become as soft as a kid skin.'

'I think you're right, John. But he seems to totter on the edge of questioning others all the time. Most of his age would be content with the first answer. But he takes it further than I had thought myself. Some days I seem to have found the answer for him only the day before and yet sometimes the answer doesn't come to me straight away. I try to think of what he might say next and what my reply will be.'

'I agree, my love. I will teach him my trade like you will teach him yours. But I confess, mine will be the easiest road to steer. Some days I find myself pulling the reins in one direction to take his mind away from where he wants to lead me; he has a sharp mind for a boy of his age. Gilbert is far behind William in those respects.'

'Yes, John, but let us keep him on our road and see where it leads. When he gets to the end he should have a mind of his own, far away from petty town squabbles if I'm right.'

The Family Business

Almost a year later, William was in the shop one day helping his father to mend various family belongings. He learnt simple, practical skills like most other children to start with and he was paying attention to the finer work his father was doing. John had recently taken on an apprentice, so he could concentrate on his regular civic duties. Preparing leather was a smelly and dirty business, cleaning and dying being one of the least exciting. Soaking leather gave off a smell as powerful as a rotting carcass, so this part of the task was performed as far away from the house as possible. John wanted his sons to continue with the trade, but to progress further and to produce more goods he needed someone to do the daily, repetitive jobs, leaving him free to do the most skilful finishing work.

'Father,' William called, looking up from repacking an old broom with fresh twigs. 'Why is it your friend Jack bought a new sword, instead of letting the blacksmith repair his old one? Why do we only repair some things and not others?'

'Ah, brooms are different than swords, William,' he said with a hint of wisdom. 'An assailant would only laugh at you if you faced him with a broom's catch of straw or an equally weak sword. A sword may look to have a good repair on the outside, but would you trust it to clash with another in order to save your life? It is better to cast it aside, or cut the overgrowth in the garden with it, than repair it and hope it works. The first bit of damage has already let you down. It is no longer as strong as it used to be. Would you be prepared to risk having it repaired and give the sword another chance, in order to prove its strength once more? It could let you down and your blows could be weakened. You see, it is sometimes better to renew than repair, depending upon how important the item is.'

'What about our boots?' William asked further. 'They might let us down in flight should our sword fail us.'

'Your point is valid, son, but boots are less important,' he said, agreeing with William's suggestion. 'Boots are used to protect our feet, but we can run without them. This is the same if we compare it to the mending of a sword. Should the sword break, we would have no choice but to run. You see, all things cost money. The whole town revolves around bartering of one kind or another. We have to buy food, the material for clothes and boots, even pay taxes and rent. Swords, you see, are not items one can wear on one's person; they are special, like thick hide boots. If a man has a sword, he is likely to have something others would want to take from him. That is why he needs it at his side, as I have one some days.'

When John finished speaking he tried to cut at William's head using his hand as a pretend sword. William responded to the challenge and used the brush he was repairing to fight John back to a stand-off position.

'So a thief is unlikely to take from a person without a sword or boots.' William let his pretend sword down. 'He would choose, instead, to steal from someone with a sword and wearing quality clothing, indicating he had something of worth, rather than one dressed in rags.'

'Yes, that is likely, but it's not always the case,' John answered. 'Some dressed in rags may have stolen gold concealed in their pockets, but their faces usually give it away – or the ale they drink.'

'Their faces?' William frowned.

'Yes, just as your frowning face tells me that you are confused by my remark, theirs tell me they have something to hide. Look in Mother's mirror and watch your expressions.' John indicated for William to look towards the mirror leaning on a shelf. 'Each face tells a story of some kind. You see, if there was a man dressed in rags with gold in his possession, one who would normally fight a dog for a chicken neck, his face would be alive with the find. Like the dog sweeping the floor with his tail, he cannot tell us he can smell Mother's fresh salted ham, but his mouth dribbles from both sides, theirs suggest to me the same.'

William stopped what he was doing and went to fetch the mirror and bring it back to the table. On his return, he pulled an array of faces at the copper mirror, tilting his head from side to side as he did so.

'Yes, Father, it is true,' he said seriously, before sitting down on the stool again. 'Words can be seen or portrayed on faces – we could almost speak to each other in silence using expressions alone.'

William continued to pull his face in the mirror and John smiled as he did so.

'There is more, William, if you are interested?' He looked up from his work again. 'There is more to the face than I have told you; would you like to know my thoughts? You seem eager to learn about what can be seen in the face.'

William nodded and looked up to invite the advice.

'Noses, William. Yes, noses,' he said quietly, expecting a reaction from William.

Instead, his face was impassive, his eyes indicating he was longing for more; or he had learned not to frown already by watching himself in the mirror?

'If you look at Mother and me,' he said, 'our noses are equally proportioned, like my best boots are matched to suit the left and right foot respectively. It is the same with other couples if you look around you.' John smiled before continuing because William had opened his mouth with surprise.

'Quarrelsome folk seem to have a different shape between them, pointed or flattened, one way or the other, never the same. Do you see, my son?'

'Yes, Father, can I look into the street now and see who's passing by?' he asked, quite excited with the suggestion. 'But you can tell now what I am thinking by the look on my face, isn't that so?'

John nodded as William walked across the shop to look out of the doorway. The head of an elder my son has, he thought, but will I regret sharing such deep thoughts of the face and mind with him? Will he look at Mary and me soon though different eyes? No – I cannot prevent my son's eagerness to learn. I will have to seek more wisdom in the future. I did not have half he has when I was his age. William will look to me for guidance. As his proud father all knowledge of mine shall be his. His eyes have always looked up to me with yearning for information and I will give him all I can. If it be the cause of strong debate, then let it be so. He is my flesh and blood. Even if I have to fight him one day with words, I will love him so. Even though his tongue may one day hurt my ears, he is still mine and I will love him for it. John's thoughts turned to feelings of dread for what the future may hold as he stared at William's hand on the door post.

Suddenly, John jumped up and lunged for the door in haste. Mary had walked in to see them both, causing a draught to push an open door towards William's fingers. William seemed to sense something, so he turned to face his father as he rushed towards the door.

'I thought you knew the secret, Father?' he asked, assuming he was coming to join him.

'No, William,' he said, holding the door with relief. 'The draught from the other door swept this one towards your fingers, but you turned in time.'

'It was the sound of your feet and the falling of the chair that made me turn, Father,' William said with a smile and raised eyebrow. 'I thought you had pricked your finger on a needle while working leather.'

Mary joined them in the doorway and then looked past them into the street. 'What are you both discussing so intently?' she asked with a hand on each of their shoulders. 'Is there a bull loose in the street or is it raining plums?'

'No, Mother, just folk with noses from the same mould as the bull; some even look as if a ring would suit them.'

His remark puzzled Mary, so she looked at each of them in turn, trying to guess what they had been discussing.

'If the folk in the street could hear you both, they would come into our shop and hit you over the head with the very broom you should have repaired for me by now!' Mary struggled to pick William up to squeeze him as if in punishment.

John relieved Mary of her burden and swung William around the room before sitting him down with the broom once more. 'That's it now, William. Game over.' John turned to kiss Mary. 'Turn your attention back to the broom now and away from the mirror. The brush still needs a new face.'

'I don't know, Father.' Mary shook her head playfully. 'Bulls and brushes, what are you teaching him?'

'Ah, my love!' he exclaimed. 'The brush must always follow the bull to catch what he leaves behind. Otherwise, the bull would chase the brush and the person doing the sweeping!'

Mary partially closed her eyes in despair and walked away with a much larger grin on her face. John winked at William to tempt him to agree with his suggestion.

The Maypole

The town's welcoming spirit was building up for the arrival of the summertime celebrations. May was by far the most joyous month of the year. Winter had been shaken off and spring growth was well under way in the countryside. On this particular day, the town had arranged a mock battle to be staged. There would be cockfights, jesters, dancing, music and a large maypole in the market square. There were also stalls selling food and drink, as well as many visiting jugglers and acrobats performing in the streets. Many people would trickle down from the hamlets in the surrounding area and swell Stratford to near bursting.

Mary was near to having her second daughter, Anne, at this time, so John took William, now seven, and Gilbert to join other children from the town around the maypole – the highlight of the year for some. Joan was still too young to go outside with her brothers, so she stayed at home with Mary. All the way to the market square, William danced between the exposed cobbles protruding from the dirt, trying to get Gilbert to hold hands with him as he did so. William had danced around the maypole for the first time the previous year, but Gilbert was more reluctant to leave his father's side. Eventually Gilbert joined his brother and they held hands as William took hold of the twine to follow the other children. The music from different areas of the market square sounded like a disorganised compilation. It had a pleasing but ill-composed tune that kept passers-by glancing in all directions with bemusement.

The day seemed more like a regular market day, with men from other villages huddled together exchanging money. John chose not to join them because the high interest rates on his moneylending were renowned. He preferred his customers to come to him if they required his services and he didn't go out looking for trouble. Only open trading took place under the public eye – he had a position and reputation to hold on to. Other colleagues from the town chambers joined the groups, but they tried to avoid John's attention. They did business with people from all walks of life, advising in all capacities.

As John watched his two sons having fun, his friend Thomas Eldman came to stand by his side, accompanied by his wife who was also called Mary.

'Ah, the other Mary in my life,' John said with a cursory nod and a yawn. 'How did you manage to pull Thomas away from his stack of silver coins, then?'

Mary Eldman lowered her head to smile before Thomas answered for her. 'I am surprised to see you at all, John. Your own pile would put mine in the shade for sure, but I do not envy your lack of sleep.'

'You talk as if I had land from here to Oxford and back.' John pointed to Thomas' purse. 'A man with a great pile already in the barn, it is you with the wealth and the time to sleep it off, not me.'

'Do not believe this man, my love,' said Thomas. 'Why, he only just managed to squeeze through the door past a bigger stack of coins. His own wife could not squeeze past because of her condition.' Thomas patted his own stomach to infer the same.

John replied with a scoff as he turned to watch William and Gilbert again at the maypole. 'That is true wealth, Thomas,' he said, looking towards his two sons. 'They shine more than any silver or gold, and they grow faster by the day.'

'Yes, you are right,' said Thomas as he and Mary both nodded. 'But they consume silver to grow and much more than I expected my six to cost.'

'But they are well worth the investment and one day they will return the favour, Thomas,' said Mary seriously. 'Indeed, they work all hours for you most days.'

'Hmm, yes, my love,' he replied awkwardly.

'Oh, the cost is a necessary evil, Thomas,' John said. 'You cannot expect a good harvest without planting with care. You have to be patient and allow growth to occur naturally, without wanting a quick return on your investment.'

'They bring food to the table daily,' said Mary. 'They also engage well in all the other tasks you set them, even if it keeps them from learning the Bible.'

'Hmm, yes, there are good points, but now I have a bet to place.' Thomas tilted his head to the side, indicating that he wanted to leave. 'I am tempted by the black cockerel. Which one do you fancy, John?'

Just beyond them an enthusiastic crowd had gathered to watch the cockfighting and to the side was a smaller group of men who had flapping birds under their arms ready to fight later.

'I will join you when I have found my two.' John turned to look for his sons again. 'But I've noticed that not many black ones ever win.'

John walked across to find William and Gilbert and take them to watch the cock fight, leaving Thomas rubbing his chin deep in thought.

His two sons were having the time of their lives, jumping and twisting around the maypole with the other children. It was a picture that would bring great smiles from any proud parent.

'Right then,' John said. 'Another cockfight is about to start. Come with me now if you want to see one for yourself.'

'What is a cockfight, Father?' asked William, passing the ropes to waiting children while steadying Gilbert.

'They peck with their beaks and spur. Just like men with daggers. You will see,' he replied, picking them both up and proceeding to run with them, one under each arm.

This made his sons laugh as their ribs caught on his arms, but the excitement soon stopped when they reached the crowd. John let the boys down just as two cockerels had been thrown from the ring; they were dripping in blood right in front of them, with one loser and one winner, but they were both finished off by a man snapping their necks because they were so badly maimed. William hadn't seen a cockfight before, so the experience was new to both brothers and so was the ensuing horror.

'What is the purpose of a cockfight, Father?' asked William, looking up wanting further details.

'Just a pastime for occasional enjoyment. It is a tradition most enjoy.' John struggled to lift his sons above the heads of the crowd to see. 'They peck and spur each other, in the belief that one of them will win the hens' favour. The winner lives sometimes.'

It was all over in a trice, but the terror of it stuck in William's mind for the rest of the day. Such a violent exchange at the happy Maytime celebration didn't really equal the excitement of tripping around the maypole. Gilbert seemed to like the sight of the torn-out feathers and the noise of those shouting around him, but children see and learn to enjoy many different things.

'Why do cockerels fight, Father?' William asked, looking down at another pair of limp losers.

'They just do. The male species of most animal species fight, just like soldiers fight in war. Cockerels are the same.'

'But they both get wounded,' said William with a deep frown. 'Why do they not come to a truce and share the corn? There are always plenty of chickens and we have sacks of corn.'

'It is the nature of some creatures not to share. This is greed.' John shrugged his shoulders, indicating his incomprehension in the matter. 'There should be plenty for all, but if one weakens, the greedy take all. That is why most folk just look after themselves. Come on; let us look for the colourful jesters. Where did I see them falling about last?' John looked around for such a group.

The jesters turned out to be much better than the cockfight. Both children laughed loudly, even though they didn't understand the adult innuendos. As the lead jester passed between the giggling crowds, he touched some and whispered to others, causing a ripple of laughter. After a short time John stopped watching the jester to look at William, who was studying the act. He was trying to compare the new words with the laughter and to see why they were so effective and what they could mean.

I hope William does not ask me what the jester was referring to when he was talking about shaking something in the morning, John thought. I hope he thinks of the jester's bells and not something else. These people should be more careful how they appeal to the different audiences. Some children are more inquisitive than others. I will just pass any questions over to Mary. She is better at explaining these things than I. She is the one with a head full of words. Her innocence drifts over these questions like fog does over still water. I get bogged down in the marsh with deeper thoughts and explanations to the lewd and bawdy remarks.

'Father,' William shouted, jumping up and down. 'Can we see the battle next? The Spanish are going to try to take the bridge, I hear.'

'Yes, and then it is home for soup,' he said, quite relieved by the innocent question as they turned to follow the crowd towards Clopton Bridge.

William looked up to the colourful soldiers lining the streets. 'Who are the Spanish? I have heard the word said many times today. Do they live deep in the woods?'

'They are from a country across the sea and they do not like us, William,' John said with tired eyes, expecting further questions. 'They do not like the English because we steal from their ships,' he added, trying to anticipate the next question.

'What is a ship?' asked William, looking at the pitiful replica of a boat on the river. 'Is it similar to a boat?'

'Boat,' said Gilbert, pointing towards the river.

'Yes, boat, Gilbert, a boat.' William turned to point one out to him.

Oh, his endless questions, John thought. But I suppose they both have to learn. It's not their fault if they are oblivious to the fact that I work by candlelight into the small hours in order to produce stock for market day. I hope they will benefit from my sleepy eyes.

'Boat,' Gilbert said once more.

'Soldiers as well, Gilbert.' William pointed towards the opposite bank. William still hadn't forgotten his previous question, indicated by his stare back at John in expectation of an answer.

'Yes, a ship. It is like a boat but bigger,' John explained with his hands spread wide apart. 'It has a pole in its midst like the maypole and from it a large sheet called a sail is fixed. From this the wind is captured by the sail and so the ship is pushed along in the water, but steered by the rudder, which is at the back, of course.'

'Does God push the wind, Father?' William waved his arms around to feel its coolness.

'Yes, I believe that is so,' he answered. 'But the direction and force is a mystery to all, and the sail has to be able to move so it can catch the wind. I have seen them turn just off the coast before.' John placed his hands upon their heads and turned them towards the battle taking place beside the river.

The mock battle had all the town cheering. It was a certainty that the Spanish would lose, but a second loss awaited them as the Spanish were all thrown in the river by the crowd. Everyone laughed as they cooled down in the river, joined soon after by the pretend English army who had just defeated them. Gilbert hadn't said much that morning, but at the sight of the river battle, he applauded relentlessly for more.

'Can we go closer, can we, Father?' he shouted out relentlessly.

'Not today, Gilbert,' John said. 'There are too many people and you might get trampled, but we will next time. We can stand and watch them for a time if you both wish.' John stepped towards a slightly elevated mound and stood his two sons before him so they could watch the excitement of the play fight which was now coming to an end.

William and Gilbert still had the battle on their minds when they returned home and so John was pestered into bringing out the toy wooden horses after they had eaten. Mary and John then watched the boys' own version of the mock battle, helped by John, who relived being young again. John had made them a leather sword each so they could pretend to fight in relative safety. They couldn't stab him with the soft swords, but they certainly managed to slap him hard, which was just as painful.

School

The first day at petty school was an awakening experience for William. Ann was the new baby in the Shakespeare household and he, like her, had to start at the bottom with a new adventure. The love and high regard he had for his family were like chapters from an old book. School was tough and punishment could be hard. Mother's lap was many fields away. William began a cautious, tentative search for knowledge with each innocent turn of the page in the book of school life. The school usher shouted out to ask all the children to answer their names, but one boy hadn't made it that day. The plague had taken another victim, but a young death was common gossip. It had the same impact as a farmer's missing sheep had. All one could do was to helplessly shrug one's shoulders. All the boys were sat on long benches, chatting together, but they were soon quietened by a sharp crack of the school usher's birch on the front table. The school usher was called Mr Dobson, a man of authority and discipline, but one with a socially conscious heart. He was short and plump with a greasy line of hair flowing down the side of one cheek and finishing under his chin.

'Good morning and welcome to the school,' said Mr Dobson with his authoritative chin pressed into his neck. 'I am your school usher and I would like you all to greet me each day in a polite manner.

'Well ... I am waiting,' he said more loudly, with a single raised eyebrow and darting glares between the frightened faces.

He can only raise one eyebrow, William thought, staring at his expression. What a character he is. He must have practised this expression in front of a puddle.

The reply from the shy class was weak as one might expect, but a further crack of the birch brought the whole class to attention sharply. 'Good morning, sir,' the children said out loud.

'That is much better, boys,' he said, smiling. 'My name is Mr Dobson and you will always speak to me with a daily introduction that is kindly worded. First of all, I would like to tell you the school rules and they must be strictly followed.' He paused for a moment and straightened his back before continuing. 'But before I do,' he said with a hint of compassion to his voice, 'I would like to say we are down in number today. One of your intended friends passed away last night, so you have an extra space on your bench. But don't use it to lie on or you will join his family in pain.'

To put further pressure on the boys, he began looking around the classroom, carefully studying each face in turn. He was looking for twitches, an early indication of future trouble, he thought. After what seemed like an hour, but was only a couple of minutes, he snapped away from his predatory stare and spoke out to shatter the quiet of the room once more. 'Is there anyone in the room not able to see my fingers?' he asked, waiting a few moments for fear to break the silence. This was an early eyesight test of his, but a pretty crude and informal one.

'My thumb then, my room of owls,' he said sarcastically, but it flew over heads; only a few children grasped the aim of his weak-witted remark.

Oh, this day will pass like worm crossing an open field, William tutted to himself. Market day in the rain is more interesting. Or even watching Mother gut a chicken – certainly more so than the *owl* remarks. But there again, if I were a worm, surely I would be wriggling up to tempt a blackbird to my early fate.

'All can see, then? Good! I will ask you all one by one to count markers on the wall here — that is if you can count.' Mr. Dobson paused before looking around for any late hands; then he raised his eyebrows to invite each boy in turn.

So this is school, William thought. It is more like Father lecturing all present after finding a badly stitched seam, even before we have so much as picked up the needle! We have not taken a single apple from the orchard, nor have we walked over precious *barley*, so why does he look down at us as if we have?

All the boys took it in turns at counting the markers on the board, but eight boys either had defective eyesight or were unable to count.

Mr Dobson invited the eight boys to the front of the class; then he made them swap places with the boys who had been sat on the front benches. 'Sit down, then!' he shouted. However, as they did, he quickly ran across the front of them and slapped their legs in turn with the birch.

'One ... two ... three ... four ... five ... six ... seven ... eight,' he said as quickly as his birch skipped across their legs.

All eight boys cried out and rubbed their sore legs, looking up to Mr Dobson. Their faces all asked, why me? But he was clearly enjoying their painful frowns.

'Let that be a lesson to you all.' He looked up to the rest of the class and waved his stick as if spreading butter. 'When I ask a question, I want the truth.' He raised his voice, 'And nothing else!'

Oh, the bully's crown is yours indeed, thought William, inwardly huffing. I would present you with a leather one if I had the chance – from the hide of an old bull's rump!

'To continue,' Mr Dobson said, now more restrained. 'I want you boys to remember the following: You must all wear boots of some sort each day – even if they are made of straw! And furthermore, you must all arrive with a clean, fresh face – not as if you had just riddled the fire. Mind you, though,' he looked up to the ceiling with a pleasing look to his face and nodded in agreement to himself, 'if you wish to come with a blackened face, do so by all means. But just remember this, with my sleeves rolled up and the trough just outside, my stiff brush will remind you of your forgetfulness in your haste to get to school on time!'

With this the boys laughed a little, helped by Mr Dobson's smile, easing the atmosphere somewhat.

Mr Dobson took in a deep breath and tapped his stick on the desk lightly to call the children to attention. 'We will start by reciting the Lord's Prayer, then later the Psalms and the alphabet from the school's horn books. But I must add,' he said seriously, with a further crack from his birch, 'that these books are expensive to replace. It will cost many a lash from the birch here if one should go missing.' He paused, glaring at them through squinted eyes to emphasise his determination to carry out the threat; then he relaxed and continued speaking. 'When you have finished petty school, you may attend grammar school. There you will learn Latin, prose, rhetoric and the art of our written language and so forth. But today, my boys,' he said with a friendly smile as a parent came to observe the class with the head of the school, 'you will all become friends. You will be strangers no more, just happy friends.' Mr Dobson lowered his head in a welcoming smile towards the two newcomers before turning back to address the boys once more.

William's thoughts began to run away with him and he felt that he had to ask a question, even though he feared the barking reply.

'Sir, Mr Dobson,' he asked politely, followed by a cough.

The sight of his raised hand caused the whole class to look at him, expecting Mr Dobson to crack his birch or even shout at William, but they were wrong.

Mr Dobson was surprised by the lone voice, but he forced a smile and leaned forward to reply to William, with his eyebrows raised and his head turned with interest.

'Stand up to speak, my boy. Don't be frightened,' he said with a broadening false smile. 'Let us all hear what you have to say.'

William stood up and cleared his dry throat before speaking, but when he spoke it was clear he hadn't spent his early life leapfrogging through farmyards.

'Sir, Mr Dobson, at what point do strangers become friends, sir? One moment we do not know each other's names and then next we are, and rightly so, friends.' William finished speaking with a sigh, his heart racing. His virgin public voice was no more. Whatever happened next he had taken his first great step.

'Hmm, good question, boy. What is your name again?' Mr Dobson nodded his head to acknowledge William before indicating that he should sit down.

'William, sir, William Shakespeare,' he said, grateful that he was once again able to feel the cold bench with his hands as he sat down.

'William, your point is well made and it is such a simple question, but one which I have never been asked before. It is simply this, my boy: strangers become friends when *trust* forms between them. Do you see now?' He nodded to affirm his advice.

William nodded in response but he waited for Mr Dobson to finish before he spoke again.

'A stranger can never become a friend until he is trusted, take note of that, all the rest of you,' Mr Dobson said with a smile towards the visitors. 'Heed what I say.'

The parent and school head seemed more than satisfied with the feel of the class, so they turned to walk away quietly.

'Yes, thank you, sir,' said William with a polite smile.

Mr Dobson then acknowledged William's reply before continuing with his lecture to the class. 'Mealtimes, boys, something you will all be looking forward to most, no doubt.' Mr Dobson rubbed his hands together with real smile, possibly to reflect his own poor diet. 'Whether you eat meat at home, or mere peppercorns, it matters not to me. At school you will all be treated the same. If the baker brings fresh or past week's bread, we will all dip into our soup with the same. No one will be treated any differently.'

For a moment he seemed to lose his concentration, dreaming of lunch with a pleasant smile, his weakness for food having been shown to the whole class. 'Right, moving on. My next point is this,' he said, turning his mind back to discipline. 'Let William be an example to us all. Having so humbly asked a question, you will now all follow his lead. Be polite, raise your hand and call me sir. Now, are there any more questions before we hand out the books?' He looked around and none came, so he continued with the lesson, knowing he had instilled fear into most, but just enough to form the discipline barrier he needed.

William's first day at school was a day he remembered above all others, especially as it turned out to feel like one of the longest. When he got home that day, he had to explain in detail what happened and what had been said. He exaggerated the size of the usher's birch to Gilbert and Joan, but it was just enough to make them fear it before he smiled at them. Anne was just a few months old at the time. She was a quiet baby and William's attention was drawn to her first when he came home each day. He was like father number two to her and she seemed to sense William's presence, often crying for him to pick her up, but cleaning and feeding duties were still left to his mother.

When William tried to get to sleep that night, thoughts of Mr Dobson's birch flashed through his mind each time Gilbert turned over in his sleep. His head was alive with pictures and thoughts of the day. He intended to study hard and question how people used the new words he came across. William often imagined he was inside himself, witnessing the world passing by his very eyes, looking forward to the future, but in his mind he was actually thinking of the past as the grim reality of the usher's birch struck home.

Oh, Gilbert's elbows digging into me feels like the painful threat of the birch. I must change my position, William thought, rubbing his ribs to ease the discomfort. William shuffled down to the bottom of the bed to escape his brother's arms, but something made him stand up and look through the window. A sudden brightness made him close his eyes for a moment and a bright orange glow filtered into the room from outside. Accompanying it were loud cracks and bursts, then more flashes of bright light.

'How large the sun is and yet it is so low in the sky. And what of the shouts and screams?' he said quietly, walking closer to the window.

The horn that was fitted into the leaded lights prevented him from seeing what was happening outside, so he pushed one of the windows open to take a closer look.

An end house behind the shop on the opposite side of the street was ablaze and spiting out fire. Several people ran about the street in panic, 'We're next, we're next,' they screamed with their hands in the air.

William had never seen flames reaching so high, not so close anyhow, but its warmth was permeating the air and through the open window onto his face. He was oblivious to the danger they were in and he didn't even think to wake up his brother. The spectacle of it kept him riveted to the spot as he studied the flames'enchanting spurts and flashes.

After several minutes, the drama and intensity of the situation jolted William to wake up to the reality of the situation and its worsening terror. The town was on fire and the roof was now burning hot! William blinked several times to check what his eyes were witnessing. Suddenly, John and Mary burst into the room. Anne was in Mary's arms and John had Joan in his.

'Come on, William,' John ordered. 'Take Gilbert and come downstairs. Fetch a blanket with you.' John kicked the door wider for William and Gilbert to pass by, then followed them downstairs with big strides.

The family had made precautions in the event of fire in that they would remain downstairs just in case the wind changed direction. Mary lit some candles in the living room and John left to organise men to smother the fire with an array of borrowed buckets. The baby began crying, so Mary tried to get her back to sleep by shushing and rocking her. After a short time the family settled quietly on the floor in a makeshift bed. All they could do was to look on helplessly and watch the vegetables in the back garden take on an orange hue. The plan was that if the fire spread across to their house, they could easily escape through the shop and into the street.

'Mother,' William said, looking up at the flames with a deep frown.

'What is it, William?' she answered, tucking Anne in who was now sleeping peacefully.

'If the burning house lights up our garden from just a few yards away, how big must the sun be to give us daylight, to see the distant sheep on the hills?'

'It must be much larger than the fire we can see. Try to sleep, William, you have school again tomorrow.' She gave him a hug. 'We can talk about the sun, and even the moon if you wish, but tomorrow evening.'

'Today was easy for me, Mother,' he whispered. 'Some of the others could hardly speak properly let alone count. I was the only one to ask a question.' William wafted a moth from his face.

'You have made a good start, then,' she said, wafting the same moth away, which Gilbert caught between his hands.

'Help the others if you are able to,' she added, shaking her head at Gilbert with disapproval. 'And with this the schoolmaster will see that you are helping him.'

'Will I learn anything from the Latin or prose he spoke of? Some are unable to speak our own language without having to learn another.'

'It is for scholars, William,' she said, indicating he should whisper. 'With this knowledge you can broaden your own thoughts further. If Father only sold gloves, we would not be so well fed, but by selling other wares we are able to supply goods to more folk. If you master another language, you will be able to speak to more folk with the same tongue. Let me give you an example. A pig can only grunt to another of its own kind and the same can be said about a cow and a sheep, but the farmer can guide them all with just one stick.'

'Yes, I see now. I will study, Mother,' he smiled, reflecting on what she had just said.

'Good. Now to sleep, both of you.' She blinked hard, indicating that they should close their eyes.

'Where do you pluck your wisdom from, Mother?' William asked, mischievously pretending to close his eyes. 'Every time I ask you something, you reply without referring to a book or the Bible, or even speaking with Father.'

'This is the last question, William,' she whispered, but at the same time leaning closer to his ear. 'It is a secret of mine I have never told anyone before, not even your father. My mind is open to anything without fixed judgement of any kind. So when I am unsure of my next step, or indeed when I am questioned by someone, especially you, I see faded pictures and hear words in my mind, giving advice on how I should answer. It is as simple as I say, William. If you can do the same you will want for nothing and no challenge should ever beat you square. But sleep now, I insist!'

William nodded and quickly drifted off to sleep. It didn't seem for long though before a sooty-faced stranger woke the family up at daylight.

John returned home just in time to wake everyone up with a handful of fresh eggs for breakfast, nearly scaring them away in doing so. Both his hands were cut and his clothes were black and torn, but the fire had been put out. The house where the fire had started had been pulled down as had the two others next to it. No lives had been lost, only possessions and sleep. Fortunately, there had been little wind that night, so the fire hadn't spread as quickly as past ones had. Mary tended John's cuts before rushing about preparing food for everyone, as well as seeing William off to school. John could hardly move he had been exerting himself so much. He just sat there with everyone attending to his every whim. They had to step over his legs to walk past him, he was that beat. John had such a deep stare that he didn't even flinch when Mary wiped the grit from his cuts or wafted eggs under his nose; he had to be prodded out of his transfixed stare.

William's second day at school seemed to pass quickly, but his return home that evening made the day near equal to his first in that it was memorable. His father was a trader in many goods, but the sight welcoming William from school that day shocked him into doubting he'd arrived home at the right place. Mary had already made known her dislike at John's latest acquisition: a stack of part-burned timbers from the dwelling that had burned down the previous evening now housed in the back garden.

Mary had been exchanging cross words with John when William walked into the room, so she presented one final statement before going upstairs. 'Our house looks like we don't know the difference between pig and pork!' his mother muttered to John. 'We have black upon black, right up to our bed sheets! There is filth everywhere.'

John tutted to himself before inviting William to come outside with him.

The apprentice from the shop had already begun chipping the burned parts away, but William and Gilbert were expected to help as well. Mary's tutting and grumbles of scrubbing her sons free of the black soot for three days soon went with the quick profit made from the beams and her dislike was replaced with a smile, as concessions from John were to her benefit.

Lessons and Games

During the holiday periods, William would often help his father in the stall under the market cross. This was a privileged position and John used it to his full advantage. On one particular day, William had wandered off to see some local players performing a watered-down version of *George and the Dragon*. However, he was so captivated by the colourful exchange that he had wandered too close to a group of tethered horses. Suddenly, a friend of John's took William by the arm and pulled him to one side to give him a stern warning. The farmer was called Bill Croach, a well-known, ruddy-faced character with leather cap and bristly hair sticking out from either side.

'You are John's lad, aren't you?' Bill asked, shaking his head at him.

William looked up and down at the farmer and then glanced towards his father's stall before answering. 'Yes, I am, but what of it?' He stepped back and pulled his arm away.

John had seen the farmer restraining William, so he leapt over his table and ran down to him, leaving his apprentice to manage the stall.

Bill looked up towards John and seeing him running towards William, he stepped back to wait for him to reach them.

'What business have you with my son?' John puffed, stopping next to William.

'Oh nothing but saving him from a good kicking, John,' Bill answered with a smile, tapping his stick on the ground.

'Oh, it is you, Bill,' John replied, realising he was not a foe. 'But what kicking do you speak of?'

Bill smiled with raised eyebrows. 'Can I take him across the square to show him what I mean?'

'Yes, you should walk with him, William,' John replied, his hands on his hips to help control his breathing. 'Fear nothing, he is a friend.'

John pointed to guide William to follow Bill, but he walked behind them to see what he had in mind. William was more hurt than surprised at his father directing him to accompany Bill; after all, this man was a stranger to him. What wrong have I done? he thought, with a look of surprise towards his father, for this man, my father, to let me go off with someone I've never even met before. Now all eyes are on my reddened face, but why? For standing still, I wonder.

'Look here, er, William's your name, isn't it?' Bill asked.

William nodded but then folded his arms to shut out the man's attempt at kindness.

'Horses kick back and cows kick forward. Let me show you, lad.' Bill lifted his stick to prod a cow.

The cow felt the irritation straight away and kicked forward a foot or so. Bill proceeded to do the same to a nearby tethered horse, but this time it kicked backwards quite violently and his point had been made, opening William's eyes to the danger he was in. William was so shocked that he leaned backwards, blinking with fear, even though he was several steps away from its hooves.

John had been watching close by, so he nodded his head to thank Bill for his trouble. It was an oversight on his part that he had never told William about it before. Although William was embarrassed by the spectacle, he thanked Bill for his trouble but it was more for his father's benefit and because it would be expected of him. This was another lesson for William, not just about horses but to look out for things other than what might be happening under his very nose and to be more aware of his surroundings in future.

After they had finished at the market that day, John and William made a slight detour before going home. John had learned that an early type of football game was taking place in town. Neither of them had seen anything like it before, so John suggested they walk to the edge of town to see what all the fuss was about. When they arrived there they stood alongside some of John's friends to witness an early and crude version of the game.

'Hello, John' said Alan McCarthy, a friend of his. 'I didn't think you would have any interest in such games as this.'

'Well, I think William should take note of new things in town. It may help to broaden his thoughts farther than our small borough. The county may have many more pastimes like this that we might learn from, but I doubt there will ever be any money to be made from predicting its outcome. There looks to be many more losers than there is folk taking part.'

'Yes, I think you might be right, John, but it looks more like a mock battle than a game. I must confess, I am unable to follow what the aim of the activity is intended to accomplish.'

'I fear the thought of being asked to make gloves for such a monster with so many hands.' John and Alan laughed a little to themselves.

They all looked across to a large crowd of people who were gathered around a pitiful ball. It was lying on the floor unattended and there was a scrum of pushing, kicking and biting going on around it. Dust had been stirred up and hands were swinging all ways in desperation. It was near impossible to get to the ball for the disorganised fighting. Young children were running around playing other games and hand carts were being pushed past those taking part.

'No, I do not see the point of it at all,' said John, sighing to himself. 'It looks like a foot fight over a swollen bladder, ready to pee over those close by if it should burst.'

Both men smiled and continued to watch with frowns and twists to their confused faces.

'Ah, I might be able to assist you with this,' said a stranger, who was already leaning upon a horse-tethering post nearby.

The man straightened himself up and walked towards them. John and Alan turned to look towards him before nodding heads to invite his comments.

'It is a game where there are two gangs who wish to control the bladder ball and they have to pass it by all means into the opposition's catchment space. There does seem to be no order to it, I must confess, and surely little in the way of rules for this type of engagement. But it does take the eyes of the crowds with it and I see that tempers often rise after many a scuffle. The young ones tend to get bruised more than the older children. Some I have seen have become quite skilful at controlling the ball, but they are often kicked out of the way by the thicker-set individuals. It takes the attentions of passers-by for many an hour as they push and shove about for the sake of getting the ball. It is a game which mystifies both those taking part and those watching. Indeed, the outcome is as unpredictable as the direction a mole might take beneath our feet in its search for worms.'

'It looks too rough for me,' said William as he looked at a younger boy being sat on by another. 'Some have no boots and they stub their toes on stones. It looks worse than the kick from a horse.'

With John being a leading figure in the town, he winked at Alan and then wore a more serious expression as he turned to the stranger. His intention was to see if the man could speak to a larger crowd after making his suggestions.

'My name is John Shakespeare; I am an alderman from this town.' He then tilted his head to the stranger to invite him to introduce himself.

'Oh, sorry,' he said, looking quite surprised. 'I did not know I was in such company. My name is Hart, Andrew Hart.'

'Mmm, so you know of this game, then?' he asked, rubbing his chin to indicate thought.

'Not to any great degree,' he said, but nodding nonetheless to accept he knew a little. 'I have seen it played elsewhere.'

'What a find you are, Mr Hart! I will stop the game and you shall tell them your rules. Step back, William, and let the games usher tell all.'

Hart blinked with surprise but then a look of shock was written on his face as John put his hands up and shouted out to bring the game to a stop.

'Listen, all!' cried John. 'There are rules to follow. Now, listen to the all-knowing Mr Hart here and he will put you straight.'

The scuffles in the crowd came to a hush and soon all the nearby eyes were focused on the stranger's face. He kept still for a moment, to allow the unrest from his exposure to settle down, then he stepped forward a little way.

'Mmm, er, right, then,' he spoke out.

'Louder,' called John before turning back to smile at Alan.

'Oh, yes,' he said. 'Well, we must have rules. To begin with, I say we must not allow kicking and using one's fists against each other. This is not a fight – it is a game. There must be no carrying of tools or blades and no items present in pockets. No biting or stamping on opponents who might be laid out hurt. Er, the longest reach you have comes from the toe, so use this to kick it with. The game revolves around a "kick and run" philosophy, so run fast and use your might and skill to kick the ball to the other end. If, er, you may get the chance to knock the ball with your heads, but make sure you have your eyes closed. You must have good order to your play and, er, the game is played best with similar ages on each side. To have big and small together must not be just and proper, so equal size and the same number of folk on each side is preferable. It has to be fair, I say. And it may be useful to stop now and again to scrape the dung from the ball.'

The crowd and those partaking in the game stood silently, waiting for something to happen or for someone else to speak. The stranger stood ready to face any mocking or challenging remarks to what he had said.

John had been thinking about it, so he began to nod his head slightly as if in thought, almost having a conversation in his own mind with himself.

'It makes good sense what he says, eh, John?' said Alan.

A group from the other side of the playing area began to add to the suggested rules, but they were intent on ridiculing what had already been said.

'No mules must take part,' said one.

'And no Spanish dukes,' said another.

John smiled and put his hand up to speak now that the crowd was beginning to laugh with them.

'It makes sense to have some guidance,' he said, smiling broadly. 'You could try your own suggestions out if you wish, but I doubt you would find either a Spanish duke or a mule fool enough to play with your stone-throwing tactics.'

'Let them try what Hart suggested,' said Colin, another friend who had stopped nearby. 'Give them a try, it can do no harm.'

John took a few steps forward and spoke to the crowd.

'Try as he suggests,' he said, indicating with a sweeping action with his hands for them to continue.

The game began once more, so John looked down to William as if inviting him to take part. William shyly shook his head from side to side and looked down at his nice clothes; he wanted to keep himself clean. The game seemed to take on a more organised feel to it, but it was still quite crude and disorganised nonetheless.

'Boot it!' called Alan loudly. 'Boot it past them all.'

'Where are you staying in town?' asked John, greeting Hart as he returned to stand by him.

'The tavern near to the bridge.'

'We will meet with you later to share a measure of ale. You spoke well then. There seems to be less chance of blood and fewer cries of pain now you have spoken out. You may have done a little good, you know.'

'I would be honoured to meet with you,' said Hart. 'Thank you kindly, Mr Shakespeare.'

Family Life

At the point where three strip fields met, there was a piece of common land just outside town that a horse and plough couldn't work. This triangular piece of land was bursting with wild flowers, tall weeds and butterflies. It was one of the most popular places frequented by the townsfolk. The family was enjoying some time together after they had been picking mushrooms a few hundred yards from home, with the exception of John, who was busy working in the shop with his apprentice. Mary sat with her eyes closed, basking in the scent wafting by from the nearby flowers. Anne was asleep at her side, so this was a luxury to savour, away from the smelly streets and bustle of Stratford for a short time. William was playing beside her while Gilbert and Joan were chasing each other across the sloping meadow. William, now eight, glanced up to his siblings, then focused his attention back on the toys he had brought with him.

'Wooden doll, you be my queen.' He tilted his head to look at his arrangement. The peg soldiers were dressed in apple green. 'Green soldiers and a golden queen, never will their blood be seen.'

Mary shielded her eyes from the bright sunlight. 'What do you mean by your rhyming verse, William, "never will their blood be seen"?'

'Well, Mother, the golden sun gives life each day to the green trees and grass. It will never cut it or harm it. So if our queen should dress her soldiers in green, she would be like the sun. Her golden clothes would be like the sun. Then all would stop fighting. Do you see?' William looked quite serious as he brushed back the hair on the doll and propped her up in the foliage.

'I doubt a queen could stop all fighting, with golden clothes or not. Some queens may even be the cause of it, but I see the light from your heart. I think you may have been studying our streets for too long. When people fight, it is only for a short time. The daylight is so we can feed ourselves, not fight! The crops need sunlight to dry their seeds.' Mary smiled and patted him on the head, shaking her head with pride.

'Mother,' he continued, standing up to view the soldiers, 'when people fight and knock each other to the ground, could the queen stop this? She is the queen, after all.'

'No, William, she would have to see it first. There are many people and only one queen. Just like with you, your sisters and your brother, I am unable to watch you all at the same time. Anne could be crying for me, Gilbert and Joan could be playing on the town muck heap, but you, William, could be fast asleep in the shop for all I knew!' Mary gave William a playful cuff to his head.

'Mother,' he replied with a frown showing hurt. 'I am an asset to the family. I sell with wit, not sleep. Many customers leave with both leather and a smile under their arm.'

'Oh, William,' she said brightly, 'it is from me your wit. I passed it to you at birth but now I have it returned. You are easily had, my son.' Mary stood up and looked over to where Gilbert and Joan were hiding, shielding her eyes with both hands from the sun.

'Mother, I trusted you, but I will learn from your wit. You will not retain victory for long,' he said, acknowledging her superiority.

William continued to play with the doll and soldiers, but he altered his verse to suit his fresh thoughts, much to the surprise of his mother. 'Wooden queen, never to be seen, now not gold but emerald green. When the soldiers hide in yonder bush, your new dress colour will make them blush.' William sat back from his arrangement looking quite proud, but he still didn't look satisfied. He had a deep frown on his face.

'You have changed your story to having the queen in a guise of green,' said Mary, looking across with surprise. 'You should advise her of it one day, William. Perhaps she has a need to hide amongst those closest to her to eavesdrop.'

'Perhaps if I became a soldier myself, or even dressed her soldiers in merry clothes, they would play and never fight.' William suddenly closed his eyes and put his arm up to his face, fearing what might happen next.

Joan had escaped from Gilbert, but her hasty dash was aimed at her ending up in William's lap for safety.

'Oh, Joan, my dear rose,' William said, holding her safe. 'You have escaped the bully boy and trampled on my queen and men, but I will protect you from the daggers aimed at your throat.'

William moved quickly to the side as Gilbert brushed past them to tumble over in the long grass.

'Let us be going home now, William,' said Mary. 'Your father will be missing us after all this time. Call the wounded soldiers to your side.'

There were many home chores still to do that day, so William took hold of the basket of mushrooms with Mary and they walked back towards Henley Street. Gilbert galloped around them all the way But Joan was only three and she was soon fast asleep on William's shoulder. A cannon wouldn't have woken her, let alone her brother's war cries.

The next day William was helping his father in the family shop late in the day. William wasn't a great craftsman yet, but he had a vocabulary sharper than any knife and he could make many simple things. John had set William a task of stacking sacks of barley neatly and rearranging some animal skins. Although children had to work from an early age, not all life was strict and disciplined. Children still had to have fun in their childhood as they approached their teens.

While William was in deep thought arranging the skins in order of size, John crept behind his back towards the roughly hewn counter. 'All your money, boy!' he shouted, using a pretend measuring stick for a sword. 'Or I'll put your skin with the others on your stack.'

William jumped up with shock having dropped one of the skins, but after a moment's thought, he turned swiftly to answer his father's threat.

'Stranger, you can have my money, but fear my boots, for one day they will tread upon your tongue and cuff your ears. And you will never speak or hear any compliment from my purse's demise!' William finished, his chest sticking out like a mighty shield, daring another advance from his father.

'Oh, brave boy,' John replied, waving the stick either side of William's head, 'you reply with only words, but you would need a stool to stand on to touch my tongue. Your words are for mice!'

'Mice cannot pull ears, though,' William shouted, jumping up to his father to grab his ears, 'or make you smile as I can, you common peg maker.'

John laughed loudly, spinning William around in his arms, but it helped take the weight from his ears as he did so. 'Your words, William, your words; if only I could sell them instead of barley. No seeds to plant, or seasons to grow and wait patiently for ripeness, just to reap each day at will. Oh, William,' John sighed as he sat him down on the counter.

'Could that be so, Father?' William asked hopefully. 'Our shop is well placed and you are well known.'

'Some truth, son,' John sighed. 'Well placed for some things but wrongly placed for others. A town such as ours is far from London. That is where words are to be sold. Your words, William, no matter how good an ear they are planted in, will never sell here.' He sighed again. 'They will feed no one in this street.'

'But I make you and Mother smile,' he said hopefully. 'My brother and sisters also.'

'William,' said John seriously, with a stern face to calm his previous wit, 'listen to the glover's poem. Let it be your bedtime thought:

'After words of rhyme and clever nature, words of wit and loving doves, what of thumbs and fingers? We fill our bellies from making gloves,' John finished with a tight-lipped smile as he patted William's head. 'Come on, Gilbert is already sleeping.'

'I know, but my thoughts are of making gloves and making those wearing them applaud. Could we eat from that?' he asked, happily applauding himself as he jumped down from the counter.

'Perhaps ... perhaps, but it is hands that applaud and it is the same hands that pay, think as I say now.' John nodded his head to indicate that William should retire to bed.

John followed William into the kitchen and watched him kiss his mother goodnight. After this he pretended to chase him to make him giggle and climb the stairs more quickly.

'We are alone again, my love.' John took hold of Mary by the waist. 'William makes me laugh with his innocent but thoughtful words. Are they from you? I wonder.'

Mary turned from her pile of folded washing to accept the embrace and answer him.

'His wit, perhaps, is from me, but he studies how we both speak, and what customers have to say. I often watch his lips mumbling out a long word you have just said. Sometimes I feel he is not like other children, with thoughts for games and the like. He stares with a fixed head for learning all there is set before him.' She gave John a quick kiss before turning to her work.

'Is his speed of learning taken from his mother's speed of retreat? I wonder,' scoffed John, letting go of Mary's waist, only for her to stumble and knock over a drying pole.

'No, John,' she said, holding her head in a fluster. 'I have so many things to do and you also. Let us finish our jobs first; then I may consider a further kiss or two.' Mary tilted her head and lifted her eyebrows with promise.

'The doors will be bolted! And the apprentice bedded away; then I will be yours, my love, quicker than a crack from my belt.' John began his own exit in haste.

'It is good that you are capable of working fast, John,' she said, turning back to smile at him. 'For after you have finished you can then help me to finish my chores.'

'Oh, yes, my love, and with equal speed, I shall.'

Like a Crow

One particular day William was making his way to school and as usual he was strolling down the centre of the street, smiling at the birds and passers-by. Sometimes he would stop to look at something, to study how a hinge moved or a wheel turned, for instance. As he walked past the farrier's shop, he stopped to look at a rotting gatepost and a spider wrestling with its new catch. After studying the conflict, William took a blade of grass and tickled another spider's web. Straight away a spider came out to investigate, but on discovery of the grass stalk it retreated just as quickly.

'So, if a blade of grass acts just like a fly's feet,' William said with astonishment, 'then it must be that a spider cannot tell the feel of grass from a fly until it faces it square. What deception. They could play a never ending game with the spider. If only flies could carry grass on their backs, they would be the finest players about.'

William let go of the blade of grass and left it swinging in the web and continued on his way, kicking a stone in the direction of school.

Observing the spider gave William an idea for a short observation exercise for the boys to perform at school. A boy had recently asked the usher whether killing someone on stage would be more believable if the player had actually killed someone in battle, having experienced it first hand. The usher decided to explain what the actors were doing without altering the school's syllabus, a sort of general awareness exercise, in which the class had to show how townsfolk were different from each other, by copying faces, actions or shapes. With paper costing nearly the same as bread, William had to explain his idea to his schoolmaster first, rather than write it down. Although not a word was to be spoken throughout the exercise, the school usher agreed to William's idea to imitate the actions of a spider to see if any lessons could be learned. The act was simple: it was to demonstrate to the class that a blade of grass could mimic the actions of a struggling fly. A spider would be tempted into thinking a fly had been trapped in its web, in the same way an audience would be led to believe the acting on stage was real. A good player would be believed on stage, just like a blade of grass had tricked the spider for a moment on its own sticky stage. To mime the actions of a spider, two boys were lashed together, their arms flailing, and the rest of the class were left pretending to be flies. This left William, who stretched out as if he were a blade of grass to try to tempt the spider out of its corner. William managed to get his point across that day; however, the school master put him in his place after the exercise with his remarks.

'Spiders and flies are for children, Shakespeare. Words and ears are for humans. You have many a web to spin yet, boy.' The schoolmaster laughed out, with the other boys following his lead.

William took the point with a pleasing nod of his head. Despite having wit that would spoil the schoolmaster's advantage, he kept his thoughts to himself. Those in the room may laugh at me, and the schoolmaster also, he thought, but it was I who told the story. Without me, there would be nothing to laugh at.

Days like this came often at school for William, a shining star dulled by ignorant boot wax. His skin was thick and supple like his father's gloves, fitting all occasions with ease.

Not all William's encounters went in his favour, though. There was one occasion that injected a note of caution before speaking his mind for some considerable time afterwards.

Many of the other boys didn't share his company for more than a few minutes; William seemed to be on a different plane in their eyes. He always glanced twice at what he walked past, unable to resist the chance to study anything new. His mind was always ready to compare a puddle to rain. Most other children wanted to play in the woods in the evening, or get up to general boys' mischief. William's interests were in watching and listening. He knew which low beam to pass each day to check his height and who might be watching him and which crack they were looking from.

William had been dawdling on his way home from school one day, while examining fresh rain splatters upon a newly painted tavern sign. How strange it is, he thought, that the rain falls in droplets, then turns to longer beads, then falls some more and makes a puddle without a join or an edge. What special glue it is this stuff to loosen as it does, then fix to form a puddle and soon a stream.

When William looked up a group of people caught his attention, so he walked over to investigate. A couple of travellers had sat down to gossip with the locals and they seemed to be telling tales which made them laugh and frown. The two, though, were really as one, for they had an act of deceit to trick ale'd-up eyes out of their loose change. One would toss a coin to bet with the other, to see if it landed either face up or face down. The second man would appear to win and money was exchanged quickly. Others then wanted to join in, so more heads looked over their shoulders. A large crowd soon gathered around the two men, all eager to wager on the fall of a coin. Tossing coins was commonplace, so the two being friends made their deception easy. One would check the two-sided coin of the other and then exchange it with another which had two faces. The men from the town were all taken in and their pockets were soon emptied. No one except William suspected that the two of them were swapping the coins between them; they were both skilful and quick.

William had to force his way through the many legs as if it were a thicket. From his new position, he studied the game for quite some time, watching the faces of the sad losers tell him of their painful losses. One thought that crossed his mind was whether or not he should speak up and tell the truth or walk away? His decision was quick, but if it ended badly he would have to accept the fall that would inevitably come.

William suddenly slipped his hand between the many others and snatched the coin as it spun. With this action, all eyes were on William's hands. Suddenly, all the legs parted as if a wolf had run through sheep. William stood there with a great space on either side. Everyone looked shocked and their frowning faces looked on, encouraging him to speak.

'The coin has two heads, look,' William shouted, turning it between his finger and thumb. Silence ensued as all eyes passed between the coin and the two men's false smiles.

One of the men tried to snatch the coin from William, but he stepped back towards the crowd. Jack, the carpenter, took the coin from William and turned it over and over in his hand. Then the rest of the crowd followed his narrowing eyes, intent on revenge.

William took his chance to head for home with his bag under his arm while all eyes were averted. I have proven their dishonesty, he thought, running faster to make up for the time spent dawdling. I have done good. These men were stealing from others.

The men didn't get away with their deception; they were both beaten and thrown into the muddy river, penniless for their efforts. However, the matter wasn't finished with. William should have known better than to loiter with the crowd, for John's thick belt was waiting for him when he eventually arrived home and this time William's words couldn't numb or escape this certain pain. A sore behind forced William to sleep on his front that night. He felt like the farrier's anvil, singing out all evening with a searing heat that lasted until the following morning.

William had to walk to school even earlier the next day, taking awkward steps with his legs apart to try to ease his pain. There were no spiders to find or birds to look at that day, just careful steps and thoughts of regret as he looked to see if anyone was watching him. He would have to conceal the pain written all over his face from whoever sat beside him at school. If he told one boy his secret, then *all* the rest would soon know. As William began to get used to the awkward strides, he started to compose himself and think about schoolwork.

Latin, he thought. A dead language but alive with the fixed-edged words of law none can escape. Hmm. And so fixed is its verse as well. English is best. Where words can flow like a gentle, swirling stream. Not forced down the weir like water with speed and a gush, but allowed to dance and skip, and sink and rise.

With William's deepening thoughts the pain seemed to ease and he pleasantly drifted downstream in his mind, before hitting a sudden rock to wake him from his daze.

Shocked, William saw a man striding towards him holding a thick piece of wood, but it was worse when he turned to face the other man. Both men were sore losers; they wanted William bruised and battered as well as the return of their double-headed coin. Their clothes were thick with mud from the riverbank and their cuts and bruises from their own beating were still swollen and sore.

The first man sneered at William, his lip curled up with hate. 'You will remember this wood, *boy*! The knots will be stamped onto your skull and the splinters will be shoved up your nails!'

William looked each way at the muddy-faced men, then clenched the leather bag to his chest and stepped backwards. My deed in helping others has already been punished, William thought, retreating fast. Yet these men have a far worse punishment than a belt could bring; their anger injures me already.

'You will bleed now, boy, and bleed long!' the other man said, moments away from his first lunge towards him.

It was a foolish act the men were undertaking. William was only eight and he was the son of a town alderman. The town was wary of strangers, but William hadn't been alone as he'd walked to school that day; all eyes were on him through the slits and gaps in several doors. Suddenly, a blur passed before William's eyes as he watched the street slip awkwardly away before him. At first William thought he had been hit by something, but he soon realised the men hadn't quite made contact with him. The farrier had reached over a water trough to take William by the shoulders and he had lifted him to the side as if he were piecemeal.

Then came the townsfolk and merciless they were – it was broken bones for them this time. The men would never come back and their cries of anguish made everyone nearby cringe. William was still shocked by the scuffle, but as the men were dragged away he looked up to follow the crowd's movements. Dark, piercing eyes were fixed on him from the other side of the street. His father stood there solemn-faced, looking between William and the crowd. At first John had glanced and nodded to the crowd, indicating that the men should be taken out of sight, then he gave another cursory nod for William to be on his way.

School that day seemed to pass slowly for William. His sore behind and thoughts of another beating that was sure to come kept him watching the sun's position. The clouds masking its progress across the sky raised William's anxiety, as whilst the sun was behind them he had no way of telling what time of day it was and how long he had to wait before he would be subject to his father's wrath. On most summer days the sun hid behind the school chapel, indicating that it would soon be time to close their books. All school days come to an end, but being the last to close his books, the last to stand up and the last from the classroom made the day last longer for William with his delaying tactics.

Fingers pointed at William all the way home that day, town gossip and folded arms in doorways accompanying his every step. William was shaking at the prospect of his impending doom. He felt like a lone rabbit, forced out into an open field with hidden foxes whispering amongst themselves, exposing his position.

Oh, how I wish for a speedy wind to close in, rain and all! thought William nastily. For mouths and doors to bang shut and break off gossip's noisy hinges!

That evening William received a further lecture from his father and his belt whipped across a table, making his mother and the rest of the family all jump.

'William,' said John in his deep voice. 'Let today be a good lesson for you. The two strangers have been dealt with like a rat underfoot. Good service you may have been to the local drunkards,' he added more quietly, 'but this is not so for us, my son. As you make errands or walk to school, your way there and back will be like that of a crow. Straight there and straight back! No branches to rest on or crumbs to feed on in between, do you hear well, William?' John reprimanded, his teeth gritted. He turned around and looked out into the back garden to let out a sigh of weakening anger.

Mary was close to tears, but the family couldn't be seen to be involved with brawls and scuffles. They had a position to uphold in the town, so she felt she had no alternative but to agree with her husband and nod her head in assent. Gilbert and Joan also nodded their heads silently; they, too, feared the sound of the belt. William, though, could still feel its burn as a reminder of what was to come.

'Yes, Father,' William asserted quietly. 'My thoughts will be kept to myself from now on.' William let out an inward sigh. He had avoided the belt once more; at least this time, and he had learnt the error of his ways.

The Green Light

The next day was Saturday and it began quite lively. There were no references to the previous day from either William's parents or his siblings. Mary and John hummed to each other and Gilbert was dancing with Joan. William was in deep thought, trying to compose himself from yesterday's lesson and recent beating. After an hour the tension seemed to pass from William's face and he seemed to lift himself up with a fruitful smile.

'Mother,' said William politely. 'May I take Joan to the meadow near Shottery to pick some blackberries? Then afterwards, would you show me how to bake a pudding?'

'Yes, William,' she replied. But seeing John's frown, she added, 'But don't be long. Your father needs you to help in the shop this afternoon.' Mary thought it wise to let William come to terms with his punishment, so she allowed him to have the morning away with Joan.

William sat Joan down on the berry bucket and fought to tie her bonnet around her excited head. Joan loved going out with William. He could make her laugh at the fall of a leaf or a self-made hiccup. She tried to carry the bucket herself, but William ended up carrying both her and the bucket for some of the way, with it banging against his knees. William soon began to whistle a tune to Joan while pushing the leaves away from their faces, and soon they were making their way down the twisted path into the lush countryside and the best blackberrying in the area. With Joan's hands pointing all ways with excitement, William took advantage and tickled her under her arms and on her sides. Joan's laughter echoed around the nearby woods, in turn disturbing a nearby fox eating its fresh kill. The fox scurried away but as it did so, the sound of its escape made William stop to listen further and pull Joan to his side. Something else was moving towards them beyond the distant trees and it sounded like women singing.

William was still erring on the side of caution after the previous day's escapades, so he decided to stand his ground and let the noise come his way. He placed his hand over Joan's mouth and stepped into some tall ferns to the side of the path. The melody skipped around the nearby bushes and trees. It was a bright, sunny morning and as the trees were grouped so close together, they prevented most of the sunlight from passing through them down to the twisted pathway, shielding the light. What light did escape between the leaves made the space beneath them glow green.

Then, as quickly as the fox had retreated, a young lady in her mid teens walked towards William and Joan and stepped into the green sunlight permeating between the leaves for just a moment. Her face turned pale green and she seemed to float along singing a well-rehearsed song from her heart. Her song continued for a moment. Both were oblivious to the other's presence as the women sang sweetly, unaware they were being watched.

With William and Joan remaining so still, the ladies were close to brushing shoulders before they noticed them in the ferns. Both ladies stopped, silently trying to cover their mouths; their secret melody had been discovered. As the ladies took a moment to gather themselves, one of them could be seen clearly beneath the break in the canopy. She appeared to be in her mid teens, but something caught William's attention and he stared back at the green hue on her face. Both sets of eyes were fixed as they stared back at each other. Her next step forward brought the moment to an end as she swayed to the side, into the sunlight, and then the pale green light was gone for good as she took another step into the shadows.

William snapped out of his trance and then lowered his head to smile and bid good day to the two. Both ladies smiled back at William, but the second turned to look more deeply as she passed.

'Come on, Anne, he is too young for us two larks,' the first lady shouted back, running away into the woods and giggling to herself.

'Yes, Elizabeth, and he is too old for her,' Anne replied, referring to his sister as she looked over her shoulder at William as she began to run.

William twisted his head in thought whilst trying to restrain Joan with both hands as she tried to wriggle free and chase after the two girls. Oh, two days and as many lessons learnt, he thought, pushing Joan forward into the green light to test its substance. The first to fly as straight as a crow without stopping and looking for crumbs. The second being to wonder why the green-tinged sunlight was more tempting than the taste of the berries we seek.

* * *

William wasn't the only one left feeling confused after the meeting. Anne, the second young lady, had her own thoughts as she paced up and down in her bedroom. she knelt down to pray beside her bed, while looking through the open window.

'I am sixteen and I feel as fresh as the meadow we ran through today, but my thoughts are of his eyes. He must have only been eight or so, but his eyes had a much older appeal to them. Mother says I must start looking for a man. She meant one a little older, but he was oh … so … and … and … he looked *into* me, not through me and down my bosom like older boys do. The boy had something to him … oh, why did I run away from him? We ran for fear of something we did. We wouldn't have sung out so boldly and bravely had we known of his presence.'

Anne's eyes watered over with regret. She could think of nothing else besides the meeting in the woods and William's smiling face. Just to be friends or ask if he passed by there weekly; but now he is gone, she thought sadly. Gone! Oh, dear Lord, forgive me for my thoughts towards this boy. I have this feeling of warmth inside, and yet at the same time I feel I have both sinned and suffered a great loss. A boy half my age and yet he could grow to double his height one day I am sure. I will dream on. Even if it is so far removed from the reality of my life. It is not as if dreaming is the same as committing murder. I have not sinned as such, but oh, how I wish I could slay years from my age. How I wish it could be so, my Lord. From this bed I share with my sisters we often see the moon. Perhaps it will be that he sees it at the same time as I do … the same source of light seen at the same time. I can do no harm with thoughts. I have not sinned, but his face will be mine till next we meet. I hope that time will come soon, before we reach heaven. Oh Lord, I truly hope that this may be so.

William's father was at an aldermen's meeting that morning and they were having a heated discussion regarding a newcomer who wanted to settle in the town. Strangers were not welcome in many parts, owing to a feeling of mistrust. Pestilence, religious differences or even a fear of taking the town's wealth and chastity from the women could cause heated debate from all concerned.

'Oh, John,' said an elder called Melvin. 'You are like an unstoked fire. Your enthusiasm just waits to be attended to. What of this man? Or would you have us puff like bellows at the problem?'

'An unstoked fire is always ready to burst into flames!' John shouted, banging the table. 'I have fuel at the ready. Don't let my faint glow and passiveness lead you into thinking I am beyond smoke! This man's lies are like a ploughman's crossed furrow, plain for all to see, no matter how much he shuffles his feet in the soil. From point to mull board his deceitful words follow the bent earth, each subsequent word brightening up an already reddened face. I will not support this man in his application. He has come here to burden us. He asks us in innocence, with his hand on his heart and yet his eyes on our purses, of that I am sure.'

'But John,' said Melvin, shaking his head with raised shoulders and hands open in hope. 'He is a young man, willing to work and pay his way like many others around here. He has worked in past weeks, not idling around, and for pittance.'

John prepared to stand to make known he was about to leave, but then shook his head firmly before speaking further. 'The glorious crop of bread grows in the field for all to see, and as it sways gently in the breeze, most can see its potential and its journey to our bellies. But I can see weed amongst this man's good seed. He is only after our charity like the rest. His eager smile soon drops when our backs are turned. His honour is as false as thin ice looks tempting enough to trick a duck!'

'Is this man a known thief, John?' asked the secretary, looking up from his papers. 'What have you found out? I see only a veil of innocence myself.'

'His tepid smile is like a trough of the same,' said John, pulling his coat on. 'His thirst will not be quenched until we are all but dry, our well then drained into his own. I have been told of his previous ways. A friend at Snitterfield says he has emptied many a pocket there. Furthermore, my friends,' he added, turning back from the door, 'with his half-closed eye and smile at my wife, would any of you here trust him in your linen box? Or perhaps weigh your corn when his finger might be on the scale.'

All the men at the table were silent as John glanced at each face in turn. Just a few papers were shuffled between hands to break the monotony of an otherwise frozen scene. The stranger had winked his last that day. Other aldermen feared their wives' good looks had been noticed by him. John had his way that time, but influence was determined by wealth generated from crops and produce. Should these fail, the wealthy would also suffer and with it their power. Several aldermen had mortgages and rents to pay as well.

William and Joan had just about finished picking blackberries for the day. Joan was holding the bucket and William was sucking his bleeding thumb when he touched Joan's nose with a berry. 'Sometimes, Joan, we have to give up our own blood in order to taste that of the blackberries.' She giggled to herself then stifled a yawn.

'I see it is time you should be in bed,' he said. 'We will go home now, but on the way we will pretend to be bride and groom.'

Joan laughed as William crouched to jump from the twines, then lifted her and twirled her around. William spoke with a deep voice like his father's as he pushed his way through the greenery with big strides. 'Hold my arm, my betrothed. I will protect you from the nettles. They may make ill of your legs and cause you to hop down the aisle.'

'Will you marry one day, William?' she asked. 'And have a shop like Father?'

'My little bride to be,' he said in his now normal voice, 'not all children grow up to be glovers or makers of the finest of jams even. A whittawer brings with him the foulest of smells, but with jam it is exactly the opposite. I think I will mix foul with sweet in the future. But marriage is for time to decide. Perhaps it may be foul or sweet also. My mind, though, is on jam for the future. Working leather or carrying wool are trades best avoided, unless you have either leather fingertips or the legs of an ox. However, my sweet sister, these things are far from my mind now and should be even farther from yours. Let me lift you on my back and let us be gone before the wasps steal our fruit.'

William helped Joan onto his back, tied her shawl around his neck and then fastened the bucket on the end, to leave it swinging under his chin and his hands free to hold her legs.

After running through the ferns and splashing in the edge of a stream, William eventually made it back home again. His partner aloft made William feel as if he had been carrying a young bullock on his back – Joan was in a deep sleep as usual.

John was sat down in the parlour drinking milk, drumming his fingers impatiently on the table. Without warning, he spoke sternly with his chin tucked towards his chest.

'Helping in the shop is more important than doing women's work which will soften your hands. You have work to catch up on now in the back room.'

'Oh, John, we have to eat as well as sell,' his mother said before William could reply.

'He will have to earn good money in the future,' said John firmly, standing up and holding his lapels as if he were at a meeting. 'Berries alone will not support a wife, even in the only month of the year they ripen. You won't earn a crust picking berries all day.'

'But John,' said Mary with her hand on William's shoulder, 'Not many even consider picking berries. But there are more hands in the air demanding to be fed than gathering birds when the pudding is ready to eat!'

Mary stepped towards John a little way before whispering into his ear. 'I take it you have had a testing day? William has taken his punishment well, my love. Perhaps we should put it behind us now.'

John grumbled to himself before turning and waving William away. He didn't see things the same as Mary. William began his usual chores around the shop and John followed him through to the shop to discuss the subject further.

'William, my point is this,' said John solemnly. 'As you grow up you will develop blisters and prick your fingers with needles, doing real men's work. Cooking and jesting around are for women, or men with feathery thoughts. The school teaches you a good source of knowledge and from this you can do great sums and run your business properly. Fancy words and play-acting has no future, like a beetle on a leaf in a stream. When the farmer's cow starts to slip on wet cobbles, the only way is down. I hope it will never be you, my son, that's all.'

'Yes, Father,' William answered shyly, 'but at least the beetle may be still upright, waiting for the right moment to step forward.'

'I agree,' John said. 'Even though what you say may be true, there could also be rough rapids or even a waterfall beyond the next bend.'

'We have spoken of this before, Father,' said William quietly, clutching his cap in his hand. 'We must still make light of the situation – life does not revolve around work alone.'

'I agree,' John replied. 'But the performances you gaze at from time to time and the words and dreams they speak of, they are a mask. Look behind the masks. See their soft hands without skill. The tools they have are nothing but imagination. What use are they but to laugh at? Show me a wall built of folly that is made to last, or a … or a town built upon a marsh.'

William nodded to show his understanding, if not his agreement. His 'will' was his strongest asset; after all, it was the first four letters of his name. William's aim was to keep his eyes and ears open and his mouth shut in future, absorbing as much information as possible.

The Catholics

One Saturday afternoon the family gathered together to go out haymaking. They owned a field nearby that had to be cut and the weather was just right. John's brother, Henry, was looking after the shop with his wife, Alice. They had come to stay because Henry had been ill for some time. The hay was to be used to feed their few animals for the winter, so it would be stored in the barn they shared with some other friends in town. The children weren't allowed near the scythe and so all they had to do was turn the grass from the previous day's cut and gather up what had already been turned and dried. The men, meanwhile, continued with the seemingly endless task of cutting down the tall grass. There were other helpers who received just a lump of bread and a measure of ale for their trouble and the day was seen more as enjoyment than hard work and would be enjoyed by all. As Joan was still not quite four, she ended up finding a little niche of her own – a patch of wild raspberries in the hedgerows – and her face showed the telltale signs, for both cheeks were covered in red stains, with hands and legs to match. Gilbert managed to catch several field mice, in between spates of hard graft, much to the chagrin of a watchful kite hovering above. William kept his head down with Mary and got on with the job; they were looking forward to bread and cheese for lunch that day.

'When can we eat, Mother?' asked William, pausing for breath. 'The more they cut, the more we turn. The end is as slow coming as winter takes its time leaving, dragging its feet as it goes.'

'The food will come soon,' she answered, 'when your father has reached the bottom hedge. And so will the milk in winter when the cows eat this hay. Come on, try a little more.'

'But I wish we could stand and watch a great scythe cut it all down for us,' he said, puffing deeply.

'So do I, William,' she said. 'And wash your faces, turn the spit, make new gloves, plough the fields –'

'And find food,' Gilbert interrupted.

'Yes, and find food,' Mary agreed, pausing from her work to wipe her forehead. 'Oh, what a day that would be.'

'Could God do all these things for us?' asked William.

'Well the rain and sun help things grow,' she said. 'They give life, I suppose, and soak the ground for rich and poor alike, so we can wash and drink. God gives us the fields, but it is ours to work and for all of us to be thankful for the food we grow and the animals who feed on it.'

'But why is it such hard work?' William struggled to throw a large pile to the side. 'With the fields and hills beyond, God has certainly given us plenty to do and think about.'

'If our lives were too easy, we could all end up big like Mrs May, the baker, tasting her wares each day. Or Mr Cartwright, the butcher, who hacks and cuts with few errands to run,' Mary said.

'Yuck!' William exclaimed. 'I would sooner be here and have backache than touch the smelly blood and those intestine things.'

'Yes, let us carry on. We must if we are ever to get finished here.' She paused to look at William who was staring at something behind her.

Mary turned to see what it was and cried out with shock. Joan had wandered back and her face was smeared with red all over from the raspberry juice. 'Oh Joan,' Mary closed her eyes with sorrow. 'I will have to scrub you near raw to get rid of those stains.'

'Mother,' said William with a mischievous smile, 'Joan has been listening close by. She may have been to see the Cartwrights. They could be real blood stains,' he added with his overactive imagination.

Mary screwed up her face in disdain, relaxing her grimace as Gilbert pushed past, chasing a mouse.

'Gilbert, let them live!' scowled Mary. 'Do your work like the rest. How would you like your head stamped upon?'

'Sorry, Mother,' he shouted back. 'But they come in the house and ... and there are even some in our room.'

'And ... and work,' she answered, pointing to the fork and hay.

Lunchtime came soon after this, so John joined the family along with two older boys who were helping them.

'I am ready for this,' said John, wiping the sweat from his brow. 'But it looks like our Joan has started already, or is her nose bleeding?'

'No, just the berries,' Mary answered. 'Good job they weren't poisonous – what a day that would have turned out to be.'

John lay down before her. 'Give me a kiss. Never mind how you look, my love.'

John got his reward, but he also got a thorn stuck in his finger for his trouble as he leant towards her. This brought laughter from the other boys watching, but they soon stopped when John turned and spoke.

'Oh Mary, it's a pity we have no bread or cheese left for the lads here,' he said, teasing.

'Ow, mister, we are sorry, too,' they mumbled.

'My wit is as sharp as any thorn.' He laughed and handed them some food. 'It'll take a lot to catch me out. Look sharp and eat it.'

Everyone had nearly finished eating, when they heard a man shouting as he ran towards them down the field. John stood up because it sounded like official business and he was still a leading town alderman.

'Mr Shakespeare,' the man puffed, 'I must speak with you. It is an urgent matter I bring to you.'

John walked away from the others where they could speak in relative privacy behind the hay cart. Here, they whispered to each other for some time. All the time the messenger was pointing sharply. The news seemed to have a bad air to it, judging by their stance. When John walked back over to the others, he had a composed look about him, albeit his face was serious.

Mary could tell by his swift advance that he was troubled and that there was some urgency to the matter, so she stood up to face him. 'What is it? Is it the shop? Your brother? Are we at war?'

'No, Mary,' he said with concern, 'but it's serious all the same. A man has been found dead in the woods. It does not sound like an accident, so I must go now. Take the children home with you and the other lads. He was found just over yonder hill.' John pointed into the distance and nodded his head in the general direction she was supposed to be looking.

'So close, John,' Mary said, clutching her arms to her chest.

'Yes,' he agreed, 'and his body not quite set.'

All present climbed onto the partly laden cart and set off for home, collecting the scythes with haste as they went. William had whipped the horse and they were soon approaching the gate.

John ran ahead to get changed. This was to be an official inquiry, so he had to look the part in his official capacity.

When the family arrived back at home, they instructed the helpers to take the hay and tools to the barn. Then they locked the back door and waited for news. Throughout the rest of the day, sergeants and other armed men galloped past the house without warning. Windows were closed and doors were locked. Each time they clattered past, Mary worried a little more, wondering what trouble had come to the district. Henry and Alice were doing their best to keep up with the gossip, asking each passer-by who dared be out for any news. Mary couldn't look outside for worry. She could feel the air blackening like an ill mood. The younger children didn't seem to mind, but even William had his head cast down as he tried to carve his name on a smooth piece of leather offcut to keep himself occupied.

Henry limped into the house from time to time to give Mary an update from passing travellers and so far three more bodies had been found. Other rumours were also heard, from Spanish spies to travellers and witches; there was even one of a dishonoured monk attacking folk.

When John eventually came home later that evening, the problem had been resolved and his official overseeing duties had been attended to.

'Oh, John,' cried Mary, clinging to his neck with relief, 'I thought you had been cut down with the other four.'

'Four?' he asked, looking over Mary's shoulder to Henry and Alice. 'There have been two deaths, my love, only two. The culprits are being hunted down as we speak.'

'Two is worse than one, though,' she said, looking up. 'What has been happening?'

'Let us put the children to bed first, eh,' he said, his eyebrows raised enquiringly. 'Then I will tell you of the day's happenings. Do not worry yourself, Mary.'

The children were soon in bed after a rushed supper. But Mary simply had to know what had happened. It was still daylight outside when she put them to bed early and they were quite noisy for some time before drifting off to sleep. Tidying away was rushed as well, but all eyes were on John as he finished his last sup of ale. When the house seemed quiet, John nodded to Henry to peep outside and see if any ears were listening, for what he had to say was to be hushed. This again brought fear to Mary's face. After John and Henry had finished checking, they returned to the fireside and John waved the others to join them, throwing a couple of wet logs on the fire as he did so, causing a spit or two.

'I will say this to you all as family,' he whispered loudly. 'But not a single word must be spoken outside of this room – ever. Do you hear?'

They all huddled together as John took in a deep breath, ready to tell them of his findings. 'The men were Catholic,' he said, watching their faces fall. 'Those involved have been cut down like weeds and their deaths will not be investigated further.'

Only the whistling logs could be heard after John had spoken; their stares were like those of empty corpses.

'There has been a hunt organised locally,' he added. 'I knew nothing of it myself. It was from a higher office, but not the queen's. They say officials have been verifying stories of secret worship locally. The dead men had all the usual signs on their personage, right down to the last detailed trinkets.'

'Who were they?' Henry whispered.

'Brooks they called them, two brothers,' John answered. 'Their family, as large as it was, is now gone.'

'Are they hunting them *all* down?' asked Mary in a loud whisper. 'They have one who can barely walk and one still on the breast!'

John didn't answer. He bit his lip and raised his eyebrows to confirm her suspicion.

'They were only young lads,' said Alice sadly. 'We knew them both. They are our … were our neighbours. They lived near to the church.'

'Yes, I know,' said John. 'They will be asking further questions and, if necessary; searching further houses. It's the priest they seek the most, do you hear?'

'Oh, we must hurry home,' Alice whispered, with slight defeat and wary glances towards Henry.

Henry put his hand up to indicate that she should calm down before glancing at the others for further reaction.

'Why now, John?' Mary asked, clenching her teeth with hatred. Her hands involuntarily reached for her brooch for something to do and the pin became embedded in her palm. 'I would like to shake hands with their God – with dung in both palms!' she hissed.

'Oh Mary,' John sighed. 'I know you feel for the children, but we are helpless in this matter. Do not speak in this way, my love.'

Alice and Mary leaned against each other, biting their lips to try to stem back the tears they felt rising to the surface as any mother would.

'We must all keep our heads down,' said John with a sly look. 'We must keep our eyes and ears to the ground and keep our tempers checked. St George cannot slay a painted dragon on some wafting flag;

it has to be faced square on. It is right that we should have fighting spirit, but in mind only. Family life should not be risked by showing one's faith; it will follow you anyway as you pray each day. It will keep you alive and it will guide you so that you may do what is right. The time is wrong to fight. It would only end up with a witch-hunt, with innocent lives being lost. So just bide your time and pray. This country's religion is nothing but a plumb bob, swinging one way before stopping and returning the other. But if you know of secret worship, whoever they are, you should tell them to hide their weapons of faith.'

'We will, John, we will,' Henry answered quietly before taking his leave.

Alice had relaxed a little, so she and Mary nodded their heads in agreement and held each other's shoulders to calm themselves further.

'Before you go, Henry,' John rubbed his knees with his palms as he stood up, 'take heed of two things our father said years ago. A clever grouse watches the arrows pass it by. It will never check to see from where they were aimed. If it did, its position would be compromised towards the hunter's eye!'

'Yes, I remember it now!' exclaimed Henry. 'But what was the other word of wisdom?'

'A good hunter keeps his eye next to the arrow's flight, but if he sees the point, his blood is soon in sight.'

'Yes, I see the wisdom of his ways. We will ignore our minds and listen to our hearts only,' Henry said.

The meeting ended that day without any further reference to the murders or religion, but it lay ill on all minds. With a sense of normality returning and a final swig of still ale, they raised their voices to chat for a short time. Things like this would happen from time to time to disrupt the balance of their lives, but diplomacy and careful thought would often save many lives. A hasty move would only bring about a sudden end. Cornered prey has to fight as bitterly as their attackers, but often it is better to gather strength and escape to live another day – and a more pleasing one, accepting all faiths and not just one.

Town Life

William was now ten and one day he was leaning against a neighbour's doorway waiting for his mother, who was inside collecting a measure of milk. Richard had just been born and Mary was inside exchanging gossip. On the other side of the road the local tavern was attracting more interest than it usually did on a Saturday. The reason for this was a travelling acrobat (some said madman), who had arrived on his yearly visit to the town. His outfit was probably a cast-off from some royal acquaintance. It was faded blue with plum-coloured edging and it was well soiled. It had been professionally tailored and looked to have been sewn together by a seamstress of great skill. At first glance he looked like a normal jester, but his faded outfit reflected his equally worn and pale-looking face. He was a thickset man, who looked capable of lifting several sacks at a time. Those who laughed at him did so from his own entertainment, rather than to ridicule, and he looked more than capable of throwing a would-be heckler over a wall.

William's thoughts were not confined to his act; they were focused on his many followers exchanging looks of amazement. Their heads moved up and down with each jump or quick turn. The acrobat must indeed be mad, William thought. His cartwheels are awkward and clumsy, but his eyes are only on the feeble reward from the tavern owner. The audience come to see his jumps and dance, but not his mind, and the tavern owner sees his pockets swell, but cares not for the limited future of the acrobat. His jumps astound all, but I see the holes in his shoes as his hands touch the earth. There is more to this man. Like lifting a well-trodden stone, there is a different louse or worm under each. To look under a man's shoes, or even at the contents of his larder, will show how he and his family really live. Perhaps he has no family ... I doubt if he would. They would have to follow him from village to village and from town to town, hiding behind the bobbing heads of the crowd, to distance themselves from what he actually was. Their heads would have to lift up and down like expectant pigs, never knowing if the hands that fed them would soon be revealing a knife.

Ale tastes foul though, the language is foul that it brews, and so are the stains from the foul men who pee against the doors and walls of the town. Perhaps its effect on their minds is the same as the acrobat's. I wonder – does it also make them mad for a time? His smile is false, but he is a man I would not trust as easily as the crowds follow his twisting body. I would follow his hands for sure if he came to our shop. I would not turn my back on him for a moment's breath, for he would walk in hungry and wobble out pregnant!

Why does Mother take so much time with the milk? I can hear who has died, who has a strong son and who has daughters with looks that can be likened to the queen. Mother replies with our own family merits. Oh, my face reddens with her words. I would rather watch the madman than Mother's contrived praise. The neighbours will think I am the next for knighthood, Joan and Anne to be princesses, Gilbert a mercenary wolf hunter and as for Richard ... well, he could be the alchemist to turn horse droppings into food again, making twice as much as he started with. How did Mother know he would not be another girl? Mother said, 'I felt a boy.' How could she know this?

Oh success! Milk at last. Perhaps my face should mask my feelings that Mother had counted it by the drop. I will smile, to conceal my real feelings. Why, Mother has that look on her face as if bearing news of a royal pardon. Who this time have the town's stones aimed at? Who will bear fruit from the seeding gossip on Mother's face?

'Come along quickly now, William.' Mary tugged him by the shoulder, trying to make up for lost time. 'You have work to do with Father next. You should have been thinking of that instead of standing there biting your nails.'

'Hmm ... yes, Mother.' William walked quickly to catch up with her. 'The madman had holes in his shoes,' he observed, changing the subject.

'Keep away from his sort,' she said, turning back to face him. 'Like soaking leather, leave it to soak away from you. The smell will seep among your clothes and come back to bite your nose before you know it!' Mary smiled then pinched William's nose and hurried away. She had been gossiping for too long.

William laughed, but he turned once more to glance at the madman and wipe his nose before following her.

When they arrived back at Henley Street, John was concentrating on some fine stitching while the other children chased a large stag beetle around the kitchen. Most Saturday afternoons the family would do the chores around the house and help Father with the shop. The mood was often light-hearted and frivolous, but always turned serious when customers were present. This particular Saturday turned into a day of confinement, for a sudden heavy rain storm had seen off all passers-by, so the children had to amuse themselves indoors.

A short time later when Mary was drafting some accounts for John, William looked over her shoulder to watch her quill stroke the paper. He followed each swirl and cross she made as the quill glided over the sheet of paper.

'Mother, how do you know what to write? Do you write as you first think?'

'Ha, ha, no, William,' she said, smiling. 'Paper is expensive. You must think clearly first, then write down what your thoughts have agreed upon. To do otherwise, well, it would be like wading through hawthorne lips first. Always think, William, always think about where your pen is poised before putting your thoughts into words. Writing should be compared to your target practice at the public butt[1], you know. We must have a clear sight of the target before we let loose our inked-up arrows of intent.'

'But there must be some construction to your aim, Mother?' he asked with a frown. 'You must surely have serious or lighter matters in mind, depending upon to whom you are writing?'

'Yes, I have,' she said, sitting back, 'and many more besides. The mind has more words to connect a beginning to an end than a bird has grass available to make its nest. They must have purpose, of course, and sentences usually follow a common form, but if the same word is placed differently, it can take on a whole new meaning, depending on the tone of our speech. You should not, of course, write as a common chicken – write as a colourful pheasant. Pick your quill accordingly. If you want to write as a chicken, observe its simple life and its actions. Its daily routine of pecking within its limited confines is easy to follow from where we stand. However, if I want to write with adventure in mind, or I have to help Father with a summary, I think of all the free meadows and woodlands the pheasant has under its wing. Each day is a new story, offering a new danger or a hidden nesting site. This is my choice,

---

[1] The 'butt' is where public archery takes place.

William.' Mary made one final comment before turning back to her work. 'Listen to your father speak. He has sharper words than most can think, and I can write them down. You will be able to do that one day if you listen closely at school and observe your surroundings.'

William nodded silently, then walked towards the front window and looked outside into the muddy street. A colourful sentence from the pheasant, he thought, but if I wrote on a day like this, it would have to reflect the rain and its dullness. Will the rain wash the foul words from the air of the drunkards? It will certainly dampen the feathers of both chicken and pheasant, both fowl and not foul. My words have a slight colour to them, I think, but by wing they cannot fly far today. Tomorrow, they may increase to dribbles, then streams, then rivers! Oh, the rain is such a mighty source of cleansing; if the Lord had a broom, I would wish it to sweep clean in all directions. The rain has no taste or smell – the well also, even the river – nothing. How can something that is so big, and which is a giver of so much life, be without these riches? The opposite, though, is as plain to see as it is piled high. Filthy black rats run amongst the muck heap and in ditches. This must be the opposite of water. Thoughts on life itself have no smell, and yet death has made up for its lacking! Even my mind can conjure the stench. If that is so, could I bring my mind to smell only water when I am surrounded by filth? I will try sometime, but not today.

'Look outside,' shouted William, pointing. 'A fish is leaping up from a puddle. Oh, but a much greater jump is needed to reach the river I tell you.'

'A fish,' said mother with a great frown. 'William, you will be telling us you have seen a duck wearing a knitted shawl next.'

'No, Mother!' he exclaimed, 'It is a fish, a moving fish with a shiny back.'

All the family except John joined William at the open window. It was, after all, a strange occurrence to have a fish in the street, splashing on its side with its mouth gaping wide.

'I wonder, William,' Gilbert looked down to his clenched hands with an evil smile, 'do fish like beetles?'

William laughed. 'I think the beetle would cause the fish to choke. It is nearly half its size.'

'Oh, let it be free outside,' said Mary, stepping away. 'Let it take its chances with the fish.'

'But it cannot swim, Mother,' cried Joan.

'Let it try,' said Gilbert, his eyes opening wider with a boy's cruel dare.

'Nor can the fish walk,' said John sternly, looking through from the workshop. 'Set it free outside this instant.' Mary didn't like creatures like this or of similar kind, and John's intervention rose above all the childish taunts.

The beetle was freed and both perished soon afterwards. A passing horse trampled the fish and the beetle was soon drowned beneath a woman's boot. William and Joan consoled each other at the window. The deaths had been so sudden and needless.

'Try not to be sad, Joan,' said William, trying to comfort her. 'The beetle gave you more than the stickleback in this life – at least you played with it for a while.'

'The driver of the cart and the woman with her careless foot,' said Joan, 'they knew nothing of what was beneath.'

'Yes,' William rubbed his chin and placed his other hand on her shoulder, 'but if the peg had come adrift from the cart's wheel, or the woman had a hole in her shoe, they would have noticed more.'

Joan looked up. 'What do you mean?'

'He means this, my rose,' John said, walking towards the window. 'People live in a higher world than fish or beetles. We always look where we are going from the height of our eyes. The fish comes from the safety of the river and the beetle the thicket, but the street is our world and meant for our wheels and feet only. We only look down when we have to. This is why the creatures were ignored – they had the misfortune of being away from the safety of their own kingdoms. Both the dray and the woman could have been stopped, as William suggested. The wheel may have fallen off in the next street and the woman could now be sat drying her soggy feet. But we may all be wrong. Why was the fish in the way in the first place? Or, indeed, why did you put the beetle into the street instead of the garden?' John looked down at William and shook his head before returning to the workshop once more.

'Yes, Father,' William replied after him, 'but I doubt if either would have steered around the two, given the choice. Our daily errands seem far removed from their simple lives.'

'They are, indeed,' John replied, 'but most only discover loose wheels should they fall off, or holes in shoes if it rains. Some, though, check what they have in dry times. These few have the ability to look ahead.'

'The madman today,' William said, 'he was the same. He exposed his true self, by not looking ahead to the soles of his shoes when he did a tumble.'

'What! Did he tread on a fish?' John smiled as he turned away to get back to his work.

'No, Father,' William grinned, 'but the beetle would certainly have tickled his feet.'

John laughed as he picked up his needle again, but he was shaking his head with a great smile. Oh, William, he thought, you see more than a hawk searching for its prey. Many will be wary of your sharp words, my son. Your eyes let nothing pass by without you dissecting it like a hooked beak.

The storm soon passed and with it went thoughts of the muddy street. There was work to be done now.

Celebrations

Soon it would be time to celebrate again. It was the eve of John's birthday and Mary had commissioned the making of a wooden birdcage. Her intention was to obtain a bird for the cage from one of the passing shows that often came to the town, but she was hesitant in case John didn't like it. Mary was smiling and squeezing her hands together as if praying when the cage was delivered. It had taken a whole year to plan and the cage had been made without his knowledge. The carpenter placed the cage down by the fireside and then retreated after payment and a final polish. Mary told the children that she would unveil the cage after supper, so William could now plan what had awakened in his mind when the cage was delivered. He had in mind a treat for his father in the form of a prank, despite the harsh words of the previous day.

John suspected something was up and that perhaps Mary had news of a possible new birth in the family, judging by the expression on her face. When the family lined up ready to reveal his surprise, William was noted for his absence. They thought he was outside relieving himself, but when Mary pulled back the cloak, William could be seen crouched inside the cage with a handmade paper beak over his nose. He suddenly began flapping his elbows about and began whistling a tune he had composed. The tune had thirteen notes cascading up and down the scales, ending with the first note again. After William had finished, he paused as he pretended to recall part of the tune once more, but he kept stopping as if he had forgotten the melody. Those present wanted to assist him and whistle it for him to help remind him, because the tune was so simple, once again demonstrating his wit.

Mary was shocked. She couldn't remember purchasing a singing bird with the cage. John just shook his head with pride. Blisters and sweat would never make him smile and love his son's wit or melody as much as this. William had made another grand entrance. The family entertainer was on his stage once again, albeit a little cramped.

*   *   *

A few weeks later William was making some masks in the garden. They were to be part of a future birthday treat for Gilbert and he was carving with his tongue sticking out, showing deep concentration. The difficulty was that William was using an adze and knife to cut out the hollows from some leftover softwood. Everyone would have to guess who the masks represented on the day.

'I wonder if God used an adze to make the rivers?' he said quietly to himself. 'Some beds are carved deep and straight, rough hewn and with stones cast to the side like shavings piled up at the carpenter's feet. The soil banking is so soft, but its grains lack the shape and hardness of stone. I wonder what glue holds the hard grains together. What a wonder the stony ground is, with soft stuff between, allowing growth to spread with roots below and greenery up top. A road could not be made of soil, nor a field of rock; the ill mix is plain to see, but still some fools try. I have seen many a plough jump when young farmers tap the horse's rump in haste! Rock beds into the soil like an egg snuggles into the safe confines of its nest; one is a wall to the other. Sometimes the cuckoo ravages the smaller nest for her own. The smaller egg cannot yet fly and will now never get the chance, for even if it hits soft earth, it may be trod upon or eaten. And if that weren't enough, the cold would ensure the same fate as the rock, only slower. The strong will always survive, but the weak will always have to put up with second taste and have little or no chance of second helpings.'

William finished mumbling to himself, having heard Mother walking down the garden to see him. Mary had made no secret of her presence and she was humming the tune he had composed for John's birthday that day when he had climbed into the birdcage.

'Who were you talking to, William?' she asked, finishing her tune. 'A flower or hopping bird, perhaps ...'

'No, not quite, Mother.' He lifted his head up from his work. 'It was just rehearsal for the masks I'm making. The characters I want to portray are so different that I find it easier to speak aloud to compose my thoughts.'

'But you have carved facial expressions.' She looked at them more closely. 'Will their faces portray what you have in mind for them to say?'

'Oh, Mother,' he said, trying to sidestep the question, 'the surprise for Gilbert is the masks, but for you and Father it is the character behind them. I cannot tell more.' William turned his head away with a tight-lipped smile and Mary accepted his answer.

'Could you surprise me in the same way?' she asked. 'Without a mask – something just for me?'

William thought for a moment before putting his adze down, then he stood up to face his mother. 'With or without a mask, the surprise should not be a surprise because you are expecting it, but you can have my heart any day you wish it. Once, you told me about a flower calling the bee with its upturned head and you said that I should smile to encourage people to talk to me. You are like a flower to me. Every day you smile, whatever the weather, like a flower smiles, expecting the sun and rain to rest upon its face. In the same way the flower bows to invite a bee to sip its nectar, I notice the scent from your bedtime kiss. It makes me close my eyes and dream of sweet-smelling meadows. Then my heart burns with content as your hand touches my brow.'

'Oh, William,' she said with a fond squeeze, 'let your lucky mother hold you with pride. I could gorge on your prose like a bee on pollen, then with my belly too full I would have to crawl all the way back to the hive.'

John had been listening to the conversation from the back door, ignoring the cries from his needy apprentice in the shop. What charm, what absolute loving charm, he thought. This bee of mine could fly away with her if he were not so old. My feelings on our first encounter were far less than the love I feel now. After we shared the longing look between us, there was nothing more for weeks. But her father kept watching me and my progress from a distance. I felt it, though, him noting my every move. Then there was our first real introduction on Mayday – oh! what smiles were seen that day. Her family were lined up as if it were a wedding, to greet me in person. They knew before me that our union was sealed. How did they know I was the one for her? Her father wanted it as much as I did. He had a smile as big as Mary's. He must have been planning the match for years before he died. His death reminded me of a torn-out dandelion – with one last burst of life, it spreads its seed before sinking to rot. He died knowing we were intended for each other. I am sure it was this that made him pass away with a smile on his face, in the knowledge we were soon to be wed. Parents can see better than younger eyes can, from a great height or distance, even, they can tell from only half a glimpse. And now I can see great things for William in the future. Please let the sun never set from this moment.

'Sir, we have a customer.' The apprentice forced the door open to make John jump.

'Oh, oh, I am there. Let me pass.' John blinked from the sun as he quickly put his hand on the boy's shoulder to pass.

Mary left William to continue with his work, but she did not sing a tune with her retreat. Instead, her heart hummed it silently with her thoughts and accompanying smile.

William continued to live his life without realising the great power of verse he had hidden in his sheath. Verse to slice through minds in an instant was a great weapon indeed, and one which could change many fixed perceptions into a more pleasing order of merit.

The leather dyes were all William had available to colour the masks, but his new-found acting skills would make up for the dull wood. Other members of the family had been invited to the birthday celebration and they were all eager to join in with the fun. News had reached them about his newly acquired gift with words and a line of aunts stood shoulder to shoulder, eagerly awaiting his performance, with the rest of the family perched in odd positions around the room. William's stage was an old rusty-coloured blanket stretched 3 feet high in the corner of the room. It was hung over the clothes horse to give him a changing space and his masks were laid out on a small, jointed table.

'Are you ready to begin, William?' John crossed his arms in fear for his son's exposure to all present.

'Yes, indeed,' he answered in a deep voice, springing out of the corner with his first mask. 'But are you ready to taste my boot?' He swaggered back and forth in front of the fire.

Mary smiled with pride. All eyes were on her eldest, but Gilbert was about to dampen the lively air of expectation.

'Fat Cartwright,' called Gilbert with a smile. But this soon became a frown as Mary's glare at his rudeness caught his attention. 'Oh, Mr Cartwright, the butcher,' he said, in an attempt to make amends.

'Indeed, young man,' said William, through the mask. 'But you will feel the horn of a dead beast should you insult me again.'

Gilbert hid his reddened face and looked at William as he rummaged around for his masks, in an attempt to avoid the glares from his mother or father.

Anne sat quietly at the side of her mother with Richard, the newest member of the Shakespeare family. Anne was often hidden from view. She was a quiet child for most of the time, rarely joining in unless encouraged.

Trying to ease the tension, William quickly donned a large doll's mask, a near copy of Joan's jointed wooden doll. John made the doll for Joan some years ago, but she was still as pretty as the day he gave it to her.

'Who am I?' he asked, bending his knees like a doll, with stiff movements to follow. 'Who am I? Oh, my bones are so stiff, yet I am so young.' He looked straight at Joan and tilted his head from side to side as if it were hinged.

Joan was hiding behind the fall of her hair with shyness. Her smile indicated she knew the answer, but the crowded room kept her silent.

'Could it be Quarmatea, your doll?' Mary whispered, pushing Joan's hair from her eyes. 'She has similar looks.'

Joan nodded her head to agree and the mask was quickly replaced by one of John, with an exaggerated black moustache.

'Let the room be quiet, my flock. Let me hear no whispers to make my crooks flutter as birds do,' he said, pruning his upturned black moustache, which he had now named crooks. The room shook with laughter, but John still had his arms folded, not quite knowing what to say at the likeness William had depicted. William then put on a crown made from old leather offcuts, which invited even more laughter.

'So you wish not to be quiet, but I will continue all the same,' he said, waving his hands to direct his speech as John did. 'My decree is this: as I am the bailiff king, I give notice that the wearing of boots will be forbidden in the town streets.'

'Oh!' uttered the guests, looking between William and John.

'Furthermore, I also decree that in their place, foot gloves should now be worn,' he said, pointing at the glove he had slipped on his foot, 'and these should be purchased from the nobleman Shakespeare.'

The whole room let out an almighty laugh, followed by applause. This time John broke his folded arms to applaud, but now with tears of happiness. When the creaking of the settle and the laughter had waned, William turned to put on one more mask, this time a mystery mask, unfamiliar to most.

'I plant fifty to get a hundred, then again to get two, then plant to get double, then ask more money from you.' William pretended to count money as he paced up and down. This time the room was silent; only whispers were louder than William's footsteps. The ruddy cheeks on the mask and a limp with his gait gave no clear indication of who he was meant to be.

'So you are had by my disguise. But if you do not pay, I will be had also; all will rot!' William finished with his head down, but eyes looking up, hoping someone would guess the character.

'Farmer Race,' called John. 'He doubles up each time. But if we failed to pay more, his price would fall and his produce would rot. Well done, William. Is it he?'

'Yes, Father,' William replied, 'and that is all the masks I had time to make.' The room sighed. 'But fear not, my face is an ever-changing mask. There are some I could copy without such props.'

William quickly turned to the fire; then turned back, imitating a chubby boy. He puffed his cheeks out and batted his eyelids to impersonate Gilbert. Even the way he walked with his hands behind his back was characteristic, not to mention the constant brushing of his hair with his hand. William then took a bow. It was his final act for Gilbert's treat and it was followed by gentle applause.

'Mother,' said Anne, peeping out from behind Mary's apron. 'Our William makes everyone laugh. He uses words like a preacher.'

'What do you mean, my rose?' she answered.

'Everyone listens to him, because his hands help throw out his voice.'

'I haven't noticed this,' said Mary, thinking deeply. 'But I can see how you might compare them. Painting in the air with his hands for the listeners to follow – yes, you may, indeed, be right.'

When the laughter had stopped, John stood to address the room and waited for silence.

'I think William has been well rewarded by your applause,' he looked around the room, 'but let us now turn to Gilbert and the gift we have for him.'

Gilbert stood up shyly, kissed his mother and went to stand by John in front of the fire.

'Here you are, Gilbert. This is for you, but you must share it with your brothers and sisters.' John turned to pick up a sack from the fireside.

With puzzlement and thoughts that no joy could come from a sack as this, Gilbert untied the binding and looked inside. 'Oh, I cannot lift it. What is it, Father?'

John took hold of the sack and pulled out a saddle and bridle. What a treat for the children; they could all ride now. Gilbert's face showed great relief – thoughts of a month's supply of flour and fears of a bag of logs had dissipated.

That evening all the children were chattering like crickets, with one speaking before the other had finished, right up to the moment they fell asleep. Excitement was the cause – tomorrow was to be a day of learning how to ride and how to look after the family pony.

The following day's breakfast was a hurried affair as the children ran about with bread in mouths and their fingers sticky with jam. John gave up trying to make some kind order that morning and he left Mary to it while he retreated to fetch the pony.

The three children were soon in place, but the new saddle was lost underneath with three aloft as John led the pony down the lane. Mary stayed behind with Anne and Richard to prepare food with the relatives. The other children would have their chance to ride next time. The pony didn't seem to mind carrying three of them; he was well fed and loved, so he was unlikely to complain.

Farmer Race let John take the children over to one of his fields, where he had just finished the haymaking on the riverside. Joan was first to try as she was the smallest, but her riding skills would need more time because John had to hold the reins as she trotted. Gilbert, on the other hand, took to his first ride with ease. He was strong for his age so the pony didn't get his own way.

Just as William stepped forward without looking, the pony quickly lifted its tail and let out bulk to make room for feeding time. William was looking the other way at the time, so the first he knew was when he felt a sloppy warmth on his legs.

John laughed. 'You will have to laugh with us, William, even if the cause of it is you smelling like an old boar.'

William turned his lips to partially smile then closed his nose off to demonstrate the awful stench.

Joan wasn't as polite, falling over onto the prickly grass laughing until William started tickling her with revenge for her mirth at his expense.

This didn't stop Gilbert and John though, who howled at him even more. Then, with a serious expression, William strolled down to the river to wash his leggings, but his face softened as his father looked at him closely with a smile.

'If you hadn't smiled at me as you did, Father,' William looked up from his cleaning with a broadening smile, 'I would have been stern-faced for the rest of the day.'

John stepped away from the river's edge to stand by Joan as William set about cleaning himself up, desperately trying not to smile in an attempt to be serious again, especially now William could see the funny side. John and his brother further diffused the situation by splashing water at him.

'Stop, I have no means of defence,' shouted William, shielding his head with both hands. 'You wet me as if I were a bundle of washing, but I know where your pillows are and I promise you an earwig each tonight.'

Joan kept her distance from the water fight, merely laughing loudly as she tried to hold the pony still. John picked Gilbert up and took him in the water with William, but he slipped with the weight and they were soon soaked.

Suddenly, the scene was disturbed as screams could be heard above the splashing sounds as the pony attempted to pull away from Joan's grasp. The sound of splashing and excited voices had made the pony agitated.

'Do not try to hold him! Let go, Joan!' John shouted, but his words were wasted as the pony lifted Joan up and tossed her to the side as quickly as he had just slipped in the water moments beforehand. Before Joan had landed on the grass, John and the brothers were scrambling up from the river towards her.

All hearts raced as they tumbled over the rocks and scrambled up the bank, each trying to lengthen his arms by 20 feet to hold her. As they ran towards Joan, they could see her still, pale face lying partly hidden in the grass with no sign of the pony. John was first on the scene, followed by William, who knelt at great speed by Joan's side. Gilbert looked over his father's shoulder as he shook her. William felt his throat dry up as water tricked from his hair and ran down either cheek like tears as they waited for any sign of movement.

'Joan, Joan,' John said in a high-pitched voice like Mary's. 'Joan, our Joan, wake up.'

William slowly took off his hat and tilted his head each way as he looked down into Joan's face. He was struck with fear that she might not pull through.

'William!' said John, his eyes now wide and his face stricken. 'She cannot be dead so suddenly. She cannot be gone yet, my son, put back your hat.'

'No, Father. There are no stones nearby that she could have landed on, only grass,' he observed, dripping water on her face as he wrung his hat out over her in an attempt to stir her.

The three looked down, speechless and with hope. Each drop from William's hat made a different path down her cheeks and a cold breeze wafted clothing and hair, but there was nothing. They felt numb and none felt the wind's grip or heard its sound as they waited and waited, watching intently for signs of life as the trickle of water slowed and along with it, their hopes.

'Why are you all around me?' Joan spluttered. 'I will not drown on the grass. Where has all this water come from?' She frowned deeply, looking up into the shocked faces that were unable to smile back.

There was no further riding that day, but there had been more than one lesson learned, and none of them would need reminding of it. All the way home, Joan was held close to John's chest and God was thanked for his intervention with each step. The pony followed almost unnoticed, even though he was blameless. The silence was in thanks for Joan's reviving breath as each dwelled in their own thoughts. John felt guilty for his own carelessness in leaving her alone to handle such a large animal, realising just how close a tragic end to the day had been.

William was in deep thought, staring at Joan as she held her father's neck all the way home. So precious are crowns. The kings beneath are nothing without them. They are the same folk as the rest of us.

William was right; the family, as with kings, would not be so complete without its crowning jewel so bright as Joan.

On their arrival at home, John told the rest of the family about the accident and the evening was spent together, Joan receiving many thankful hugs and warm pats on her back. This was followed by an early bed for the children, who whispered beneath the sheets for quite some time. An hour or so later, John sat down, gazing at the nearly burned-out fire. He seemed to be carrying a heavy burden of guilt. He was present in body alone that evening, his thoughts distant as others tended the fire.

Mary came to sit by his side as the fire lessened its glow. 'John, the blame is not yours,' she said. 'We are all safe. Let a lesson be learned by that. It is a warning to all to be more careful, not a judgement on you, my love.'

'But she could have been taken from us by my carelessness. I will not take my eyes away from her again,' he said, staring into the dying embers of the fire. 'Never again!'

Mary turned to throw a couple of logs onto the fire. 'We must, as life insists, carry on whatever the day brings. We still have her and we have learned our lesson. If it were pestilence preying upon our worried minds, then what? She has become part of life's trips and falls we all learn from. We must be thankful that she lies sleeping upstairs and must take comfort from the fact that we may kiss her any time we wish.'

'You are right,' he said, taking her hand. 'The day has ended as complete as it began, but with steps of regret between. I will let them pass. You are right once more.'

Granny Arden

One day the Shakespeare family had travelled up to the Arden farm at Wilmcote to help out with the harvest. William could not help with the rest of the family because he was nursing a sprained shoulder; he could hardly lift his left arm without yelping out in pain. He had slipped down the steep wooden stairs at home the previous day and also had a cut and bruise to his head. William was eleven at the time and whilst he couldn't join the rest of the family, at least he would have the benefit of being looked after by Granny Arden for the day and it was to be a day of great intrigue for him. Granny had overseen the upbringing of a large family; she had been present at many births and deaths and was often looked upon as the one with great wisdom. She had a rounded face and was quite short, and she always wore a fresh bonnet each day, with layer upon layer of wrap-over garments.

From an early age, Granny had observed William's constant frowning and search for answers, so she had a lesson or two in mind to tease into his consciousness as she looked at him up and down.

At first William was a little uncomfortable at being left alone with his grandmother for a whole day and the sounds of spits from under the cooking pot made him jump and then freeze again, as if expecting a sudden burst of fire. Granny had given William the job of turning the spit and basting the joint with his good arm.

'The crack from the fire is only noise, William. The dry groans are from the driest of wood,' she said, trying to calm him a little. 'But it, like many things, can also be construed as a warning, like a falling tree cries out to warn of its creaking death.'

William nodded shyly and looked up into her smiling face. She tilted her head to encourage him to come to stand next to her.

'The crop we reap today is set in rows, Granny,' William said, turning his head to look through the back door. 'And yet half the home field is strewn with bushes, weeds and trees.'

'Yes, it is, William. One has been arranged to suit our needs and the other arranged by God for lesser creatures' needs.'

'What do you mean, Granny?'

'Well, it is like this, William. The setting of all life is just God's way of challenging us. All men and women live from the land, so we take the fruits and seeds we choose, then plant them to suit our needs. If we did not do this, we would have turnips with cabbage, raspberries with barley, apples here, beetroot there and eggs hidden amongst the blackberry spines. They would all ripen on a different day and we would have to harvest them like a wild bird, hopping from bush to ground to tree in search of them.'

'I see now, Granny.' he said, nodding his head. 'Our heads would be up and down all day, picking here and there like a chicken pecks at fallen crumbs. We would have to carry more baskets than our arms could thread; it would make our lives difficult.'

Granny took hold of William's left hand. 'Show me how far you can lift your arm.'

William lifted it about a foot, but then his face contorted against the pain.

'Come here; I will rub some goose fat into your shoulder. Take off your blouse.'

William turned and did as he was bid, revealing the bruising. Granny rubbed the warm goose fat into his shoulder and watched William bite his lip a little to hold in the pain.

'Oh, Granny,' he said, gritting his teeth. 'Has father made you wooden gloves? Oh! it hurts more than the fall itself.'

'You will fall again if you cheek me with that ill-set tongue of yours,' she replied, pushing harder than before. 'The wooden gloves you speak of have good intent!'

'Oh, ow!' he yelped again.

'You will be loose enough in a day or so. Just relax and let me ease the pain. Try to think of something pleasant whilst I do it.'

'Gloves made from mushroom skins and padded with dandelion seeds, but no. I feel they would be stitched together with fish bones!' William sensed he had gone too far, so he lightened the mood with a less challenging suggestion. 'Er, roast chicken, Granny. Yes, the leg from a chicken. Eating this would make me happy.'

'Yes, of course it would, but what about playing with your Gilbert in the street?' Granny was smiling to herself at William's remarks, but she retained her still face of authority.

'Oh, Granny, this will make the pain much worse! Although he is more playful, he is as rough as a bull's hide, with hardened scales of dung on his clothes and painful fingers like a bull's careless horns.'

Granny just smiled and then she began to change the subject to distract him from the pain.

'What questions do you have then for your granny, William? You must have something you would wish to ask, now your mind is clear and we have only the simmering pot and spit for company.'

'I do not have any, Granny,' he said, rubbing his chin. 'Have you something in mind you wish to speak of?'

'You and I always speak of things away from ordinary town gossip,' she said, smiling. 'You cannot have all your questions answered, surely, William. Do you know all there is to know since we last spoke?'

'No, Granny, I think I will never know all. But a thought comes to mind as we speak. What would happen if we did know all? What then? Would we die because of it? Or just before we discover all?'

'Do not think of dying when you are still growing, William. We cannot possibly know everything; otherwise we would be bored, having nothing new to learn,' she replied, tilting her head slightly and turning towards the window. 'For if we did, we would not be here to experience what each day presents us with. I'm sure God has set mortals upon the land in order to find something out, but what that something is ... well; it is a mystery to me. I did not discuss this with your grandfather when he was alive, of course. He had a mind for the workings of the farm and steering what God had bequeathed him. But my mind is free from any landowner's whip and any king or queen's rule. It belongs to me and yours should belong to you, William. You are right to question and right to answer when you feel able, but great wisdom comes from listening and thinking each way. Taking not for granted what people say as truth, but thinking about it first and questioning it. This is true wisdom William. Listen as the seller's tongue wags at you, but before swallowing its belief. Question where their loyalty lies and what they might like you to believe in order for it to be of benefit to them. Think of where their intended meaning has come from, and whose belly it is destined to fill.'

'I can see now, Granny, why Mother is so wise,' he said with a half smile. 'You both preach from a quiet lectern, you think deeply and keep it to yourself, merely observing from the outside. Father sometimes speaks like an angry dog and grandfather Shakespeare grumbles and shouts, but this they wear on the outside like a loud cloak! It is not from within.'

'Well, then it is clear that we do have things to discuss, don't we?' she said, returning his smile whilst pinching his cheek.

'How did you know you would marry Grandfather? Was it by chance or by dreaming of an image of him?'

Granny smiled, then took a ladle, filled two cups with broth, handed one to William and then encouraged him to sit back in his grandfather's chair for a short time. This, of course, was an honour; children were seldom allowed to sit in elders' chairs at the time.

'You do ask the most prying of questions, William. The answer is this: you never know if you will meet someone from a large trading town or a five-door village. It just happens. Our way crosses sticks with others, depending upon the path we walk.'

'I understand some of what you say.' William paused, then added, 'So you could have married anyone, depending on the path you have chosen or a decision you have made?'

'No not quite, William, I said the path we walk. You cannot expect to meet a king on our paths or, indeed, water your cow next to a duke's horse. We meet and marry our own type, on our own level. A fish cannot jump up out of the water to choose a goat for its companion.'

'Ha,' William scoffed. 'But it could jump and kiss its nose ...'

'Oh, be sensible, William. I speak to you as if you are six years older; be mindful of your wisdom's destiny. You speak and act like a young man, so you must prepare yourself for the consequences of your jester's tongue, you know.'

William composed himself to match the impassiveness of granny's face.

'Why do you think God has set us here to discover something, Granny?'

'It should be plain enough to see, William. Look around this room ...' Granny looked up towards the open windows, then glanced around the room from side to side. 'All we have, all we use and all we see here comes from the dirty earth. The soil hides the creatures living below, the rocks we crush for copper and the clay we use to make pots. All this stuff and more is just lying about for God's creatures to find. We have hands to make and mend, but animals have hooves or paws and they live amongst the parts we leave wild. We decide the fate of other, lesser lives and have rules and order they do not have. This melee we are all born amongst improves as we learn the new ways of others. We have new cloth to weave, and weapons and tools to make, but the forest's creatures have only their skins and kin to think of and their next meal.

The secrets of the earth cannot be here alone for the fox to yelp at, the badger to fight or the owl to hoot at; it has been laid down for man to dig up and use. And we have conflicting religions telling us the same but different. God save the King and the Bible this and that ... What book do the birds and deer read from? I wonder. Have you thought of that?'

'You could not preach this in church, Granny,' William said, looking quite shocked. 'We would all be stoned into the Avon if you did.'

'Yes, William, you are right, the laity has always to bow heads and follow the preacher's lead. But the mind can think as it sees right. Remember this: a bowed head does not mean a lowered mind. We are all born to think as free individuals as the wind chatters through trees. But we are not free to blow hither and thither, turning leaves one way then the other; we are fixed until the autumn rest.'

William frowned at this, so granny helped him to tease the answer from his mind.

'The wind blows, so the trees and leaves follow. The preacher blows and ...?' Granny raised her eyebrows to encourage him to think out for himself.

'Oh, yes, Granny, we should nod our heads and let him believe we see his truth,' William sighed. 'You have great wisdom. 'Even when I think I have thought of everything, you show me another gate to the truth and give to me the great meadow beyond to compare it with. I will be mindful of what you have said, and of course what you may not have. I want to discover many new things and these will be more than I can think to speak of. Before a bird is taught how to fly, it must first grow feathers. Chirruping about flying just after it has broken the shell would be a true sign of impatience. When I speak, I will do so as if I am a bird first discovering that it can fly, soaring and twisting, taking great gulps of air and swooping down for its first plunge from its nest!'

'You and your words, William. But remember not to put voice to your thoughts unless with family members. You should keep them to yourself, for not everyone will think the same as you do.'

What pride he invokes in me, Granny thought to herself. What grand conversations we will share some day in the future. I look on him with pride. He is as sharp as an axe needed to cut the hardest oak, but his mind is best sheathed for now. If he were a colt, I wonder who would dare to try to ride him first!'

'Run along now, William. When you reach the others, tell them food is on the way.'

'But my shoulder,' he said with a frown; he had forgotten he had been waving both arms about whilst talking to Granny. 'Look! I cannot feel any pain now, Granny.'

'Yes, William,' she said, beckoning him to flee. 'The pain went some time ago when your mind was elsewhere. You see, the mind can both give and take pain away, you just have to believe it.'

William trotted away to find the rest of the family, rubbing his shoulder in an attempt to locate the pain as he went.

Granny smiled to herself and continued to stir the pot and baste the pork, whilst looking down at the glowing fire.

'Seeing William as bright as a stream's clean pebble makes me wink at death's face and fear nothing of its glare,' she said, sighing happily. 'When my time is done I will go willingly and with pride, for what I leave behind will be a joy and a legacy for all!'

Squirrels

A feeling of envy struck William's imagination one day. A lady friend of Mary's had been into the shop to show off the new hat she was wearing which had been made from the skins and tails of red squirrels. Her son had trapped the squirrels in an area not far from Stratford, specifically to make her a hat. Mary tried the hat on and admired it longingly as she twirled around, stroking it. William had always wanted to make his mother something special, something she would be proud of and be able to show off to the whole street, so this gave him an idea and he resolved to give her one similar. With this in mind, William asked if he could go to the nearby woods to collect some fallen timber for the fire. There were no objections to his suggestion, for the family needed wood as much as food, so he put on his boots and prepared to leave.

His family watched him as he proceeded down the street in the direction of the forest. Requiring no tools for the job, William merely took with him a pole of about 6 feet in length and a bag full of stones, his intention being to knock the squirrels from the trees and then tie them to the pole. It seemed a simple enough task, even though he had never killed so much as a chicken yet. William had wanted to go alone that day, so he'd made the excuse that he didn't want any fallen branches to fall on anyone's head. Both Joan and his brothers wanted to come with him, but there was plenty of work to do at home, so his parents were happy to agree that they should stay behind.

The afternoon started out sunny with dark clouds looming in the distance, but his parents weren't too concerned, for they knew William wouldn't stray too far. The pine forest William had heard about was on the way to Bideford, another town on the Avon farther west of Stratford. As William strode away from the town, the sun warmed his back and his thoughts were only for squirrels and his mother's new hat. The first part of the journey involved walking down the main road from the town and there were lots of passing carts loaded up with stones. Repairs were under way farther down the road, so workmen were labouring hard with barrows and tools scattered around. William soon turned away from the road and walked down a pathway toward an area where he thought he would find the squirrels. It wasn't long before the noise of rattling carts disappeared behind him with the distance he had made. Then he saw what he thought was his first squirrel on the low bough of a tree. William crouched down and took a stone from his bag, then paused to calm his racing heart before stalking towards the tree. With his body leaning back, William let his arm swing back before unleashing the stone with force as he propelled it forward at speed. He missed his target completely and the stone crashed through other branches and headed for some bushes lower down, startling a rat, which just looked up before going about its business. A cry was heard on the stone's impact – a further indication that the stone had been poorly aimed.

'Some blasted fool has just thrown a stone,' a young man shouted from beyond the bushes.

'Oh, let them be, David,' the woman answered.

'That I won't. I will take my stick to whoever it was, the woodland is for gathering wood, not stones.'

This was the task William was supposed to have been doing, but now David's temper was raised, the stone having hit his knuckles. William had already started retreating along the path, but as he turned to run away he saw horses thundering down a lane towards him.

I wonder how many more people there would have been had I made a hole in someone's thatch. Why do so many people seem irate at a poorly aimed stone?

With haste, David ran from the bushes to try to catch William, but he soon slowed when he saw the horses galloping towards him. Katie had also pushed her way through the undergrowth, in an attempt to stop David from chasing after William. As the men on horseback came closer, William slipped into the fields, abandoning his pole as he ran.

They were actually tracking the couple down because they owed money to the local landowner and they had run straight into them. After sighting the men on horseback, David and Katie ran back into the bushes and across the fields towards their cottage. This was a wasted journey, as the horses soon caught up with them just outside the door.

William realised he was safe and emerged from the bushes. God, he thought, was with him once more, so he decided to turn back and see what the group of horsemen were doing. The thick grass he was trudging through was trodden down by rabbit trails, leading towards the now distant shouts which could still be heard. From a gentle hillside overlooking the cottage, William knelt down to listen as one of the men smashed things and banged about in the cottage.

There were four men with horses, but one had a deep red coat, obviously the landowner. This man kept looking up at the dark clouds looming above, but William kept his eyes on the men. He had never witnessed anything like this before. One of the men emerged from the cottage empty-handed, so the landowner signalled to the others to take hold of the couple. Then he slipped from his horse and took a dagger from his waist as he walked towards them.

Katie was held by the men as the landowner cut off her hair. Then he slapped her to the ground. David struggled as she cried, but he could do nothing with a dagger quivering near to his throat. With another burst of hatred, the landowner kicked Katie's side and she curled up in instant agony. She lay still, winded from the blow, so the landowner turned to David and kicked him with his heel. Then he turned to pick up a hand-sized stone and pummelled David's chest with it as he screamed for forgiveness.

Both David and Katie were writhing with pain on the ground, but it didn't end at that. The landowner and his men set about smashing their belongings and tearing their clothes to strips. Following this, they made a bonfire with all their ragged clothes and what was left of their furniture, throwing everything onto the blaze.

William watched silently from a distance, fearing for his own safety, for the men were still not finished with the bloodstained couple. This time the landowner looked as if he was going to strike them with a much larger stone, which he lifted above his head and took aim.

William was only eleven, but could not bear to witness any more horror, so he took three stones from his bag and threw them wildly in anger. The stones were well aimed this time, one of them striking the landowner's horse. Another hit the cottage door and one struck one of the men's backs.

William feared being seen and so just in case he had been, he crawled back down the slope to find a cart track, oblivious to the mud and dirt.

The landowner dropped the stone and stumbled over as his horse reared up in temper. His men dashed forth to help him to his feet, but he pushed them away as he turned to the hillside. The landowner did not want witnesses of any kind, so he looked in all directions for signs of any onlookers before turning back to David and Katie, who lay on the floor whimpering.

Hatred boiled to the surface, taking his mind away from the couple. He was looking for another quarry. The line of the trajectory was now in the landowner's sights as his men pointed across the valley to the slight rise in the landscape.

William had a cold, muddy face and clothes, but he lay still and quiet, planning his next escape and listening for signs of any movement in the undergrowth to indicate they were getting nearer. It was frustrating and frightening, for he couldn't see anything from his position because his head was down, but he could hear the unsettling clatter of hooves, snorts and whips cracking coming his way. With an animal's instinct for survival, William tried to think back in haste to his previous steps. Which way could he run now he was the prey? Where could a horse not go?

Yet again my nose has delved into the business of others, William thought. But my heart told me it was the right thing to do. If I am punished for this act, then let it be so, but I would do the same again, given the chance.

With hooves pounding closer and his heart telling him he should be absent from this place, he stood up and ran for cover. Not for the tall grass this time, but for the gooseberry bushes near the cottage, which looked much safer with their prickly spines. David and Katie watched the boy they had chased, who was now running from men for the same reason they had met: throwing stones.

'Help the lad, David,' Katie cried, sniffling as she felt around her for a stone to launch at them.

'He will be safe,' he said, holding her hand to stop her from aiming at them. 'The boggy land will stop the horses from advancing further. Let us hide until they have gone. We cannot help him now.'

'Help him, you selfish man.' She pushed his arm away and threw a stone just a few feet in vain. 'The lad has saved our skin, but now he runs in fear for his own life.'

David just sat there and watched Katie throw another stone towards the horses, but it was a weak and half-hearted attempt.

William soon weaved his way through the gooseberries and made a dash for a nearby thicket with all the haste his fearful steps could lend him.

The angry landowner was close behind, thrashing through the bushes with his sword. He cursed William as he got nearer to him. 'I will cut your ears off, boy!' he yelled as he charged towards William.

His men followed closely behind, with swords at the ready but not yet drawn. They were paid followers and some had their own children. With quick-thinking initiative running alongside thoughts of desperation, William threw his bag of stones down a slope before taking a weakened cutting through the bushes. Then, with head down, William foiled the hunters with his speed. He stood up to indicate his false intentions and then crawled on hands and feet at great speed in the opposite direction, treading a second trail which would hopefully lead him to safety this time. The men thrashed in the bushes wildly where William had disappeared, but he was resting three fields farther on.

Perhaps it was supposed to be like this in that I would learn what it was like to flee like prey. Had I not chased Gilbert on all fours pretending to be a wolf, would I have been so fortunate this time in my escape? Did God play a hand in this in teaching me how to be swift? Would I be trampled upon now by this man's anger if I hadn't yet learnt to crawl so fast?

Eventually the men decided to give in and retire for the day, encouraged by the fast-approaching black clouds and the fact it was now starting to spit rain. At this point William realised it would be best to make for home, but he decided to wait a short time in case they were waiting for him on the way back, though the rain would soon make him change his mind. William sat down quietly to catch his breath, but after only a few seconds he heard a scratching noise coming from behind him. Thinking it could be a dagger scraping on a tree, his fear increased. He imagined whoever it was saying 'I have found you, boy!' with an evil glint to his eye. But when he found the courage to look, he saw a red squirrel sat there chewing at the fallen nuts from a chestnut tree, scraping them up from the ground with his paws. He watched it going about its business for a while and then he lifted his eyes to the sky in acknowledgement to its freedom.

How much better it looks whilst it is alive than worn on someone's head, he thought. Oh, if only I had thought of this before, perhaps I might not be here now, running from these people. Was my being here by chance or steered by a higher source?

William glanced up to the heavens and then watched the squirrel a little more. It wasn't taking any notice of him and neither was William taking any notice of the rain, which was now getting heavier. Never mind, he thought as his mind turned back to his immediate surroundings. At least I am safe and the clouds will soon pass. I would rather be wet than bruised, or worse, both! I will rest awhile and enjoy the nature around me. I have no fire to warm me now, just the thought of standing in front of one with its pretend glow upon my face. The damp grass and slimy bark is mine to touch. Nature is at my fingertips. No fire to warm me, just thoughts of being at one with nature, which pecks, stings, spins a web or hangs from a tree, burrows, digs or nibbles freely as my new friend the squirrel does ahead. But men, they stab and destroy all they can with hatred and anger.' William glanced at the ground, but then something made him look up to the pouring rain. He seemed to have been in a trance-like state, not hearing or feeling the downpour.

Home! he thought as he looked around for the hunters once more. I think I will take a circling detour to conceal my whereabouts!

William started to make his way around them, keeping well away from the cottage, but what he didn't know was that he was heading south towards the river. The rain was falling quite heavily and William was soon soaked through, squelching with water. The squirrels were far from William's mind now as he thought of a warm, spitting fire and a large bowl of lamb soup.

Gradually he struggled through the undergrowth as he neared the river; a path rarely trodden by townsfolk. The riverside was left to grow wild because the soft bank beyond the bushes was a danger to straying cattle and couldn't be used for grazing. Unknown to William, he had wandered too far, so when he noticed the Avon ahead, he felt elated and thought he was near to home. He turned to his left and pushed at speed through the bushes, but he was wandering towards a muddy bend in the river. To worsen his plight, he ran straight into a thick bed of mature nettles. 'Oh, this is my hell,' he shouted. 'Springtime is here once more and I have the task of collecting fresh nettles for the pot. Being the eldest, it is always I who must bring them. But oh, how they hurt!'

With both hands covering his face, William continued stamping his way through the nettles towards the shimmer of water beyond them. As he pushed his way out of he saw large puddles ahead of him and assumed they were from the constant heavy rain. But they weren't puddles in front of him – it was the shallow mud-covered bank of the river, and he was taking great strides towards it. William still thought he was following the river leading home, so he ran faster towards the tempting puddles. After another half-dozen strides, he was up to his waist in muddy water, but as he began to sink, he realised he was some way out into the middle of the river.

The rain was relentless, but William's main concern was the rising water around his fast-sinking body. In addition, he felt a pull against his stomach from the sideways current of the river, cautioning him not to struggle. It was a frightening warning, like the silent heat from a baker's oven never telling of burned bread. The great force of the river current pulled his body gently, firmly and silently.

William's quick mind had seldom let him down before, but it had never been tested to this extreme and his life had never been hanging in the balance before. There was clump of rushes nearby, so he clutched at them helplessly, though they were partly decayed, and dragged himself forwards towards land. Then with the last reserve of his energy, he twisted his legs whilst on all fours in the mud, dragging himself forward with both hands in a desperate fight to live. As his energy drained so the current pulled him back and checked his brief moment of freedom. Then came his second burst of energy – and it would be his last, as William paddled with haste to reach the side. With a final lunge from an outstretched arm, he took hold of some thick new shoots on the bank and rested for a moment until they started to bend with his weight. William grabbed wildly at a further clump to anchor himself to the safety of the edge. Now, he was wet and muddy, and miles from home, albeit afloat. The rain was still thrashing down around him and the river was rising steadily, so he didn't stop in the water to rest for long.

A warm fire was still at the forefront of William's mind, but the image was beginning to dim as he was weakening fast. All the energy had nearly been drawn from his slender body by this time – another slip like the last one and he would perish. With great caution and through experience of the soft banks of the riverside, William stepped away from the edge of the river and tried to follow its path from a distance as he made his way north, with even more obstacles to conquer before him, his energy weakening as he came across each one. Thick nettles, blackberry twines, wild roses and boggy areas put even more strain on his numb legs. He had to lift each leg in turn to aid his progress. He felt the cold more as his pace slowed, the rain cooling him further still.

The ebbing daylight was the next thing to test his resolve, forcing him to move more slowly over the rough ground. The cold and wet began to take hold of William, who had been weakened for too long. His movements became stiff and his steps feeble and then he stopped, unable to move. William closed his eyes and blinked hard, trying to will his limbs into action, but he was beat and collapsed to the ground.

Stopping and being unable to move seemed to give him a little reserve strength to lift his head in hope at the distant cries that made him listen intently. 'Could it be the peacock from South Farm?' William said with near his last breath as he sank to a kneeling position.

He blinked again and looked towards what seemed to be giant fireflies ahead, accompanying the cries and muffled shouts. Is it the horsemen? he thought. Have they been seeking revenge for all this time? Oh! they can have me for all I care. He tried to shout defiantly, instead emitting silent words. 'You can have me. I will await your sword, you villains,' he whispered.

A sudden clatter of lanterns like opposing swords gave notice that William had been found, twenty or so people having been searching for him late that afternoon. John was some distance away before he reached William as the news came in that he had been found.

'Never give in, son,' John said softly to him as he picked him up in his arms, 'not until the breath before your last!'

The search for William had been a success, but he was cold and lifeless, despite his efforts. William was settled in front of the fire he had been dreaming of before long, but his body was limp and waxy with the cold. Huddled up in front of the fire on a makeshift bed was the nearest William got to seeing the first of the snow, which settled on the ground the next day.

The family adjusted his position and tucked him in as they came to check on him at frequent intervals, but only time would heal his fevered body. John and Mary took it in turns to stay up with him. He had to be kept warm through the night. The family believed strongly in their faith and eventually William was able to sit up a little for short periods. He was still weak, but at least he was now able to eat a little food and build up his strength.

Joan kept him company for a while, chatting to him though not expecting an answer. 'The snow has made the street appear like the river, William. Mother says this winter will be a hard one and that the grass will be hidden for a long time. You like the grass, don't you, William? I wish the snow would melt so we could play outside in the garden.'

William returned a slight smile as he sipped more of his turnip soup and looked beyond her towards the garden. He had strength to eat only, but it was growing with each day.

'Mother laughed at me today,' she said. 'We were walking across the road when I pointed out a melting snowball on a horse's rump. Mother just laughed and laughed. "The melt is from a bird, not snow," she said. But I had to laugh with her. How could it be?'

William tried to laugh, but coughed instead. His stomach heaved with laughter, but his lungs could not comply. William's painful wheezes brought the family to his side, expecting him to expire or vomit. His lungs hurt and a look of pain soon returned to his face. This reaction gave the family a faint hope that he was getting better, because he was now at least smiling, albeit weakly. He had a long way to go before he would be allowed out to play.

A few days later he was starting to get some colour back in his face and he had progressed from lying in bed to sitting in a chair, covered with blankets. His first signs of communication were by means of groans. It was as if his body wouldn't let him waste any energy to speak.

One evening soon after this, John had taken his turn to stay up and had made use of the light from the fire to practise writing a little. Mary had been teaching him late in the evening, so he was using leather offcuts to make swirls and crosses, in a similar way that William had done with the honesty seeds.

William was watching him for quite some time, tracing each dip and stroke in his mind, following the shadow from the quill as he scrawled. After some time William swallowed a little to lubricate his throat and then spoke for the first time. 'Father,' he said quietly.

John looked up from his work with surprise, wondering if he had heard right.

'Father,' he said again, but this time John stopped and quickly knelt by his side. 'As you write with the quill, your strokes should be as graceful as a bird is in flight. Flying to the paper as gently as a turning bird disturbs a wandering dandelion seed. But all I see is a duck's clumsy waddle.'

'Ah! You are well again, my son!' John cast the quill aside with joy. 'You are well, indeed. You notice the pheasant's colourful strokes and in the morning you will taste it!'

John gave William a hug to welcome him back to the world as he prayed silently in reverence for his son's safe return.

After William's recovery he studied the wonders of nature with intent. Squirrels' tails were safe now and envy had been brushed aside with his experience, now no longer important. All else was just a thing of the past. Punishment was harsh for non-payment of goods and rent and he felt sorry for their plight, secretly pleased they'd only had a beating and not ended up dead in some ditch.

Fighting

At 12 years old, William was just like any other boy of his age with regard to scuffles and fights and he was now growing into quite a slender young man. Whilst his brother Gilbert was the same height, he was much stockier in appearance. William avoided fights where he could, often talking his way out of them, though inevitably there were some who could see through William's expressive arm and face gestures and who were set on conflict at whatever cost.

After one particular bruising encounter, William slipped into the house with one hand holding the side of his face. Mary noticed him as he tried to sneak upstairs to hide his wounds. She was sharing conversation at the time, so she waited for a moment to find an excuse to follow him.

'What happened?' Gilbert turned William's head to the side to look. 'Have you met with a bullock along the way? Your face certainly looks as if it might have.'

'Oh, just another encounter with the rough set.' William held his jaw as he spoke. 'It's nothing. I have no wish to fight them, but they mock my walk and long hair.'

'I am younger by two years,' said Gilbert, his teeth clenched as tight as his fists. 'But I can make up for it with a stone in my fist, brother. I will fight for you.'

'No, Gilbert,' he said, smiling at him in an attempt to dismiss his offer gratefully. 'Be an example to Joan and Anne. Ignore them and let them better their fighting skills for war, for our hearts be better placed away from them. They fight as dogs over a maggoty bone – all they can see is the bone, never themselves.'

'No!' said Gilbert loudly. 'I will give them a more poisonous venom than the adder. I will make them bleed like Cartwright's pig last week. They will bathe in it!' Gilbert finished angrily, turning to look at Mary who had opened the door.

'What makes our family speak of making others bleed?' she asked, with an equal glare at both of them as she closed the door. 'Gilbert, William, what it is that you feud over this time?'

'It is my fault,' said William with his eyes cast down. 'I could not take the mocking any longer. They pulled my hair and called me a yellow goat. Gilbert only seeks revenge for my bruises and scuffs, but it was I who was weak. I could not bring myself to walk on and ignore their taunts.'

'Mother, William always takes the bullies' scorn.' Gilbert pointed outside. 'I will not lie down and watch him take it unnecessarily. I can fight as well as they do. They need to see we are more than kid gloves. I want them to feel the fists inside them, like they did to poor William here.'

'William,' she lifted his chin, 'lift your head to follow your destiny, not point your nose down to outline your grave. Look and face me. I am not they. My hands chastise, yes, but they also love you and wipe the tears from your face. Although you did not win the fight, at least you have not sinned. But if you let them throw jest like stones, their pile would cover you for sure. Let them know you will fight if cornered, but avoid the path they prey upon. Let them fight amongst themselves.'

'Mother,' he said tearfully, 'I do not wish to fight. I am not as strong as Gilbert. I know my weakness.'

Mary turned to Gilbert to advise him in a similar way. 'As for wanting to defend one of the family, by the same token I will not have you seeking out trouble. The best way to fight and protect one another is not to be there in the first place. The next is to walk the other way or to step aside and let the assailant fail in his attempted blows. If you must fight, then it must be your last act when the wall is behind you and there is no other way. Let your blood cool to patience before it boils in haste. My mother once told me this verse and I think you should both listen patiently and try to see reason:

> Fighting with conkers, a hard one you chose.
>
> Fighting with fists, you more often bruise.
>
> Fighting with sticks leaves cuts and breaks.
>
> Fighting with words gives ear and heartaches.
>
> Fighting with sword you lose only once –
>
> A burned-out candle with only the sconce.

'If you go out to fight them, Gilbert,' she said, 'you will end up as one of them. Then another will want to fight you to claim the bully's paper crown. Distance yourself and look at what you have and where you are going. We are a family – William excelling with words, Gilbert with strength, Joan and Richard are gifted with their hands and will learn our trade well and our Anne is a rose we must all help to blossom. We have to hold our heads high as a family and see what he or she will bring to the table. Others can fight, but we are as one. Remember, Father was the town bailiff. We have a position in society to uphold.' Mary finished speaking with an equal stare for both, her hands on her hips and a sad, forced smile on her face.

The boys nodded their heads in submission. William's pain was now dissipating as his thoughts turned to the construction of the verse his grandmother had recited. Gilbert, though, was still of the mind to spoil for a fight. Her words had passed through him and were lost through the window. Mary left them to talk further, turning away with a warning glare before she closed the door after her.

'Let us go for a walk in the town,' said Gilbert, turning to look down to the street. 'I need to think more deeply about what Mother has said. We will still have to go about our business whatever she says. We will not be rats hiding behind stones and burrowing in holes.'

'Yes, Gilbert.' William stood up and rubbed his now aching head. 'But let us not steer towards the rapids. Let us find stiller waters. My head feels like there is a dagger embedded deeply in its crown.'

'Do not fear them,' Gilbert whispered. 'I threw a dead pig over a wall last week. It took two men to move it further. You are my brother and my blood. You are as much a part of my life as your boots are a part of your feet.'

William and Gilbert announced their intentions to go for a walk, to which Mary agreed, but Anne and Joan also wanted to join them. Mary thought it would keep them from trouble having the girls with them, but hopes and thoughts are futile when minds are already set as sun-baked mud.

Mary watched them leave, holding hands, through the open shop window. Don't they look a picture, she thought, happiness now spilling to the surface as she looked on with pride. I hope they return without any tears on the canvas. My words instead of oils should keep them good in the frame.

Shortly after they set off, they were confronted by the perpetrator of William's bruise, Melvin Boot. Gilbert had already smelled trouble. His fists had been clenched from two houses back. Anne and Joan were holding hands; they had only talk of mild things to think of and they didn't give a second thought as to why Gilbert was walking in front. William's eyes were preoccupied with his surroundings and this time he walked straight on, not fearing any conflict this time.

There were four boys from the rough set approaching fast and whilst they were four against four, it was not equal in any way, for William's group was at an unfair disadvantage. As the two groups came face-to-face, Gilbert spoke first, but not gently. He intended the waters to ripple.

'The dog has returned to feast again,' he said, enticing a fight. 'But not on tender steak, for a hard bone awaits you this time.'

'On goat meat will that be?' said Melvin calmly, his friends laughing at his taunt. 'We were only talking to your elder sister, William, earlier. She lashed at us.'

'You purvey false talk to all,' said Gilbert as the other boys spread out to intimidate them with their presence. 'You bend someone's ears for a while and then put your boot in them with your snail-crushing hatred.'

'You speak the same as your silent elder sister,' Melvin mocked, now with his fists clenched. 'Hard words with nothing but soft fruit to throw, you will feel Boot again soon, and not the one on the end of my foot.'

Gilbert was poised to hit the boy and lunge at the others, but William put his hand up to hold his arm. 'Gilbert,' said William, stepping forward, 'let me speak to these pitiful few. They should be turning their attentions elsewhere rather than brawling with us here.'

'What has the yellow goat to say now?' said Melvin, still grinning. 'Speak, little girl, while you have the chance.'

William had to restrain Gilbert but he wasn't about to leave it there. 'I am not a fighter,' said William quietly. 'You all know I study and think about life rather than play or fight. However, as I walked with my loving family today, I noticed other dwellings not as happy as ours. Yours, my friend, your house is saddened now as we speak. Your time with us is wasted; it is they who need your fighting spirit now, to lift them out of this mire.'

'You insult my family, you goat,' shouted Melvin, stepping towards William. 'You will feel my anger now and you will taste your own blood!'

William held Gilbert more firmly and carried on speaking as the boy's fist came closer. 'Your door has a red cross upon it; your father is dead, will you be next?' He braced his head for contact and turned his face to the side.

Melvin knew William was speaking the truth; this was the reason he was fighting. His father was dying, so he had been taking his anger out on weaker boys, but now his father was dead. It was over now. Melvin was as weak as the rest – his wrath was without its supporting flame.

Joan came running up to William's side, but her generous offer of support was not needed as Gilbert also relaxed and calmed down. Melvin's anger had been extinguished without further bloodshed. It was finished.

Gilbert, now robbed of his defence, stared with cold will as the boys stepped away in turn, eyes fixed in one position, waiting for the slightest wayward movement. The boys wandered away one by one, with heads held down and hands in their pockets. William looked across at Gilbert.

'You gave me courage to speak my mind by standing firm as a brother should,' said William, resting his hand on his shoulder, 'but do you see now how words, like the beat from a gentle dragonfly's wing, can stop an ignorant boulder in its path?'

Gilbert raised his eyebrows to agree with William, then spoke quietly, staring into nothing. 'Yes, family is like an ox and plough. Together they turn the soil, but when separated, one eats the grass and one rests upon it.'

'What are you talking about?' asked Anne cheerfully.

'Oh, just how lucky we are to have each other,' said William, smiling at both girls.

The children continued on their way, enjoying the quiet afternoon's stroll they had previously intended to take. There was still life to see in the countryside beyond petty fights. Their every stride seemed to lift them as if the whole exercise had been about progressing through change to reach this point where to fight was futile. Even the streets seemed cleaner and the townsfolk happier. A great pressure had been lifted from their minds, but like all cycles in life, the demise of others had been costed into their benefit.

Well, Well

One of the most common duties for the children of the household was bringing water from the well, but sometimes it would take all morning, depending upon what it was for. William had the task on one particular day. It was washday, so a ferry load of buckets had to be brought from the well. With wash morning being well under way, William set off for his sixth journey to the well, which turned out to take the longest. On William's arrival at the well, two apparently drunken men were sprawled out at its head. The men weren't villains, but they appeared to be celebrating something.

'May I pass you my bucket to fill, please?' William asked a dark-haired young man whose eyes appeared to be wandering.

'Eh, lad, 'ave you more ale fer me? I 'ave a new son,' he slurred. 'The birth of a child is cause for celebration.'

'An' fer me,' his bearded companion added, lifting his head from the side of the well, an echo resounding out behind him as he disturbed a loose stone, which fell to its depths.

'No, only water. Would you care for a bucket?' William asked politely.

'Did you hear me twice, boy? My echo, my echo, my echo,' the bearded one added, laughing.

'How does the ale make you feel?' asked William, turning his head to look down, 'You can hardly speak properly and you are unable to stand.'

'Ha, ha, we had you, lad. You thought we were a pair of drunkards,' the bearded one said, jumping up. 'My name is Abel and this is Hayden, my friend.'

William was shocked by the appearance of the two of them, but he smiled as they both stood up to greet him with a handshake. There were other townsfolk nearby, but they only glanced briefly at the men because they were both well-known.

'I thought you were town drunkards,' said William, setting his bucket down to rest. 'I thought for one moment you might throw me down the well.'

'We perform on stage,' said Hayden, kneeling down at William's side. 'Players we are, lad. But what is your name?'

'William,' he answered, looking up at both men.

'So, William, what brings you to our stage today?' asked Abel. 'Have you come to watch us?'

'No, it is washday,' he answered. 'But it has the same sounding, wash and watch, so I will watch more of you.'

'Stand back, William of Stratford,' said Abel, wafting his cape at Hayden, 'and wash our show.'

'Yes, be patient and think of our *well*-being,' said Hayden, building in pun upon pun. 'Your appetite whetted, let us pull you up the shaft of the well to our show.'

William sat down on his upturned bucket to watch the comical pair. They seemed to draw him to watch them as if he were hypnotised.

'This hole, Lord Hayden,' asked Abel, pointing down the well before whispering, 'is this the lair of the dragon?'

'Yes, legend has it so, my servant,' replied Lord Hayden. 'But it has a mighty belly by the look of it. I saw it a moment ago.'

'Yes, my lord,' replied Abel with a finger to his lips in thought. 'What could satisfy an appetite as large as this creature has?'

'Boys, yes, the beast eats boys by the pair!' exclaimed Lord Hayden, shielding his eyes, pretending to look for some.

'Must he have two?' asked Abel, walking around William. 'Are there any other ways to get past him? I fear we will die of thirst if we are not able to feed it something. The dragon may even burn the rope so that all the inhabitants of the town will be thirsty.'

'Yes, my servant, there is a way round it,' said Lord Hayden, shaking his head with concern. 'There is but it is so dangerous, none have survived the look.'

'Oh, Lord, I beg you tell,' Abel asked on one knee, with his hands clasped before him to pray. 'My thirst, it is as dry as blowing leaves.'

'Hmm, I will tell you, but first find me a single boy,' said Lord Hayden, waving his hand in dismissal for Abel to find such a boy. 'A shiny-faced boy who can be trusted deeply and well.'

At this point William remained still, but with a big smile of expectation that he might be sought upon to help.

'You, young man,' Abel bent down to William. 'Will you help us with our plight? I can see your leaves are in need of softening with the empty pail you sit on.'

'I will, but what do you want of me?' asked William as he was being led towards the well by Abel.

'Nothing but help, young man. Step here and look, but keep your head low,' said Lord Hayden as both he and Abel lowered their heads to William's height.

The three crept to the well and paused before Lord Hayden whispered to William, 'My friend, do not fear the beast. He eats pairs only, but you must glance down to give us his position, then we will drop a stone on his head. Not to kill him, just to distract him from our rope awhile; then we will thirst no more.'

William was now taken in by the plot, so he carefully started to peep over the side of the head of the well.

'Farther, William,' said Abel with a wink to Hayden, 'farther, my friend.'

'Yes, farther but quietly,' said Hayden, poised to pounce.

'There is nothing but water and rope,' William whispered loudly. 'The dragon must be sleeping.'

'No, keep quiet and look further,' said Hayden before taking hold of William's side.

'William, the dragon is behind you, oh no!' Abel said out loud.

'Grrr, supper at last,' growled Hayden, gripping William's side before laughing.

William suddenly jumped with fright. 'Oh, oh, help me. Oh, you had me, you fools.' He turned to the smiling faces of the two men before him.

'I was right.' William shook with excitement. 'You did intend to throw me into the well, but with fingers for a dragon's teeth in my side. You have tricked me well, you two.'

All three sat near to the side of the well and laughed, two of them with old tricks in abundance and one with much yet to learn.

'Where have you staged all your plays?' William asked his two new friends.

'Bristol, Nottingham, but London is by far the best and biggest,' answered Hayden, stretching his arms wide to emphasise the size of London.

'Are there many playhouses?' asked William with further excitement. 'What are they like?'

'As tall as the Guild Hall and as round as a river bend,' said Abel, standing up to face William. 'No, no, as round as a great henge, but packed with folk all laughing with the foolery. But you are too young yet, William. We will see how you grow and develop over the years when you learn more.'

'Do you perform often in London?' he asked. 'I mean on platforms or decks to masses of folk?'

'We have many times,' said Hayden, looking to the sky. 'But most times we earn our crust from the innkeepers here and there. There are plenty in London. All you need is a multitude of faces and expressions: serious, witty, happy ...'

Abel continued, 'Then a sad face, a mischievous face, or even a face full of love and radiance.'

'I have practised the same in a mirror,' said William hopefully. 'And I have made masks for my brother.'

'Mirrors and masks, eh?' Hayden rubbed his chin with a glance towards Abel.

'Mirrors and masks,' repeated Abel. 'Yes, my friend, I have an idea for a play, a new play.' He turned around, rubbing his chin further.

'Is it a play I can help with?' asked William, jumping up with excitement.

'Er, no, William,' replied Abel. 'It is for older men and women. You have years to go before you can hear of the plot.'

'William, our new friend,' said Hayden, holding his hand out to say goodbye. 'Thank you for both your time and your ideas. We have to go to prepare our wagon now.'

'Will you be back some day soon?' asked William, rolling his bucket to find the handle.

'Yes, oh yes, William, that we will,' said Abel.

The pair of them waved before rushing away. Their thoughts were sincere because he had given them an idea for a future play, but sadly for William, he was left with his bucket and an excuse to find for his tardiness at the well.

'You see, Abel,' said Hayden, turning to wave again, 'where our ideas come from is down to a matter of chance as to where we happen to be at the time. The boy being there was down to luck and we will all benefit from a little of this in the future. I would say it was what one could call an opportune moment or fate.'

Hayden explained the simplicity of his new idea, briefly drawing his explanation in the air to indicate what would follow. He looked to Abel for his opinion.

'Given us a masterpiece, so he has.'

'Yes,' he replied with raised eyebrows of hope. 'Masks and Mirrors will be our making.'

Every year the two returned to the town to present a show and both men drew William's attention. Although they weren't the best of actors, nor even gave the best of plays, they were the best William had acquainted himself with to date and they stirred his mind, and seeded his imagination even more. Hayden and Abel were like a thin spider's web to London. If thickened and worked on or added to each year, it could one day turn to rope.

Foxed

Sometimes the Shakespeare family fell on hard times, mostly because bad crops affected the spending habits of the town. To help with any shortfall from income, William and Gilbert had to work at nearby farms for wages in the form of a supply of vegetables, an early form of payment in kind. Gilbert was picking peas one week and William had a gruelling time picking turnips, but his efforts were worth it because of the promise of a sackful to take home that day. He was on his own because Joan had gone with her father to purchase some kid skins from a nearby town. William intended to carry the turnips home after work, but he had been sidetracked along the way by something glimmering in the distance. He put the sack down on the dray and shielded the afternoon sun from his eyes, trying to make sense of what he was looking at.

I believe the lake beyond the woods is new, thought William, looking across toward it. Fresh and new, but the rain must have crept there each night without wetting here in order for it to have formed so quickly. This is wonderful. We will be able to fish in its clear waters, if it is still there, mind, for it may vanish as quickly as it appeared. The lake has filled up in only a week of evenings, but its ripples invite me to look closer. I can hear it calling, enticing and luring me to the water's edge.

William climbed on top of a nearby gate to look from a higher point. The daylight will be here for hours yet. I must go and find this new lake, he thought to himself, casting the thought of turnips aside with the time.

The other pickers had dusted themselves down and were heading back to town. William, though, had been drawn away from their retreating line. It took him about an hour to climb to his mystery waters. He had to pass over low farmlands and then climb through thick woodland, at the top of which was just one more obstacle to pass through – masses of wild dog roses – which was not an easy task away from the normal path. When the last of the sharp bushes had been conquered, William climbed up a tree and stood on a low branch to view his lake. The branch dipped with his weight and William leaned the other way to compensate, but his mind was everywhere, looking for the orange white-tipped tails of a fox; slyness had tricked his mind, he thought.

'I have been foxed,' he shouted. 'I have been foxed by this blue foxed-field. Waves, indeed.' William then began to speak quietly to himself as his shoulders relaxed in submission to his loss. 'But not wet; they are merely ripples of wind, stirring up the landscape. Why do I not listen to simple gossip? Gossip that would have saved scuffed boots, torn stockings and cuts. I would rather Father's iron buckle had injured me than have inflicted this upon myself unnecessarily. Linseed! Linseed oil! What a fool I am. I am my own judge and I sentence myself to more cuts on the way home. Never will I be a great hunter. If I ever lead a hunt, I would probably end up chasing a well-used broom or leading my men to follow our own tracks. If I was to lead an army to water its horses for the night, my rank would soon be lower than the lowest of fruit pickers. Laughter from my own ranks would frighten the enemy more so than the Scots. No one must ever know of my mistake. If I dare tell even Joan about my blue foxed-field, my face would turn a similar colour from embarrassment before reddening. My stupidity must pass now. The walk home will be punishment enough. Oh, the turnips! What a fool I have been. What further punishment awaits me now? But bad things usually come in threes – there will always be three punishments. I hope Father's belt is well secured today.'

William shook his head and smiled to himself, then took one more look into the blue field and turned to trudge back through the rose bushes. He had little speed but great haste as he tried to out-stride the springy twines. The way back to the turnip field seemed much quicker than it had in coming. William's eyes were on the field only. His feet, though, had to take chance after chance as they strode out the distance. With eyes focused on both the dray and the sack of turnips, William vaulted the last gate and ran like the wind. His run to victory ended with another hasty jump in mid-air. Then William twisted with the skill of an acrobat, to land in a sitting position. The third punishment stared William in the eye. Unbeknown to him, the farmer had let his bull into the field and it now looked up, having been disturbed by his movements.

'I thought my cut legs and torn clothes were to be the second and third punishment together,' he sighed, sitting down with despair on the dray. 'Either that or the third is to be my father's wrath with the promise of the belt. Oh! how my wounds hurt, but they are not half as bad as those the bull could inflict.'

William sighed and looked around before speaking again. 'The sky is darkening and the sack feels so heavy. I could never outrun the bull with this in my arms.' Glancing back to where he had just come, he realised that the blue foxed-field was on a slope. I should have known that water was flat and saved myself the journey! I wish the bull would look at it and not at me. 'Look away, you beast!' he shouted.

The bull didn't move a muscle, it just stared even more, but William could do no other than stare back at it.

'Third punishment will not be so. I am not ready to take the third punishment in this way just yet.' He looked in all directions to find the shortest route. 'There must be a way to escape. Thankfully, no invading archers trying to aim at me, just a black and sweaty boulder with four legs that can roll any way it wishes and through anything, including me.'

William then found what he thought would be a solution to his problem, but he decided that it might work better if it was helped along with a prayer.

'Dear Lord, I beg so humbly of you, distract this beast away from my tempting hide.'

William took the turnips out of the bag one at a time and then proceeded to throw them over the nearest hedge into the next field. The turnips could certainly outfly the bull, but William hoped to try to outrun it next. It took only a few minutes to empty the sack, then a further five to flex his muscles and summon enough courage for the run. Then, with sack in hand, William made the sign of the cross and then jumped from the dray and ran with great leaps from furrow to furrow. Even a hare would have envied him that day. He made it to safety and undertook the second picking of the day with the turnips, before realising the bull was safely tethered up and that he needn't have gone to all that trouble, delaying him yet again.

'So they come in fours to me. At least I have had my fill of bad tidings today. Tomorrow, I will act with less haste and take an hour to tie my laces.' William shook his head and started walking home with the sack over his shoulder.

The next day the family were sat down to an evening meal, chatting after they had eaten a helping of meat and the turnips William had picked. That morning John had taken the boys down to the public butt, so they had plenty of excitement to discuss.

'Oh, the meat was cooked to perfection. It was as tender as Anne's smile, my love.' John smiled at her and Mary. 'And the turnips were so lovingly picked and prepared ...'

'What about my peas?' spluttered Gilbert while eating.

'And what about the apple pudding, Father?' Joan asked, also with a mouthful of food.

'Yes,' said Anne, 'I also helped.'

'But we haven't tasted any yet, my sweet doves,' John took another sip of ale, 'but it smells as good as your mother's bread.'

The week's takings reflected on John's mood and the amount of food on the table, for a London banker had recently bought thirty leather money bags from the shop. They had just been through a difficult period, but with good fortune such as this, they would have plenty to feed the family for some time to come.

'How was the morning at the butt, John?' Mary asked, handing out a portion of apple pudding. 'Have we a Robin Hood amidst our family?'

'Well, William did get a bull's eye.' John looked around at the smiling faces at the table.

'And what else? Judging by your faces, you have more to tell. Did William hit a goose?' she asked, looking at John and then William.

All at the table started laughing, even William; although the jest was aimed at him.

'Well, my love,' John laughed, tapping the table, 'William did hit the bull's eye, but it was on a target 25 feet or so from the one he was aiming for.'

Mary joined in the laughter having seen that William was also amused. She had to balance things with all the family, so if William hadn't been laughing, she would have merely smiled politely.

'I pulled with great strength and aimed well for the target in question,' he said as everyone laughed even more. 'But I admit my arrow may have had a slight bend in it.' Everyone laughed even harder.

'You may even have used a bow, mistaking it for an arrow, William.' John added.

'Perhaps ants were moving the target as you took aim?' said Gilbert, nudging William. 'Or the wind might have blown your target away and you skilfully followed it.'

William could only smile and let their mirth continue, for his mouth was full and so he couldn't speak to counter his demise. It was rare for

William to be at the blunt end of ridicule, but he let them all have their say good-naturedly.

'The wind couldn't have blown it that far,' said Joan seriously. 'The targets are too heavy.'

'We are only joking, my dear,' said John before taking another sip of ale. 'William has no eye for archery. There will be no legends written about his good aim and skill with the longbow.'

'Who is Robin Hood, Mother?' asked Joan as she tried to cram more food into an already full mouth.

'A famous outlaw from Nottingham,' Mary replied as the laughter died down. 'He robbed from the rich and gave to the poor, and his mouth was always full of food, too.'

Everyone laughed again, but Joan didn't understand the root of the humour. It had gone straight over her head, just like the arrow had missed its target with William.

'Returning to more serious matters, Mary,' said John, hushing all at the table with his hand. 'The banker yesterday, he said something interesting that I have only just remembered.'

'And what was that?' asked Mary, finally sitting down to eat her pudding. 'Did he baffle you with numbers?'

'No, what happened was this. I asked him why he had come all the way to Stratford to buy his leather money bags. He then turned to me and said quite seriously, "Never wrong the fruit, Shakespeare." I have been thinking ever since what he could have meant, but I didn't want to lower the status of my intelligence by asking him at the time. I just nodded my head to agree. The quote had me thinking for some time, I must admit.'

As John finished speaking all heads turned in William's direction.

'What do you think it might mean then, John?' Mary asked, glancing at William for his input as she ate.

'I thought this would be a test for William,' he replied. 'He is the dreamer of the family. What do you think?' John looked straight at William as if he had just found him guilty of a crime.

'Well ... at first ... er ...' he said, once again with a mouthful of food, 'I thought that he meant that we shouldn't kill too many cattle for the bags. We may run out of cattle. But then the cattle are not fruit and we also eat meat from this beast. His education must have depths further than cattle. His meaning had further depth to it.'

'I thought that also,' said John, rubbing his chin. 'But it isn't so, is it? There's something else.'

There was a slight pause as all seated at the table remained silent, waiting for William to speak. He put down his trencher board with both hands and thought some more for a moment.

'I know what he meant now, Father. Never wrong the fruit. It is simple now I taste the fruit we are eating. He meant this: the fruit has seeds and all fruit gives us tasty flesh alongside its seed. All animals, birds and people eat the fruit, but if we chew the seed to nothing, that would be wrong. To throw the core of the apple on the fire will burn the seed and therefore not casting it aside to rot before it dries is another. So by saying that you shouldn't wrong the fruit, he meant you not to destroy the seed, because from the seed trees can grow to give more fruit. The banker came from London. He came here to spread his money, which was his seed. In other words, from him casting his seed in a monetary sense, he meant that business will grow in between.' William stopped eating with his eyebrows raised, waiting for a response.

The family were all open-mouthed, unable to eat their pie and shocked with the simplicity of the answer.

'That certainly makes sense.' John lifted his goblet to finish his drink. 'You can see so much. I was on a different path, in a completely different direction. Even though you are not going to university, you will still do well in the future. You have a different way of looking at things than most folk and some would swap a horse or two for what you have.'

'William?' asked Gilbert, looking across. 'Why do people talk with secret meanings? Why could he not say what you have said, then we would all have known what he was talking about straight away?'

'It is simply this,' said William. 'It is like another language. The banker was a well-educated man with a good income. He talked to Father on a level a London businessman would have understood. He thought he had an equal level of understanding with Father, but it was actually one most townsfolk wouldn't have understood or even remembered. If he had met them, he would have only passed the time of day, just to be polite, but the conversation would have trickled away to nothing. I think the banker will be back. He was telling Father as much by what he was saying; only next time he may come out with something else. You see, they are from different backgrounds. The banker obviously thought Father to be of the same kind, with the same level of thought, that he had been educated with.' William finished with a smile before looking down to pick up the last of his now cold pudding.

'If that is the case, William,' said John, nodding his head and smiling, 'then I hope you will be in the shop when he arrives. If we are unable to understand the next riddle, perhaps you could give him one of yours.'

Grammar School

A memorable day at school for William was of a verbal exchange between the schoolmaster and him during his last term at grammar school. The schoolmaster was called Thomas Jenkins, an academic with a good reputation who had recently joined the school from London. Mr Jenkins was renowned for both his immaculate dress and the success of his students. He could iron the wrinkles from his clothes quite easily, but William was a bumpy cloth he desperately wanted to smooth over to towards his way of thinking. His ploy was not to chastise William, but to beat him with words. He sought a verbal victory, not one of caning.

The rest of the class seemed to sense the conflict. As soon as the first exchange started they kept their heads down pretending to read.

'Today, boys,' said Mr Jenkins, 'we are going to imagine that we are all on one of the queen's galleons out at sea and are planning to capture a sleepy Spanish port. We are just about to slip alongside their moored flagship. What flags must we not fly?' When he had finished speaking, he looked around the room for a show of hands.

William was first to put up his hand, so the rest of the class gave him little competition. The floor was his. 'Our own red cross on a white background, sir,' called William.

'Yes, Shakespeare,' Mr Jenkins said, his nose twitching while looking down, 'but there is one other flag we must not fly and it is one that would cause the Spanish to smash our mast to pieces with cannon fire.'

'Perhaps a paving flag, sir?' suggested William with a cautious smirk. 'A paving flag would certainly have caused our mast to both fall over and smash.'

This comment made the other boys look up again from their work. They could sense the tension building, but they kept glancing at Mr Jenkins and William in turn.

Mr Jenkins held his next words back, but his thoughts turned towards switching the humour and giggling pupils in William's direction. 'Good point, Shakespeare. Instead of raising the skull and crossbones, you suggest a paving slab. The obvious answer is not so, as indeed I had thought.' With this, Mr Jenkins turned around on the spot before speaking further, but his tone of voice was now lowered, to emphasise his authority. 'However, all-knowing lad, could you explain to the class just what a paving flag should be doing on Her Majesty's galleon?'

The class tittered at Mr Jenkins' wit; he had William backed against a corner. He lifted his nose and lightened his voice. 'Are we to suppose our galleon was on a mission to hurl these slabs at them to sink them instead of using cannon fire?' He looked up with a victorious smile to the class.

'Well, sir,' replied William, 'instead of hailing to the skull and crossbones, they were actually pirates in disguise. The paving flag was booty, sir!' William tried not to smile and the other boys followed suit; they knew the schoolmaster had the cane at his disposal.

Mr Jenkins was agitated by William's reply, but he remained calm and nodded his head with a smile, giving him time to think. 'Booty, you say. But what a booty, Shakespeare! A paving flag? These pirates of yours would be well rewarded by the queen I am sure for bringing her stone flags.' Mr Jenkins smiled, thinking he now had William like a cornered prey. But this, like Hampton Court tennis, brought a smile to the class once more, ready for the ball to be hit back square. 'Yes, Shakespeare,' he continued, 'I can see the queen's face now. Her new gold orb and state crown, both lined with chippings of polished flagstone. She would either knight you or have your head before nightfall!' He finished speaking with his arms out, waiting for the applause that was sure to come.

The class gave it, but only in the form of polite laughter, for they knew the reply would be quick.

'The paving flag was indeed booty, sir,' answered William without expression. 'Indeed, it was of the finest quality. It was the base of a statue of the Spanish king we had just stolen from them. They would not dare fire on their own. This was our safe passage to escape the port, sir – a far better flag than all the rest.'

William dared not humiliate his teacher with laughter. He had tomorrow to think of; but closer to his mind was Mr Jenkins' now twitching face. The rest of the class had their heads down hiding their faces in books, but their ears were still with the plot.

Mr Jenkins had lost the exchange, but to steer them away from the loss, he asked William peripheral questions to distract them. 'What would it be like on board a modern galleon then, Shakespeare, compared to our simple lives in Stratford?'

'Well, sir,' William said seriously, 'it would be clean as if Mother were there. I would be sweeping the deck just like she sweeps the house out at home.'

'And what would sweeping the deck be like on board a great vessel?' he asked further, but now with a more serious expression.

'Oh, much different from Mother's easy task of sweeping the flags, sir,' William said with hidden reference to his previous victory. 'As one swept up dirt from the deck, the sway of the vessel would make it roll away. It would be a constant worry for me, sir, chasing it about the boards. I would wish for a storm.'

'Indeed you would, boy, indeed,' said Mr Jenkins quietly, but now biting his lip.

Williams reference to "easy, and hinting of victory" had been noted, so Mr Jenkins turned to walk closer to William, ready to emphasise his authority. The class feared each step he took and they could see the shadow of his stick following on the wall behind; in their eyes it looked like a great sail!

Oh, I have been too cutting with my remarks, William thought. Once again I have chosen the easy path of winning today, but tomorrow will be a loss; hard work with sore legs I now fear.

'Sir, one more point if I may?' he spoke out, in an attempt to deflect the hurt from Mr Jenkins' eyes.

'What further insult do you have?' Mr Jenkins asked with frustration in his voice. 'What other words do you have in your repertoire? Words that make a cockfight seem as pleasant as the down we stuff our pillows with.'

'My thoughts now are with a serious aim. I must confess my ignorance, sir,' William said, with his eyes gradually lowering in order to look weak. 'I am not at a level as great as yours. Forgive my foolish words. My knowledge of galleons is none such as yours, sir. I have only seen small boats before.' William now spoke quietly, with his head held down in shame. Mr Jenkins was only steps away, so he humbled himself further. 'The only part of a galleon I am familiar with is the plank, sir, for I fear that my first time on board would soon see me walking it. My words to the captain, if the same as here in class, would not return me any great favours – the only benefit being to learn how to swim, sir. That I would have to if I was to survive.'

This act was in the face of a mighty armada. All humiliation had to be put aside now; the other boys prodding his sides later would be a pleasure compared to what he was experiencing now. William braced himself for a blasting cannon ball and thoughts of an area of caned cloth he might soon be rubbing. Mr Jenkins still had his cane behind him, but as he walked nearer, William's defeatist words had snubbed its fuse.

The victorious Mr Jenkins leaned forward to a point where he was nearly touching noses with William, with both hands resting on the cane. 'Yes, you are right,' he whispered. 'With your retreating words, you lose, like you would when walking the plank. Yet your words seem to win. You turn near insult into your own gain. How do you do this? You are not like the rest. Your eyes tell of knowing more from your twisted words. You have much to learn but I, too, must learn from you, boy. My stick nearly had you then. But getting back to what we were talking about, we have smaller ships than the Spanish.' He stopped whispering, raised his voice and turned towards the class. 'We know, though! Inside, we know we can always beat them. We have confidence. That is it, isn't it, Shakespeare? You know, don't you?'

William didn't answer him; he just lowered his eyes and shuffled the papers about in front of him. He wasn't about to admit he could win a war of words and so he accepted defeat rather than experience Mr Jenkins' wrath and a sore behind.

Mr Jenkins' stomach was tensed from nearly losing his temper. His guts were digesting the verbal menu he had just tasted. With the boys in the class not hearing the whispering, they were in awe at the schoolmaster's explosion and at William's now lowered head.

William was silent. He had avoided the cane and had learned just how far to stretch his words. Not all schoolmasters would have tolerated him, or could have seen further into his eyes.

The Passing of a Rose

One particular day in 1579 was a morning William remembered well. The day began with an awkward feeling in the air. Something felt wrong that he could not place. The normal sounds he was used to seemed almost muffled but he could clearly hear sighs and groans coming from upstairs. He was recovering from some kind of fever and dizziness at the time but his senses were able to cut through the usual morning sounds that normally ran through the house. Despite his dizzy feelings and lack of enthusiasm for the day ahead, something made him turn to look upstairs. He heard his mother whimpering and so started to venture upstairs.

Mary's head was buried in her pillow as she lay on the bed face down with John's hand resting upon her weakened shoulder. Anne had passed away in the night. Joan had woken her mother after realising her sister was colder than stone. Mary had lost her first two children, so loss wasn't something new to her, but this time she had all her children to explain this to. It was unfortunate but not unusual at the time to have a child as old as eight pass away without good reason.

Tears came swiftly to all the family, but life in the Shakespeare household had to go on and they still had to make a living in order to survive. Bread still had to be worked for and tomorrow's chores would still have to be taken care of. This tragic day would soon fade away, leaving them with happy memories of Anne's short life. William was particularly affected by her passing. He loved both his sisters dearly and he felt he had been robbed cruelly.

After a short time John came downstairs with a tight-lipped expression and his cap clenched in his hand. He looked at William and shook his head slightly from side to side. He didn't speak straight away. He just stood still, listening to Mary's whimpers and the other children's shocked exchanges.

'It was not our wish for tragedy to strike today,' said John solemnly. 'But we must rest our sad faces and allow life to continue as before. None of us knows when our souls will be called by God, or even why, but we must not blame him or each other. What has happened has now passed and we are powerless to do anything about it. Reasoning or debate will not bring warmth back to her body. We have hard lessons to learn sometimes, but with our Anne we will share the loss together. What would heaven be like with no babies or children? We must hold on to the fact that we had some good times together and we have been left with some loving memories. A changing wind may knock a nest from a tree and the eggs from within it, but it is not for us to blame God or challenge His direction in our minds like a court.'

William was having none of it. He looked at his father with restrained anger for defending God, thinking he had indicated that it might be acceptable to have Anne taken away from them like this. He turned away from his father then cut away his polite family reins and let his anger gallop loose. We have all been tricked by God, he thought. There was no wind in her room last night; this nest he speaks of was lined with daggers. Huh! this bladed nest is little enough compensation for the bough of deceit upon which it rests! Called by God? I do not believe that is true. One of our innocent family roses has been taken away without question or blame. No! I will not listen to any more of this soft, rhetorical language. My … our Anne is dead but why us? We are a good family with good thoughts – well, until now. My faith in God is dented and like the scuff from a sword upon new armour, polishing it with polite words will not make it better. I wonder if you can really hear my thoughts. But what if you can? So answer me this then, God, why Anne? Say it, shout it, let me know now, I demand this much of you!

William glanced at his father and then went to stand in the open doorway. He didn't speak; he just wanted a moment of fresh air to help relieve him of her death.

William waited for God's answer just as John waited for William's outburst. He knew it would come soon, because he knew his son's mind had some anger to express. He knew he would seek solace in words, for that's where his gift lay.

'Father?' William turned his head back to John and indicated that he should join him. 'Do you see what I see?'

John came to stand by William, but he could see nothing in particular out of the ordinary to focus his attention upon. 'What is it?'

'Nothing, Father, nothing at all. Do you see it, too?'

John looked past William once more, but shrugged with indifference. As far as he could see, nothing had changed.

'Do you see, Father?' William pointed here and there, 'There is nothing. Nothing has changed with her passing. No one cares. Townsfolk go about their lives as they did yesterday. Only we know of our loss. God has not told them of our loss. Indeed, why should they know? They are of their own minds, fixed on their own problems. It is for us to mourn, or to believe the ancient stories going round as to where we came from and where we might end up. God, perhaps, is a word used to cover up many a sin in ignorance. What words would we use if we had not this one so carefully placed amongst our vocabulary? Forgive my words, Father. Perhaps God is not to blame for our loss. Could it be our lack of faith, or others' faiths being stronger than ours? I doubt we will ever know.'

'I expected harsh words from you,' said John, without mentioning the blasphemous outburst. 'Not as cutting, mind, but an outburst nonetheless. I guess I should have expected you to act differently to what one might expect. Like you, there are times when I doubt the versions of hearsay and speeches of clergy alike, but the laity have to have something to belong to, so I suggest you keep your thoughts to yourself until you have compared their lengthy meanings further. Then you may speak your mind, but I fear if others overheard your words we would be facing a much greater loss than Anne. You must remember our position in society, William.'

'I understand.' William stepped out further and pushed his foot into a hardened cowpat. 'Father. I know you and Mother have suffered loss before. But in times of anger and pain, who is to say which way your defences will make you stand. My tears still have a salty taste and the cow muck underfoot still smells as it does, but now we are all sentenced to look upon her vacant seat at supper and wonder which visitor's ignorant rump will sit upon it next.'

John put his arm around William's sunken head and spoke at last to end the matter. 'Oh, William, let your words and thoughts rest awhile now. Debate either way will not bring her back to us, so let the fire on the tip of your tongue hiss to a quiet. Let no more be said about the matter. She is gone now, son. Try to be a better brother to your siblings, for you are the eldest and they will look to you for guidance. You must set the example. Rest your wounded mind and help Mother and me take the strain. Your whiskers are growing more each week now, so allow the man inside to grow with them and soon your boots will be as big as mine. Then, perhaps, you will have all the answers.'

William then broke from words to tears as he leaned on his father's shoulder and began to sob.

This was a hard lesson for William, but he did learn from the day and he also gained greater strength from it. The rest of his family was still alive and he could love them as he had loved his sister Anne. At least they had not been taken away from him, too.

Daydreaming

William was late out of bed one morning and the rest of the family were already going about their usual daily chores. It was the morning after William's fifteenth birthday. Edmund, the Shakespeares' last child, was to be born this year, but William still had passing thoughts about Anne who had died suddenly. As William opened the bedroom window he saw it was a clear day, so he breathed deeply, absorbing the atmosphere with a pleasing smile. His hair had developed a style of its own over the past few years through constant combing and wetting. But William was now allowed to let it settle into its untidy, unruly locks, not straight and parted like the rest of his family. Indeed, he was developing his own style both on the inside and the outside.

Oh, what will today mean to the rest of my life? William thought. I was fifteen yesterday and now I look from this window towards my sixteenth year. Huh! There are two dead bodies lying on a wagon outside in the street; they must have died yesterday. There will be two less mouths to feed and two less to bring in an income and yet their rent will still be the same. My thoughts are cynical, I admit, God, but I still have no answer as to why our Anne was taken and so suddenly. It doesn't make any sense. Was it to make way for the new baby? I wonder who chooses their names – is it you or us? He turned to look around the room with his back to the window for a moment. This is the largest upstairs room in the house. It feels like it was meant for boys to run around in. The girls' room though is dressed with lace. Oh, how I wish I could put my poem on their chimney breast for all to see and in memory of my sweet sister.

He whispered the sacred verse to himself as he turned to look through the window again, but his eyes had a lifeless gaze about them, without any particular focus:

Lace covers my love's feathered rest, bouncing locks,

Soft-edged frocks, with eager looks to drown her stare.

Singing and prose is like a butterfly's fleeting waft,

the meadow ours to dance in – it is for others to read what
is writ.

Some future shadow will kiss her and charm,

but I will hate him and compare him with a goat.

Consoled with our shared blood and looks,

her love will come from another book not yet wrote.

I don't think Mother would allow it to be placed on show in their
room, especially as Anne is still in our minds.

William looked up to the buildings and down to people walking by
in the street before turning back to check out the same walls he greeted
each morning. He sighed and then turned towards the window once
more. Mother would think I was perverse if I should write the rhyme
down, or even repeat it, he thought further. Joan is such a love, even
though I had them both in mind when I composed it. I hope she will
meet a man with wealth and a good position, someone to care well for
her. The verse will stay in my head for now, though. No one can read
my mind; they can only have suspicions if my face reddens when
questioned. I blink once and then I am fifteen, again and then I am
thirty, but two more blinks and I may need a stick. Life is one quick
blink. I stand here and touch the frame and the sill today, but one day
others may be doing the same and thinking of my passing. Perhaps if I
died and came back from the past, why, I could even wave up here to
whoever was watching my funeral! They walk past going about their
simple lives, treading the same steps on the same path. They only know
one way – there and back. They know no different. My favourite tree in
the distance, dead of course, looks just like a mutilated witch's hand.
The yellow hand of lightning that struck from the sky left us with a
blackened, charred one in its place. But as I look at it, I see past the toil
to form the lead and cow-horn diamonds on the window frame to see
the beauty beyond. Time and care were needed to make these two, but
like most I have opened it wide to view the woodland beyond. Perhaps
the windows keep the plague from our house. Most have boards or slits
for windows, but those with the cross on their doors smell vile when I
walk past. Oh! look at the crows on the roof opposite, tilting their heads

one way and then the other in their quest for food. It must be bread-making day, for the baker is sweeping out his early crumbs. I have been poised as they are now, ready and waiting, only mine is to speak out at the injustice and theirs is to fly and swoop upon their quarry.

'Your way there and back will be like that of a crow!' Father had said firmly with pointed finger all those years ago. I cannot fly, though, or jump the rooftops, but birds don't think as I do – or do they? They may even be looking at me now, wondering what I am about. I can hear my brothers playing below. They love their skittles, but I favour different games or players on a stage. Knocking the same thing down over and over is too small an aim for me, not to mention monotonous. Like my school equals, they study what is right under their noses without thinking what might lay beyond the game. Just like skittles, all eyes follow one ball, but their appetite for study is less. I feel like a crow watching people below in the street, wondering if one day they will ever look up. Football is the same, kick about from here to there, no order or aim, nor indeed any skill, required for this game. Kick and run and all the same fools end up in a tumble. It is good to watch their simple aims, though.

William whispered, 'Wake up, world! Look up and smile at the sky. Don't just follow your feet all the time.'

He noticed a passer-by with a mule, similar to the one his father had recently acquired. Father swapped a pair of gloves and an apron yesterday for a mule. A nice pair of ladies' gloves they were, too. If only the animal knew its equal worth when it was born unto this world. Would it think it was worth a coat and a trunk, perhaps? I wonder what status the mule has in the stable. Would it rank lower than a mule if Father swapped one for a pig? Or is it just that we barter with goods for what suits our needs most?'

'Step away from the food, glove-mule,' the first mule may say. 'I have the first taste. I was swapped for a pig that had twenty more piglets – a fine swap, indeed.'

'The gloves I was swapped for were made from a piglet and the apron from a kid,' the second mule replied. 'These cost far more, so my worth is higher still. You have been cheated, pig-mule. Old pigs are plenty. This is why you were swapped – we are worth the same.'

'Ah, but we are not the same, glove-mule,' the first mule replied. 'The piglets were worth much more than one scruffy young mule.'

'But this is where you are wrong,' said the second mule. 'Your previous owner was a fool to swap you for a pregnant pig, so you come from a fool and so should take second place.'

'Oh no,' said the first mule. 'I was here first, this is my stable and so it is my right to be first to the food.'

'Wrong again, pig-mule,' the second answered. 'You will be first, I agree, for a pair of cheap boots. But I am quite fit, you know, and certainly as soft as gloves are. I will be the last to be taken because you are an old hide!'

'What a put-down for the first mule. Animals could be like that, I suppose.' William said to himself. He had enjoyed acting the scene out. They could be as bad as us if their thoughts could be read, he surmised.

Father will be moving his wares about now, so as to look busy in the shop and so people might think he was doing good trade and so entice more in. A poor crop reflects on his manner in that it is written all over his face that he is too eager to sell, especially when women come to browse in the shop. So desperate is his smile that I wonder if they can read his feelings like I do. My wish is that we can eat plenty all the time, much better than plain Monday scrapings. Sunday leftovers should be a thing of the past and left behind like a footprint in the mud. Last Easter we had but scraps come Monday with hardly a smile to be had. I want to enjoy next Easter with a happy family, firewood up to the eaves and uncles and aunts aplenty with piles of fresh pork to fill our bellies! We could have fine clothing to wear and sit Joan and Richard in front of the fire on a bearskin rug Oh! how I wish it could be so, my lord.

Let me think of the good things from Saturday, by far the best day of the week, with Mother's fresh-bought bread. I can smell the loaves now. It makes the wares in the shop smell good enough to eat. The smell of fresh-baked bread from the back of the shop, emanating from the house, makes folk in the shop breathe it in with a smile. But if a bakery was to smell of leather, surely all would flee in haste!

'William, come down. There's work to be done,' Mary shouted up the stairs. 'I hope you aren't staring out of the window again ...'

'Yes, Mother,' he called out, dragging his feet across to the door. 'I was trying to fasten my trousers when I realised they were Gilbert's.'

William was full of ideas and excuses, but his mother just tutted to herself. He was looking out of the window again, she thought. The boards were creaking in one place but his lies came from another.

'Don't lie, William,' she called back. 'Your truthful feet which tell of your whereabouts should be connected to your lying tongue! It would certainly learn a thing or two.'

John was hurrying to a meeting that day, so William was in charge of the shop. When he came downstairs, he grabbed a piece of bread before strolling into the shop, but he was followed by his mother's glare for his lateness.

'Good morning, Mother,' said William with a smile.

'Yes, I believe it still is morning ... just,' she answered before turning to go outside. 'It is nice to see you before the sun has dried the morning's washing.'

William didn't pursue the argument and left her to go about her morning chores. As he walked past the apprentice's room, he looked in on him. Thomas had been busy, having worked since first light.

'Good morning, Thomas. How many is it today?'

'Oh, I have sixty to sew today, Master Shakespeare,' replied Thomas from beneath a pile of straps of some kind.

William didn't answer, because he was only making polite conversation. He had things on his mind other than soft leather to make belts from.

I wonder what custom we shall have today, William thought, chewing his bread and looking out of the open shop door. I hope some of the passing young ladies come in to enquire after our kid gloves. William continued to smile and greet passers-by, enticing them inside to look at his wares.

'William,' Mary snapped with her head poking through from the house. 'I have washing to do. Gilbert is trying his best to cut the grass with Richard. Joan is helping me and we have another on the way. And yet you have time to stand here and watch the street go by. Think of something useful you can do, like sweeping out or arranging things better on the shelves. We have no time to stand and gawk outside!'

'Yes, Mother,' William sighed. 'I will tidy up as you wish and make as many sales as I can. I was doing just that when you stopped me. I was trying to entice the ladies to purchase our wares.'

'Do not sigh when I speak to you.' She closed the door with a slight bang in temper. 'I don't want to hear any more of your lies. The sound of the floorboards handed your guilt to me on a plate!'

William lifted his eyebrows and tutted to himself. Oh! the stress we invite to our lives. There is work to do but with it we must think, for without it we would all be cutting grass or washing for the rest of our lives.

Just as William finished tutting, the door opened from the house. This time it was Joan.

'William, Mother says the pegs are in here. Do you know where they are?'

'Oh, Joan,' he replied, sinking to a bended knee. 'For you, my lovely sister, anything. If I am unable to find the pegs, I will command them to come out from their hiding place and dance at your feet,' After William had finished his verse he gave an exaggerated bow and smiled.

'William, just the pegs,' said Joan, blushing with embarrassment. 'The washing will not hang itself on your gentle words alone.'

'No, but the heat from his breath with his tiresome words will dry them,' shouted Mary through the partly open door. 'Perhaps we should all come into the shop and hold the clothes in front of him. Why look for pegs?'

'Yes, yes, yes, I will find them,' William snapped as he knelt down to look under the counter.

'Be careful, William,' Mary added with a wink at Joan. 'Be careful how you speak. The shop floor is so dusty that the pegs might sneeze as they march out from their hiding place, for all the cleaning you've managed to get done today.'

Just then a well-rounded farmer came into the shop, giving Joan and Mary the excuse to exit and quit while they were ahead. They were both biting their lips, trying to hold back the laughter at William's expense, especially considering he usually had an answer for everything and he had just banged his head.

'Boy!' the farmer said in his deep voice as he waited for William to turn. 'I require a leather apron. Show me your samples.' His belly shook with each word.

The man's rudeness didn't escape William's notice, but he couldn't afford to lose a sale and so he attended to the farmer's request. But, as William turned to look for an apron that was capable of covering such a large belly that had been seasoned to drinking copious amounts of ale, he noticed the farmer's dog peeing on the goods.

'Mister, with respect,' he turned to look down, 'your dog, could you tether it up outside, please?'

'What? Get on with your work, boy,' the farmer replied, looking cross and patting his belly to hide his frustration.

'Mister, your dog is wetting our skins,' William said with a concerned frown.

'To pot with your skins. They are only cheap hide,' he said with a glance down to his dog. 'I am a busy man, so get on with it, boy.'

This was the breaking point for William. His head hurt, he had been caught lying and had been outwitted by his mother and now he had received an insult to crown them all. 'These hides are expensive,' said William angrily, 'not cheap as you say, unlike the dog hide over there which is now leaking on our quality goods!'

'You foul-mouthed youth,' said the farmer, his top lip curled in anger, 'if you were my boy I would beat you and throw you to the pigs for your insolence. There would be nothing remaining of you, boy.'

'If I were on your farm, mister,' shouted William, with an equally rising temper, 'I would certainly not wet your fresh produce the way in which your dog wets our goods. Put the dog outside now and then I will serve you.' William stood firm and pointed with his finger.

The farmer stepped back with shock at William's remark and grimaced at William before kicking his dog. William was nervous, but his blood was boiling now. He would not back down, even if it meant losing a sale, so he followed the farmer to the door, pride now overtaking him.

'It is your dog, mister, but the dog is blameless for you bringing him in here. It is you that should be kicked.'

As the farmer reached the door, he turned and pressed his sweaty head towards William's face. 'Perhaps you are right, but I'll not be booted by a shiny-faced boy. Your cheek, boy, has just cost you custom,' hissed the farmer.

'Your dog has just cost me good hides,' replied William bravely, but with feet primed to run and his hand ready to prevent a possible blow. 'Perhaps you would like to pay for these soiled goods, honourably!'

'If I see you on the street, boy, I will pee on your face and crush the devil in your throat with my boot.' He straightened his back before turning towards the door and grabbing a nearby apron on his way out, intending to leave without paying.

William sighed with relief as the farmer made to leave and was equally relieved when his father's frame blocked the exit.

'Oh, John, my friend,' said the farmer, lightening up with a smile.

This brought a frown from William. The man has the horns of his bulls, he thought. Innocent until riled.

'I did not see you approaching the shop,' the farmer said with another forced smile.

'No, Edward Fox, I see that you did not,' John said with determination on his face. 'I have been at the other side of the door for several minutes. Indeed, enough time for me to see both yours and your dog's behaviour and the little wetting problem he seems to have.'

'Oh, er, were you? It was only a misunderstanding, John. We are still friends.' Edward humbly removed his filthy cap.

'He said ...' William began, but John put his hand up and shook his head.

'Go and help your brothers cut the grass, William. Go now, please, my son,' John said without taking his eyes off Edward. 'I am pleased the meeting has been adjourned,' he said, stepping up to Edward's face. 'I forgot a piece of paper I needed this morning, but my previous ill fortune has turned into a fortuitous return.'

Edward sucked his cheeks in and backed away from John's advance.

'And speaking of good fortune, you owe me four sacks of corn for eight spoilt kid hides, I see,' said John, looking down at the wet patches. 'And you have threatened my eldest.' John raised his voice and shouted, 'How dare you threaten my son, you ill-mannered hog!'

John's face had warmed to a glowing red and Edward began fumbling with his coat buttons, trying to think on the spot. 'I will pay, John, but I need time to gather the money owed.'

'Yes, you will pay hard for your actions,' said John with a piercing stare. 'You have until the end of the week. Go and find your money and I suggest you curtail your spending until your debt is paid off in full. Perhaps you will have to forgo purchasing your daily ten loaves for a while.' After John had finished speaking, he gave Edward a fierce prod in his wobbly belly.

Edward backed off a little to let John step out of the doorway so he could pass, but his dog growled at John after he made contact.

'I cannot help the dog's actions, John,' said Edward, with a half smile and slight tilt to his head.

'Then when you come to pay me, I suggest you leave the animal outside or my boot assist you both, being as you are unable to control the beast,' John said before waving Edward to pass him.

Edward smiled nervously and nudged his dog out as he squeezed past John to escape. But as he did so John whispered, 'I could have sent you to the stocks for what you said to my son. A week, I say, a week.'

Not a minute had passed since the incident when John banged his stick on the shop counter and called all the family to attention. After a few seconds everyone had made their way into the shop, followed lastly by William, whose head was down, avoiding eye contact with his father.

'I will keep my words short.' John bit his lip and paused. 'You will have heard the exchange of words between us. Fortunately, I misplaced my paper. When I leave this house and shop, I wish to leave it in good, strong hands. Customers are important to us if we are to survive. We must bow and listen to their every whim. With all their gripes and worthless gossip, they appeal to our listening ears. They are customers and we must treat them with respect.'

William feared his father's next words. Had his cheek and lazy start to the day cost the family custom and led to bad town gossip that could damage their reputation?

'I am needed elsewhere for a while, but I will leave you this thought: well done William!' he said with a smile to the shock of all present. They all looked surprised, but none as much as William.

'William used his words wisely and well, standing up to the man for what he knew was right, but he should not be so complacent with all our customers, I must add. We must be tolerant of all who come here, whilst at the same time not letting folk tread on our wares as they tread the street.'

Mary handed him the piece of paper he had returned to collect with a kiss. It was a copy of the Lord's Prayer, which he liked to have with him for all his meetings.

The family waved him off to his meeting, but William was more pleased than any of them. He was relieved as he was as happy as he could ever have wished. This time William's maturity had been recognised and it was the first time his father had accepted his eldest son's lead.

For William, this was not just about the argument with the farmer, for if he had been cutting grass or helping with the washing, the goods would have been both unpaid and spoiled. His mind was growing sharper and more tuned to his environment, but he was never the first in the queue when it came to volunteering his help. If there was a list of chores to do, he was always the last when it came to a show of hands. John once said of William, 'If you want to find William, just look for the work and then look in the opposite direction, but one will invariably find him daydreaming at the window.' But it was said with tongue in cheek, even though he was reasonably accurate in his analysis.

All is Not Lost

After a spate of burglaries in nearby villages, John came downstairs one morning to find the shop door forced open and a quantity of goods missing. His apprentice, Thomas, had not locked the door properly, so the thieves had made an easy entry. The latest addition to the Shakespeare household was Edmund, who was fast asleep in the corner of the lads' room.

'Mary!' John shouted out angrily, but then realised that Edmund was directly above him. 'Come down and see what others do while we dream.' Then he said quietly, 'The fools, I will see them swing by their ears for this. Our stock is near quartered, but my rage now is ... ooh, doubled!'

'Thomas! Thomas,' he shouted urgently.

'What do you call for?' Mary ran down hurriedly into the shop. 'Oh! Who have we sinned against to deserve this?' she said, not knowing where to put her arms, by the side or holding her hair. But it didn't matter – the goods were gone and there was nothing they could do about it.

'People steal more from this kingdom than virginities are lost to homecoming soldiers,' John said, shaking his head with a great sigh. 'They have wronged us, Mary. They look at our position and stock, think we have a prince's allowance, then take what we have without a thought for the consequences of how we are to survive. They want a taste of what we have for their own sour pockets.'

'Yes, sir,' answered Thomas, standing up from the corner with sleep in his eyes.

'Oh, you're awake now, I see.' John scowled. 'The door not double-bolted and you asleep. If I could find a bucket big enough, I would put your head in it!'

'I ... I was working late,' he answered, cowering with his arm covering his face.

'Oh, oh, your costly sleep,' said John more calmly. 'There is nothing you can do. But when we return, you'd better make up for your careless dreams with a pile of fixed buckles, do you hear!'

'Yes, Mr Shakespeare,' Thomas said, fearful of a possible blow.

Mary hadn't words to say with the shock, so she walked up to John and held his tensed arm firmly.

'Look, my love,' said John sadly. 'They have even taken my measuring stick. How can I cut the leather when I can only guess an inch, or weigh corn with the same absent scales?'

'Oh, John,' said Mary, trying to turn his head to the side. 'They have stolen our goods, but thankfully you did not lose your life fighting with them. It is not a woman's job to hunt men down – it is yours. I am happy you are here to talk to. And I am grateful that the children, now awake by the sounds of it, are unharmed and we are still one. Order the hunt, my love. I will make order here and we will all be here when you return. If I have to skin carcasses myself, I will. We will carry on and live with what little we have.' She squeezed John's hands, forcing a tight-lipped smile and nod of agreement from him.

'You are right,' he said. 'You tend to the clumping footfalls on the floorboards above. I will find these fools and catch them while they are dreaming.'

'Remember, less haste, John.' She turned towards the stairs. 'They will be looking over their shoulders as well as forward; but you only have to look for their backs. They are at a loss to begin with.'

'Yes, Mary, I will heed what you say,' he said, before turning to take another look at the empty spaces where his stock had once lain.

John took moment to himself as Mary attended to the children chattering and running around upstairs. He wanted to calm his anger so he could direct all his energy towards the hunt for the culprits. A few minutes later he took Thomas with him outside into the street to see what all the fuss was about. William was looking through an upstairs window at the wild arms flailing and gesticulating from the growing dissent in the crowd which had now gathered outside. Other people had suffered the same fate, only theirs were lesser thefts, but a feeling of anger was building rapidly.

Mary came to the window and put her hand on William's arm. She knew he was studying the gathering, but the worry he had for his father equalled hers.

'What are they doing, Mother?' William glanced up to her then down to the street again.

'Deciding which way to go,' Mary sighed. 'The villages or over Clopton Bridge towards London. They all have conflicting opinions, trying to send Father in different directions.'

'Some have their arms folded and want to stay put,' said William, pointing. 'Look, and many others are waving knives, but surely they would only cut butter if they were faced with a thief.'

'They may,' she said with a sigh and a forced smile. 'But I hope some folk who mean well ride out with Father. We want to catch the lion at the point of the sword, not with a cob.'

Within a short time several of John's friends had gathered to help, so he could rely on real intent rather than the weak will from those who hadn't lost anything.

Gilbert had just been out back to pee, but he could sense the air of excitement as he raced up the stairs to the bedroom, two steps at a time. He pushed through the doorway and ran over to the window, eager to look out to the street below. 'Are they fighting?'

'No, just fighting in their heads and with words,' said Mary.

'Can I watch, Mother?' asked Joan from outside the door of the lads' room, knowing it was not allowed for her to enter.

'Yes, come here, my love, come here.' She waved for her to come and stand by her side. 'Edmund is still sleeping, so don't run and wake him.'

Joan walked over and put her head with the rest of the family.

John seemed to sense their presence, so he looked up. Not to wave but to tut to himself and raise his eyebrows to emphasise the complexity of the argument around him.

'Mother,' William looked down to his father's face, 'tell him London. That is where all goods are bartered. Such is the size of the market that our stuff will soon be lost with the masses.'

Mary turned to William, but she was still in plain view of John, so she turned her head back to him and pointed left, down the street to the bridge.

John looked to his right, then back up to his family at the window, before directing the men towards the bridge. 'London it is. This is where we will ride,' said John, the control of the crowd now returned to him again.

The group of horsemen galloped away down the street towards Clopton Bridge, watched by the townsfolk until the last one had disappeared.

Mary ushered the children away from the window and tried to distract them with chores. She knew the day would pass better for everyone if they had plenty to do.

With ten men and their borrowed horses, John would be able to make good time. He was soon on his way with his head down and leading the hunt. After an hour the morning sun had started to light up what the moon no longer could, so they could now let the reins loose to the full. Shortly after they had set off, a group of travellers were sighted near to the road, so shouts and whips were raised high in excitement. The thunder of horses soon encircled the travellers, but they turned out to be a family moving from town to town. There were no thieves hidden amongst their sleeping children and neither was there any quality skins baled up from within the confines of their cart.

John and his riders set off again, cracking their whips as they went until they came across another two wagons: one containing wool and the other completely empty. They still had faith that they would find them and so they carried on, even though their hopes had been dashed several times on the way. The next person the riders came across that morning was a farmer with two calves. He seemed to be quite happy considering it was still so early in the day. His self-made laughter and dancing made John suspicious. The farmer was singing with all his heart and his cart was drifting from one side of the road to the other.

'You look happy, farmer,' John said, fighting to keep his horse still. 'Have you lost an egg and found a pig?'

'No, sir, no. I have just exchanged the little silver I had for spirits and quality hides. The men must have been fools.' The farmer lifted a sack and displayed a pile of hides.

'A bargain, indeed, sir.' John glanced at his men. 'How far have you travelled since?'

'I will sell you some if you wish, or the spirits I have here?' said the farmer with a big smile.

'I will ask again, foolish farmer,' said John sharply, waving the men to his side. 'How long have you travelled since?'

'Only a mile or so, two at the most, but why do you ask?' He looked up with a beaming smile. 'Are you sure you haven't anything to barter?'

'I am John Shakespeare, an alderman from Stratford and the former bailiff. Furthermore, I am the owner of the skins you believe to be yours!' John turned his horse around and raised his hand. 'Thomas!' he called. 'Take this man and the goods back to town and then do your buckles, lad. One more question, farmer – how many are there? Speak or I will implicate you further.'

John sat back in the saddle in a more regal position and waited for the answer with piercing eyes.

'Forgive me, Mr Shakespeare,' said the farmer, taking his hat off. 'I will tell all. If the goods are yours and you return my silver, I will be thankful to have known you.'

'I will decide what, if anything, should be returned. You have received my goods for an unfair exchange that could be likened to the queen swapping her sceptre for stale bread.' John scowled and raised his voice, 'You have been so gullible that I do not find you deserving of any reward yet. Now, how many?'

'Three, sir, only three,' said the farmer, kneeling down to grasp John's boot. 'I beg you to forgive my greed.'

One of the riders roughly pulled the man to one side to let John and the other horses past.

As John sped away, whipping his horse with anger, he passed a dead rabbit on the roadside and a thought came to him. A snare was still clamped to its rear legs, so the creature must have died recently in its panic to escape. John remembered what Mary had said earlier. Less haste, he thought, as his nose brushed against the sweaty horse's mane as he patted its side. Suddenly, an obvious thought came to him, so he signalled for his men to slow down, pulling his reins firmly as he did.

'What is it?' shouted Jack, the carpenter, as John waved the hoof-trodden dust away. 'Have you sight of the thieves?'

'No, Jack.' John lifted his head to take in a breath of the cool morning air. 'Let us trot on and give them a chance to drink their fill. They will soon be ours to catch as flies are without wings.'

'Oh yes,' replied Jack with a smile. 'The spirits, of course. Let us enjoy the morning air and listen to the birds, savouring the moment. We can rest the horses' tired legs awhile. You are right.'

'Less haste, you see, Jack, less haste.' John touched his head indicate his thoughtful wisdom.

John's thoughts had been true to him, for half an hour later they came across a cart and two other horses, but it was their singing gave the thieves away. The nearby bushes were quiet from the lack of bird life but loud with slurred speech and merriment. John's men smiled at the ease with which they would now seize back their property. They had been instrumental in their own demise. It was as if the thieves had been drugged by the Lord. The riders wished fishing or hunting was as easy as catching drunken thieves. They were soon bound up and taken back to town on their stolen dray. John was fortunate enough to recover all his goods that day. Some local folk had lost their livelihoods through theft before. A stolen cart of barley, or even theft of livestock, could mean starvation for some; it was all they had.

When the riders returned to the town later that day, they were hailed as heroes and backs were patted. The sharp edge of theft had been blunted for a while, until the next one; but many lessons had been learnt and they would be sure to lock doors next time before retiring to bed. The evening meal was a happy one, although no great sales had been made that day,;but at least their stock was intact once more.

'So, my love,' John threw off his long coat. 'What made you decide that London was the right direction to take?'

'I didn't decide it alone, my love. I had help.' Mary glanced towards William.

'It was our Joan that decided it, really,' said William. 'She had to ask to enter the lads' room, whereas thieves ask no one, they just take. As Joan came towards Mother, she waited with her arms open to welcome her and to stand with us. The thieves must also go where they can be rid of their stolen goods as easily as Mother welcomed our Joan.'

John smiled and nodded. I should have known, he thought, but I was too angry at the time to be able to think clearly, unlike William here. John knew William was worthy of credit for his hand in deciding what direction they should take, but he also knew William would be embarrassed by any attention.

'So, our Joan is the hero, then.' John sat down and raised his tankard. 'And that being so, you have to kiss everyone at the table, including your brothers, who fortunately for you have not yet started shaving.'

Joan complained bitterly, while dodging everyone's arms as she passed out the food for them to share. When she kissed each one in turn, they each thanked her in a different way. Mother gave her a hug, Gilbert a kiss at arm's length, William a responsible 'Hmm' sounding with his and then finally Father, who offered her his rough chin. Richard was no wiser; he just went along with all that had been said before, hiding under the table. And Edmund was fast asleep in his cot. The day began with a bad start, but finished on a lighter note. If all their days ended like this, going from despair to victory with little or no gain, then why should they worry about seemingly bad days?

Money Matters

Going to church every Sunday was a ritual that was strictly adhered to and all the townsfolk were expected to attend the service, though some occasionally chose to stay away from the gathering. Bad debts were often the cause of this, rather than doubts about their faith.

The Shakespeare family wanted to keep their distance from certain people and so one day they decided to take their places early to avoid coming into contact with them. John was notably absent again, his excuse being that he had to catch up on his work, but Mary knew the real reason behind it. Debt, avoidance of their creditors, a bad harvest and lack of general trading had left them with a thin return on their investments. Alongside this, John was under suspicion for lending money at high interest rates and he would often put pressure on people to lessen his own expenditure.

William looked around the quiet church and his thoughts strayed to the supporting arches and stonework. He decided the stone angels were looking down at them with a shield before them, or was it a book they were reading? Perhaps it was the Bible. Either way, both would seriously hurt someone if they should fall from position, if they were to be invited by someones lack of faith. Mary nudged him to remind him where he was.

'William,' she said through gritted teeth with a quick glare.

My face must have given me away. Perhaps I was not penitent enough. The angels are still there, though, looking down. Perhaps they are laughing at me now. It is better that Mother's hand gave the punishment than to have one of them drop a stone shield or a Bible down upon my head. Hmm, the main door still looks ill-placed, with square panels fixed together in front of a plain frame. My fear of dark shapes is still with me, I feel. It has the likeness of a portcullis, but they go up and down and are not hinged like the door. I wonder if God hears fleeing souls lifting its great door knocker, but they would need His help to push the heavy door open in haste. My question of years back surrounding our Anne is still not answered, perhaps it never will be. Maybe I will find the answer within my own mind. Looking for answers could be our real destiny. Find the answer yourself, success or failure, who will know? Only my mind helps to compose my thoughts. Our door at home is of the same wood, black and thick with rough boards and nails. It is far stronger than it looks. My bruised arm often reminds me of this.

Oh, I hear a dreaded whisper. A Christening will follow the service. Time will pass slower now I fear. We arrived early, but now we are to be kept late. My hopes are that Mother will not read my next wicked thought, one which would be enough to make the preacher panic as if his roof was burning. If his font should leak at the same speed as six horses were to drink from it, would that make him rush his speech? His words would be lost in the tower, as his hands hastily tried to cup the water in desperation.

The thought makes me shiver, but not smile, of course, for I fear a slap next, or even a kick from the side. Father has made Mother new boots recently and they felt hard and thick to the touch. My shins fear meeting them. The church is filling up like market day as we all gather to praise the Lord. Not that I am against the gathering, but I just wish it would go quicker. Joan looks so accepting of the church. Her head is always pointing towards the front; chatter or chime, she never moves her head. How I love her dearly. My brothers, though, huh! They are different, likened to common cattle scratching on posts. I do love them, but with it comes knocks and tumbles, and more laughter, I hope. Oh, the preacher is here at last. I can see the boys all waiting to follow him down the aisle as we townsfolk eagerly await his words.

The procession had indeed started as William's thoughts were brought back to the present with another nudge from his mother. The preacher emerged from behind his young men and walked forward to take his position, then paused before opening the Bible.

'Another three souls have been taken from us,' said the preacher, without waiting for silence to descend.

His high office needed little introduction, but it had a sudden effect on all present. All the whispers were silenced to just one – that of a child's whimper. It was expected that everyone attend the service and listen to the preacher's sermon, but it kept the community whole.

'We will rejoice their lives for as they part from our world for heaven, they leave with us a legacy to remember and cherish,' the preacher said.

'We must pray for their souls and for three more births to take their place. We must thank the Lord that we are still here on this earth to praise Him in His great house. Let us pray.'

The service was now under way, but William was still observing his surroundings with inward comments, albeit he had a great respect for death. He closed his eyes and swallowed back the tears at others' loss. He had experienced a loss of his own not long ago when his sister Anne had passed away. These three the preacher spoke of had died both tragically and suddenly. A recent flood had claimed a wagon and its occupants when the cart had floated into the Avon. It was made even more tragic because they were children and none of them could swim when the wagon overturned in the strong current. Tragedy's rule book has no lines to follow, just blank pages ready to be written on, William thought. It is free to claim without payment, deed or asking – it has the power of the queen! I think tragedy often lies in wait, hoping complacency will look the other way for a moment.

The preacher said prayers for the three children, naming them all individually. They were known to William: Sally, Edward and John from the Pemberton farm. I only saw young Sally last week! he thought to himself. The flood took them so suddenly, leaving them all regretting that they did not know of the impending danger in which they found themselves that day. I wonder if they passed the church outside and screamed out to God for help. But they are gone now. They could even be in the heavens listening to the sermon and kind words on their behalf. Perhaps they are with Anne, keeping her company. It is comforting to think that she is no longer alone.

Shortly after this sad thought William let his mind wander again. His sin was not for taking as some did by theft; his sin was watching others and not listening to the preacher. He had to think further than what was presented to him.

I know him, William thought, looking at a familiar face. He had an argument with Father last Tuesday, money I think. Perhaps this is why we are without Father's presence again. This man has a look similar to a wild hog with a tooth protruding from his mouth. He could scrape mussels out with that! Ah, another of Father's enemies – but Father is a man without a hog's teeth. I wonder if he has a greater bite. Teeth are not set straight in most people's mouths. The same ones that smile at you could also bite you hard the next time. I remember Mother's words of long ago so clearly now when I look at the cold backs turned against us and their bared teeth. It was a summer's morning and I was sat in the corner of the garden without a friend. The others I was with had twinned up in pairs to play soldiers. 'Look up, William,' she said. 'Only sad flowers look down. Lift your head up and wave to attract a bee. Smile because it is an invitation like the flower is to a bee.'

After that day I did smile and it worked. People talk to me more now my face offers a degree of invitation. Mother knows the rules of life better than I do. She is a deep soul with hidden patience and knowledge. I like her wisdom, but she hides it well under her hat. I am sure most folk think she is quite dull but they are quite wrong in their assumptions. I think this is what she wants them to believe. Father reminds me of a great plough horse, but Mother is the reins guiding him. Gilbert and Richard are so serious; perhaps I should set the example for them to follow. That young lady, he thought, his mind straying again, I know her from somewhere. My gut feeling inside is to kiss her beneath her bonnet. I wish I could touch her warm cheek. If we could only stand wherever we chose and not be here in the usual place, then perhaps I could catch her eye. My warm hands and heart are all I wish to touch you with. Both are yours, Miss Bonnet. Yes, that's it. I hereby name you Miss Bonnet.

Mother nipped her nails into William's flesh again, but this time a polite whisper followed. 'This house is not somewhere where you can stand at the window and dream. It is the house of God,' she said, her lips hardly moving and with a surreptitious glance at the preacher.

William brought his thoughts back to the present and he looked attentively at the preacher.

Immediately after the Christening, Mary hastily guided the children away from the church. A bobbing head from behind the crowd gave notice that someone wanted to speak to her. Mary avoided eye contact and continued on her way home via a short cut. As they walked with a quickening pace, William waited for the inevitable lecture.

Soon enough it came – aided with a smack to his arm. 'Wandering thoughts again, William. You have been to church and you have wandered to who knows where,' she said firmly, encouraging the family to walk faster. 'Your mind has been everywhere but where it should have been. Times are bad enough without you adding to them. The peace and tranquillity of the church confines allows us to rest from the torment of our daily worries. Let go and pray with us sometimes. Still your wandering mind,' she chastened.

'I do, Mother,' he answered. 'But when I look at the folk who stare at us I want to turn their heads back around and nail them to a barge heading downriver.'

'So do I,' she said sharply. 'But do not think like this in God's house, where all our thoughts should be equal.'

'Equal for some, but it doesn't stop them from staring,' he said, trying to justify his actions.

'No more, William.' She indicated that he should stop with a lowered hand. 'I have said all I am going to say. Your conscience is on your own pillow. Let your thoughts rest on it now, but if you plump up thoughts of rocks, you will sleep on the same.' Mary sighed before lifting her head up proudly. She didn't like arguing and usually avoided conflict.

As she looked up, the man William had seen in church had run down another street to head them off. He was tall and well dressed and he now blocked their path, his stick held in one hand and tapping on the ground.

'Oh, do not run away so fast,' said the gentleman, gasping for breath. 'You will burn your boots to a smoulder if you carry on at that rate.'

'Why do you advise me how I should use my boots?' Mary asked, knowing full well what he was after.

'Ah, and new boots, indeed,' he added, looking down before waving his stick about. 'I hope I haven't had a hand in paying for them?'

'What of them? Would you like to buy them?' she asked bluntly, holding her four children close to her.

'No,' he shook his head, 'I have no desire to purchase the children or the boots, but I would like you to settle up on a debt that is owed to me.'

William was raging inside, desperate to defend his parents and make a stand for the family name. He studied the enemy, inwardly seething. His venomous language tempts my own poisonous reply and his smile reminds me of unpleasant smouldering skin. I cannot endure it for too long. I can only beat it away with my tongue as if it were a stick. There could be danger here from his fiery words, but mine are glowing from his bellowing tongue. Another blast and they will leap out in flames!

William eventually spoke out firmly, praying he could win. 'We are not for sale and neither are my mother's fine boots,' he snapped, coming to her defence.

Mary held his arm firmly, but she could feel William's heaving breaths, ready to let loose his anger once more.

'I would not pay a pebble for any of you,' the man said, looking down his nose as if they were dirt. 'Neither would I put the boots on a pig.'

Mother was hurt by this comment, so she took in a deep breath, ready to answer, but William's quicker thoughts blasted back at the man.

'A golden pebble from your wealth would not even buy my nail cuttings,' he said firmly. 'Neither would it buy the crackling we throw to the chickens, sir!'

Again, Mary tried to restrain William, but more gently this time. She wanted him to expel his anger and defend the family name.

'Oh, a young man with wit and the capability of stringing more words together than ... hmm ... his mother's washing line on the appropriate day.' The man's head swaggered with the mouthful of seemingly well-articulated words.

'More appropriate than your rude approach,' William hastily retorted. 'And they are far stronger words than the cheap stitches holding your clothes together.'

Mother pulled at William, thinking he was going to strike the man, but his body was taut and his chest muscles were primed for speech. Gilbert and Joan were behind Mary, watching William's hand as it lashed back and forth like a sword, emphasising his words, but Gilbert predictably had his fists clenched at the ready.

'You fail to impress me, boy,' the gentleman said. 'I have a debt to collect from a man, not a mere boy with manly intentions!'

'Is that why you approached my mother with your pointed stick and tongue to match? An apology, I demand!' said William, with arms out to stop Gilbert from moving forward.

'The debt is so, lad,' the gentleman said angrily. 'And it is for two marks more than you will ever be worth. And as for an apology, this is the closest you will ever get!'

'If wealth brings a foul tongue with it, as yours does, then I do not want it,' William lashed back. 'Your accusations are built on foundations of feathers. Why, the breeze from the half beat of a wasp's wing would make them scatter.'

'Feathers, you say, boy of filth with words to match,' he said angrily, his lip curled with hatred. 'Sit back on your feathers, boy. You will need them when you are thrown into the street.'

'Sir, the venomous ink galloping through your veins and passing out through your ink-stained fingertips and tongue is unchecked. If you thought more deeply before you spoke and wrote, a more pleasing end would come for all on this day.'

The man didn't have the words or the articulation to form a reply, but his face twisted and writhed as if he were trying to chew a holly leaf.

William paused in his attack while taking the strain of Gilbert's arm. Then he composed a quieter and more patient speech without anger. Any further attack could lead to physical conflict, so he decided to alter his words to agree in principal and lose the gentleman with them.

'Push or pull the heavy cart, sir, you do in haste.' William let go of Gilbert so he could gesticulate with his hands. 'Your sweat is wasted with the sole attempt. Share your load with compromise. The sweat from conflict adds up to only a drop from each of us, and not enough to drown a fly, for five weak arms are better than one tired strong one. Do not whip a tired horse; help it to regain its strength.'

'What is this riddle, boy?' asked the gentleman as he pulled his head back in alignment with his spine in disbelief at what he was hearing. 'Your talk of carts and five weak arms – this will not settle a debt.'

'Neither will your single arm push aside five smaller ones such as we. Or will your insults pluck the settlement of debts from the sky by the cartload? Share with the pull and equally so with the push. Wait a while for your payment, but do not try to push a strong cart like our family. Let us help you to pull it. You will get your payment, but not with insults. It will come from compromise and talk, without the need for our tongues to clash in the street.'

With this the gentleman was beaten, so he held his cape together and walked swiftly away with gritted teeth at his loss of ground. His head was full of thoughts from William's speedy articulation.

The children jumped excitedly at the change in circumstances, but Mary was a little more composed, merely smiling to herself and encouraging them to walk on.

When the family was safely back at Henley Street, Mary wanted to tell John about the confrontation and ask him about debt. She quickly dismissed the children, because her words were for John's ears only.

'Richard, Gilbert, take yourselves off for a while and help out a little by sweeping upstairs. Now, please.' Mary turned to face each of them in turn. 'Joan, go and fetch the milk with William, please.'

The children disappeared quickly, leaving Mary alone in the room with John. He was expecting harsh words, so he put his hand on the fireside to wait for what was to come.

'Who is the tall gentleman from church, John?' asked Mary, holding her head in thought. 'His name escapes me.'

'Oh, you have met him, then? It's Turnbull.' He looked up to Mary and she nodded before turning away, near to tears. He walked over to Mary and offered his arms to give comfort to her. He could do nothing other than wait and hold her until she was ready to speak again.

Mary knew this, but her tears had to come. The stress of owing others had to be kept inward for the children's sake. The family had a high position in town to uphold and they tried to keep all their business activities hidden away from the public eye.

'We have a little to pay him. Could we not give him at least something to stop him hounding us?' Mary looked up at John through her tears. 'We still have assets.'

John wiped his rough fingers across Mary's eyes, and she squinted to his touch, her own skin far more tender. 'My dispute is this: the debt has been taken on by him from another. It is his high interest I will not pay. It has not been agreed between us. We have assets, but we are short on cash, as you know, my love.'

'But just a little? Surely that would keep him off our backs at least for a while,' she asked.

'No, my love, I will not bow down to him. Giving him a little now would be as good as accepting his terms. We must wait for the courts to settle this.' He embraced Mary. 'But we have money owed from others in the same way. We must all be patient. It will be paid in good time, but food comes first.'

Mary sat down with John to talk more before the children came back with all their chores finished. 'We pray to God for our crops and for profitable sales, but sometimes it is our turn to wait for good fortune.'

'Yes, we are all given life and are shown the rules to follow,' he said with shrug and sigh at the same time, 'in the same way that the wheelwright sells his new cart with instructions for its use. Do not race across the stony ground. Do not let it rest in water or dung. Do not throw boulders from a great height into it. This is the same as the word of our God. His instructions we all know; but men break them like they break the law and the rules given with the cart. Every day someone commits a sin or abuses instructions and flouts the law. It is the same for God and the wheelwright as it is for us right now.'

'You make the problem seem so simple to bear,' she said with a smile, her head raised with hope. 'William spoke of a heavy cart today to the Turnbull gentleman, but he was not as soft with words as you are to me.'

'Oh, what happened?' he asked with his hand up to stop the answer. 'Don't tell me – William turned thoughts of the blacksmith's big hammer to an insignificant tap from a shoemaker on his tacks.' John turned away with a smile before drifting away in thought.

'Did William use abuse?' he asked, turning to see Mary's expression when she answered.

'He replied only to protect us from the insults he gave to the children and me. He stood firm, my love, that is all,' she said. 'He knotted the man's mind worse than an over-tied sack. He will have to think deeply before he tries to cut his way into Shakespeare's flour; he will have to work out the ways of the knot.'

'I follow his arguments with interest, but sometimes I worry about him.' John and Mary stood up to face each other. 'Just think of this, though. When children fight, they become better at it until one day they lose to a bigger bully. I fear we should question William's sharp words sometimes, for they will bring mobbing crowds to his heels if he's not careful.'

'Yes, indeed they may,' she said. 'But as you once told me, when you were given your father's belt it would have fitted around three people. Surely his words with a happier thought behind them could charm three people to his agreement, as well as turning insults on their heels. I wonder some days, could his words end up having a threefold benefit in the same way as your belt?'

'I think you may be right.' John stepped aside to await the noisy return of Joan and William, who were both singing. 'But if one was to compare my belt to William's words – it would encircle the Guild Hall.'

The Dream

A few weeks later John took the children with him to help at the stall under the market cross. William was capable of looking after the shop alone, now. He could hold a meaningful conversation with the customers and use his charm to sell. Mary stayed at home as well that day. There was always housework to do as well as seeing to relatives who had called to see her and the baby. Edmund was still nursing, so Mary had plenty to do at home.

The morning started off quietly with William attending to his general duties, but he had something pressing on his mind. A strange dream he'd had the previous night kept resurfacing, forcing him to stop and try to solve its meaning. The shop was usually quiet first thing in the morning, so he dusted the stock and generally tidied up where he thought best. He placed various bales and sacks outside the shop and then sat down to start edging a new pair of gloves. While William was concentrating on his work, he looked up to watch a funeral procession pass by. The funeral was for an otherwise ordinary man who had reached a good age of fifty, so none of the mourners looked too sombre. William knew of the man who was known as Ben. He normally worked for ale and a few coppers to give his sister for food. It was a cheap procession, with a plain box without fittings which was laid on the back of the cart. The carpenter walked in front of the cart, leading his horses past the small line of onlookers who had gathered to watch the proceedings, most of whom tipped their caps as they passed.

Death again, William thought, leaning back to watch. It comes to us all. He was a poor man, but he was equal to the wealthy in character. Old Ben leaves his sister only the cart tracks behind, for all his wealth, what little there was, has gone on drink. She must live on, though. The carpenter looks proud in a way, but with slight embarrassment. It looks to be a good, strong box, but I am sure he would liked to have shown off his expertise with one with a raised lid and better wood.

William then stood up to follow his thoughts into the street, taking the stitching work with him as he kept looking around.

What is death? Is this what I stretch leather for – to one day have a wife and children, then perhaps a polished casket like his? Not for me. I want to stretch myself away from the circle of town life. I want London. I want more than a small-town ending. The box goes on, bump after bump, stirring all the beer inside him. The gas will surely make him emit a final belch at the graveside. Then below he goes, to hell or towards a lightened pathway up to heaven. Whilst we can't see them, I am sure they exist, heaven and hell.

But what is hell? A black hole below in the ground, they say, but is it really that bad? If it is black, presumably one would not be able to see one's badness. Neither do I really know what heaven is. Perhaps I have been looking in the wrong direction? Could this be the answer to life? Find hell and then look the other way?

What we already have around us may be heaven. Perhaps it is here and now. We could all be looking for something we already have. We may not need eyes in hell, like the blind woman there, just feeling around each building. Yes, hell could be the same as the life she now has. Oh, the thought is pure horror. I must turn my thoughts back to heaven – but that worries me also. Father says the church was changed from a beautiful Trinity, to a plain, painted canvas. How can we change religion so fast? One can be Catholic or Protestant, depending on the monarch's mind. With crown support they order so, 'Pull down the fancy praise in the church. Cover the old; paint on the new.' How do they know God prefers plain things to colour and gold? The king likes gold and colour, yet now the queen insists on plain and flat. Oh! what would real life be like if we could change our skins in the same way? God must be a mix of colour, I think – berries, woodlands, crops and gentlemen's clothes. If not with colour, then how would we tell one fruit from the next? I think it is the ones who tell us about God who cannot make up their minds. If they could, we would not have had the changes forced upon us.

But my thoughts must be of the present. I am still here in Stratford, looking at the funeral tracks of another. They will soon be trod upon by folk not knowing it is all that he leaves as they go about their everyday business. But he leaves us in heaven – if only they knew this, the ones tipping hats.

Mary had seen William looking at the procession from an upstairs window and he was in such deep thought that he hadn't noticed her waving her duster. She hurried downstairs with questions in mind, but when she walked into the shop, William was already back inside and hard at it.

'William,' said Mary in a worried tone, 'are you alright? You look as white as a sheep. You always look beyond today. The man was old, so why do you mourn for him?'

'Oh, my mind drifted to thoughts of death,' he answered. 'I am not mourning for him. I am sorry, Mother. I have my duties, but I feel as small and as insignificant as a hoof print.'

'It is like that sometimes. But one should only mourn only for a short time. Do not think too much of death, there are a plentiful supply of both worries and joy in life to be had.'

'Worry, Mother!' he exclaimed with shock. 'Death means the prospect of darkness for all time. I fear it more as each year passes. I am sixteen and a half, but I fear halves, for one day they will become whole years and before long, ten more will have passed and soon, my own ending! Each year goes faster with each passing.'

'Be calm and think of living,' she said, lifting his chin. 'Come inside the house and let us talk further.'

William shrugged and then took one last look at the distant procession as he followed Mary into the living room. He sat on the side of the table to listen to her advice, but his arms were folded.

'Green, William,' she said. William relaxed with surprise. 'Green and black, they are the colours to think of. Green is lush and signifies growth and from it comes fragrance, food and the life that it supports. But after the crops are harvested or die back, they turn black before they return from where they started. This, though, is not the end. Next year greenery is plentiful once more and the fact that they die back is once again forgotten by all as they reap and breathe in the new life. We are similar in respect when compared with our daily chores. All men and women must pass through life in the same way, flourishing as we progress. Our seed grows with teaching in mind. This knowledge is passed on so others can better themselves and so everyone can share in the profits.'

'I see your point,' he said, letting his arms relax. 'But as other people walk about, I know they do not think this way. They pull at bread to get the biggest lump and even in the shop they check that they are getting the thickest leather, but their mind is purely on size and weight but not for quality. We know the softest leather is not the heaviest, yet they still want what their greed tells them to take. Thick gloves will last the longest, but they will still have to take them off to pick up a coin. They would be better off with their hands in pockets, for all the good they would do.'

'That may be your problem,' she suggested. 'You might be looking at folk and their lives, without concentrating on your own. You are aware of what passes by, but do not let your awareness of it allow your life to pass as theirs does. Study and reflect, by all means, but you must aim for what you want to achieve in life and live your own life. You should not look to the side or behind but ahead. Do not look at the stream in front and worry about getting wet. Think of the dryness at the other side when you have crossed over and the enjoyment you will have had in between.'

'But I do think ahead, Mother,' he said. 'It's just that days like this bring me back to the reality of the stench in the town, worries for crops and an empty board without bread to cut on it.'

'Yes, I agree, but this is our life. We were not born to be kings or queens. This is our lot and ours to plant and reap,' she said. 'Try to look beyond others' lives and not at your feet. Look up, William.'

'Your wisdom, as always, has won me over,' he said with a slight smile. 'My day started with a dream and whilst it was not morbid, it was this that started me thinking.'

'I will listen,' she answered, 'but my years as a parent have not given me the head of a dream scholar. I am not as wise as an elder, who may be able to answer you better.'

'I realise this,' he said. 'But can I tell you anyway, just to shed it from my thoughts? It was such a strange dream.'

'Yes, we have time now. Your aunt and uncle are in the garden resting; the baby is asleep and the shop is quiet.'

'It was short but vivid. I was walking through a drifting fog, but there was a dim candle flickering ahead of me. I followed it for a while and the fields I was walking through became clearer. Then I turned and climbed over an awkward stile. My next thoughts were of bees, a thousand or more, but I pushed my hand through them, without fear of getting stung, to taste the sweetness beyond. I could really taste the sweetness. My face was sticky with the honey. The bees did not sting me; they just followed me as I walked backwards away from them. Not over the stile though, which had now gone. Then I turned and walked farther down the same field, but I found myself holding the candle. As I walked farther through the fields, the day brightened up and the candle seemed to grow. It grew so big that it turned into a torch that I was unable to hold. I could feel the oil from the fat-soaked rags burning my hand as it dripped, it was so real. I held it high above me to see farther ahead. Just after this I seemed to trip. The torch fell over and I stood and watched it land on a pile of large rocks. The rocks lit up and a great warmth spread to my face. Then many other folk appeared, all lined up and looking at the flames with me. They knew of my presence and they smiled at me, applauding my sudden fall. I stepped away from the pile of flaming stones to walk backwards again, but the folk kept looking at the fire. The bees joined me again as I stepped farther away from where I had started. Then, just as I came back to the drifting fog, it cleared away. My hands were open wide and then I woke up.'

'I am still not wise enough to interpret dreams,' she said with both hands under his chin, turning his face towards her. 'But I am sure of this: it felt like a nice dream to me. Do not worry.'

'I feel much better now,' he answered. 'Ah, the door, I think we have a customer. Let's hope it's not a salesman selling candles.'

William smiled as he turned away, now a little happier after his chat with his mother. He had a brighter smile and Mary hoped he would now have a better day ahead of him.

When John and the other children came home from the market they, too, were happy. Joan was jumping up and down before her mother with the flowers she had picked, while Richard had just seen an owl catch a sparrow and wanted to tell her all about it and Gilbert had a pocket full of sycamore seeds that he was keen to show. He intended to throw them through the bedroom window to watch them spin, with the hope of one landing on someone's head, rather than plant them out.

'How has the day been?' asked Mary, looking at John. 'Did they all sell a belt apiece?'

'Yes, we had good sales today, my love,' he said. 'I shared so much laughter with these three that I nearly lost sales from laughter. I could hardly look someone in the face without smiling.'

'What have they been doing all day to make them laugh so?' she asked.

'Eating pears,' he replied quickly. 'Eating pears, my love. Yes, that is all they have done today.'

'What about the purse I showed the lady?' asked Richard, turning from the window.

'Oh yes. You mean the one with dribbles of pear juice on the leather,' John laughed, now looking past Richard who was distracted by something outside. 'What are you looking at, Richard?'

'The spinners. Gilbert is throwing them from the window upstairs,' he answered.

John tutted to himself and turned towards Joan, who was pulling his arm for attention. 'How was your day, Mary?' He pulled Joan to his side to invite a kiss.

'Not as fun as yours, by the sound of it,' she said. 'We had the funeral pass by this morning – old Ben it was.' Then she smiled. 'William sold twenty sheepskins this afternoon.'

'Who to? You should have sent him to fetch me,' he said with surprise. 'A sale like that and all on his own! Have they paid?'

'They were for your brother, Henry,' she replied proudly. 'He says he is selling them on for his own profit.'

'I hope he brings us the money.' He shook his head. 'It took me six months to get it off him last time.'

'He told William he would bring the money tonight,' she said. 'What else could he do?'

'Hmm, yes, he is family, I suppose,' John said, now in deep thought. 'But I would still like to have been here. Where is William?' He put Joan back down.

'I have sent him for some more milk,' she said. 'The goat is unable to provide for all of us.'

'What will we be having for supper?' asked John.

'Beef tonight, I told you this morning,' she answered.

'I remember,' he nodded. 'But it was before daylight. I am tired now. How do you expect me to remember details like that after a hard day? Have we enough meat to last until next week?'

'Yes, plenty.' She glanced out of the back door. 'Then we will have to see to a chicken, I think.'

'No, not yet,' he said. 'I have enquired after half a pig today. I reached a deal with Thomas, so let them lay a few more yet, eh, love?'

'As you wish,' she said, smiling.

He smiled with her. 'I prefer chicken to pig, for the latter does not lay eggs.'

'If they could hear your reprieve, they may be tempted to lay even more for you.'

The back door banged open, letting everyone know that William had arrived home.

'Hello, Father.' William burst into the kitchen. 'Amy has given me some honey with the milk.'

'Well done, son,' said Mary with surprise. 'Did you use your charm, or had you met her in a dream before?'

'I ... I ... oh, I ...' William tried to say, stumped for words and with a guilty look on his face, thinking his mother had been speaking about his dream.

'Are you all right?' John asked. 'I have never seen you at a loss for words before.'

A Day Out

A letter arrived for William one day from an old school friend of his called William Smith, Will to his friends. The two had only shared a casual acquaintance at school, because both seemed similar in their quest for knowledge and saw each other as having similar philosophical interests. Will had been fortunate, for his parents were quite wealthy and they didn't have to rely on an irregular income for their survival, unlike William. A lack of money had stopped his education, which was why he was now working in the family business. However, with Will attending Oxford University at the time, he had both the funds and the time to write to William.

To receive a letter in 1581 was quite rare, but for a young man of seventeen it was even rarer. John brought a letter back home with him one day which had been given to him at the guildhall. He was concerned by the unusual seal, for Will seemed to be showing off the new writing techniques he had learned at college. Will had replied to William's letter of two months ago, asking him to write and tell him of university life compared to their lives at Stratford. He had asked Will to use words carefully, because the letter would no doubt be read by his mother. And William was right, for when he was handed the letter in front of the family, he had to read it out to the many excited ears gathered before him in expectation. It was the highlight of the day but one which should have been personal to William. But with his parents and his giggling brothers and sister listening he was glad that he'd had the forethought to warn young Will.

'It is from Will, Will Smith,' William announced with glee as he carefully broke the seal.

'Do you mean William Smith?' asked John, emphasising his name in full while rocking back on his heels. He hated to hear people shorten a good Christian name.

'Yes, Father,' he said, hardly able to contain his excitement. 'Look, his handwriting is so bold and fancy now. It looks as if a monk has taken time off from writing a bible to write it.'

'Read it to us all then, William.' Mary shushed the children and waited expectantly.

'He says that he has mastered Greek, but not his Greek-looking lecturer,' he continued with a laugh, but then he became more serious when the family didn't follow his wit. 'Oh, then he speaks of the fine buildings and great walled gardens with vines. He has friends, more so than he had at school in Stratford. And his elder sister is getting married.'

William was skipping words, so John interrupted him. 'William, read it out in full.'

'Oh, yes,' he said but then thought for a moment before speaking. They will frown when I read young lad's things out, but I must do as I have been bid. Mother will read it next – how I hope his remarks wash over her head.

'From the start,' he said to begin once more:

With bountiful joy, dearest and gracious friend, William,

From this Greek fortress I have conquered, but not its captain. I send you this letter, but away from lecturing eyes. I am held prisoner in these aged buildings, but should I escape, there will be more toil, I think, with these walled confines with twisting vines, letting all know who the walls belong to. There are few pleasures here. The maypole is considered common folk's play. Anything of child-mindedness is frowned upon. These Latin and Greek men are sombre folk, almost military-like, keeping strict order with a cane – a thick, polished cane, I say. It is not so bad, I must confess, and the food is as good as home, but women are as plentiful as swan is on the menu.

William lowered his head to hide his embarrassment at Will's words before continuing, but his mother putting her hand to her mouth to stifle a giggle didn't escape his notice. She followed the thought and knew what he meant, that much was clear.

'And more,' he continued:

There are some women, though, but they are often hiding in the shade and certainly not enough to go round. But I confess that I prefer to write and have simple chicken or beef with my bread, rather that than chase through the hedges for wild pig like village life demands of us. I have tasted good ale, but only a little. We both know what vile antics it stirs up in men and spews out to the rest of us after copious amounts.

My sister is getting married to a rich farmer, so I will have to throw dried flowers at them. Had we thrown corn, I fear he would bend down to pick it up if we threw and wasted as much as we normally do.

Without languishing further, my friend, would you care to meet at Banbury some time? It is just a short ride away for each of us. Oxford is a long way to travel in just a day without stopping at some inn. Is a fortnight from the sixth any good to you?

I take it you will say yes, so I suggest we meet up next to the water troughs in the town square at midday.

Your honoured friend,

Will.

William offered the letter to Mary, but she knew he had read it out in the full, so she shook her head to refuse the offer.

John looked at Mary to see what expression of judgement she had as to their meeting so far away from home.

'Are you going to meet him then, lad?' he asked.

'Well, may I? Will you let me?' William asked, knowing John's question had humbled him into asking.

'He is your friend; do you want to go?' John asked.

'I do want to go, but I would like your approval,' he answered.

'He is still your friend, William, I take it?' John enquired further.

'Yes, but I have no means of travelling there. I can only walk.'

'How important is it to you that you go?' asked John, still standing firm.

The others had started to filter away at this point, though Mary remained in the room, with her hands closed in front of her. She had her head down, waiting for John to have his say before she passed comment.

'I have known him since school,' said William, both hands open in submission. 'This is a chance I have to see more of the land. Not many will be offered in Stratford.'

'We will see,' Mary intervened. 'It depends if we can spare you. You know we have to live.'

'Yes, we will see, William,' John nodded with approval. 'We will see. If you continue your good work and bring in more customers, then I think we could find a mule for you to borrow – depending upon your future conduct, mind.'

Mary and John smiled; they had no intention of letting William loose on a mule, but he still thought his parents were serious. John turned to Mary and whispered loudly into her ear so William could hear it, still testing and teasing him.

'On second thoughts, I think I have enough leather for some new boots for him. He will have to set off early, though; it is a long walk.'

William turned to the side to stop himself from protesting and thereby dulling his chances. He pretended to read the letter again while they discussed it among themselves, but secretly he had decided that he would be going whatever decision they reached. Even if I have to make gloves for an army first, I will meet you, my friend, he determined.

The child–parent stand-off had been exhausted fully. Neither would give in to certainty either way. John was holding the reins back from his son. He wanted him to stand alert and not chase head-on into the world. He wanted to think about his decisions as he had cautioned him so many times before and not act in haste. William knew he could not go without help, but he had manhood growing inside him, pulling him away from the order of home, ready to carve out his own life.

William soon got his way and his attitude turned from looking down to the glover's donkey[2] in submission to looking towards an adventure and beyond. His spirits were now so high that even John noticed William's attitude towards work changing. With it, his disciplinarian side mellowed and he left him to it more. He had even arranged for William to travel on one of Thomas Eldman's heavy barley wagons. This of course was a twofold tactic – to help William to see his friend and to keep him safe on his journey to Banbury and back.

William thought it was a great personal victory. His wishes had come about and he would be free to enjoy his first day away from Stratford.

---

2 A device to aid the making of gloves.

Even though it had been a test for him set by his parents, he had passed it quite easily.

The journey didn't seem to take too long, but he'd had to get up so early, so he slept for most of the way. He arrived early for the meeting and sat on one of the horse troughs for almost two hours waiting for his friend. When Will arrived he had another surprise for William: he brought one of his friends with him.

'William,' said Will, tapping William on the shoulder from behind.

'Oh, Will,' he turned to say. 'With that new beard of yours I could not tell it was you.'

'Wit as usual,' Will replied, laughing with his friend. 'This is William, as you can see.'

William shook hands with Will and turned to shake hands with his friend.

'And this, William, is my friend Simon Cranbourne.'

They exchanged handshakes and walked across the newly cobbled square towards the nearest inn for lunch. Simon and Will looked like brothers, apart from one having a beard and the other being clean-shaven. They also had similar likes, dislikes and opinions and each one knew where the other was coming from. Simon must have had to sit at the front of the class, for he seemed to need to tilt his head to see clearer as he walked as one of his eyes wasn't so good. The three young men were smart and well-mannered and they seemed to strike up a relaxed friendship straight away. William had only been acquainted with Will on a few occasions, because Will's family didn't want their son having a strong association with William after he finished grammar school. However, what little time they had spent together in the past had bonded them together like beetle glue. They needed little time to get to know one another again, although it seemed like it was only yesterday when they last met.

'Are you studying with Will, Simon?' asked William.

'Trying to,' he answered with a further smile. 'He argues with me all the time, testing me as if I were in court.'

'Good practice, though,' said Will, as he missed a step. 'But I have taken note of the wear you inflicted on my boots just then when you tried to trip me up. I do hope the wax is still good.'

Simon laughed. 'Do you see, William? He eats lecturers by the month. I fear the rest of the class will have to join together and pay for a woman lecturer. He is like a melting candle when women are about. I tell you, this is the only way we will get one to last a term.'

'That is not so,' said Will, taking the bait. 'But I have speeches in mind to make them blush.'

'He has, William, he has, believe me,' said Simon, ruffling Will's hair. 'But with his well-rehearsed sentences and longer words than their dresses, well, they never fall out. Like the ruffles they wear, his brave words are still laid out neatly on his tongue. He fights men with words like a soldier, but his mouth is closed for all women.'

Will could only smile to hide his embarrassment, but William had to take a helping for himself and join the debate. 'Perhaps if you coughed, Will, the words would fall from your tongue, then somehow you could arrange them in front of her very eyes; the right way up, of course.'

'Enough of your wit,' said Will. 'Have you two been writing to each other behind my back? Your plot is as weak as cheap ale.'

William stepped to one side to look behind Will, before continuing with the onslaught. 'It looks as if someone has been writing on it, though. Have you not the luxury of a blotting rag at college?'

The three of them entered the inn in jovial spirits and they found a vacant seat under a window. The quick-witted conversation soon ended when a lady, showing more than William had seen before, delivered an armful of food to a table of heckling men.

'Seriously, William,' Will closed his eyes to turn away from the woman. 'What ale do you prefer?'

'I ... I have never sat in an inn before,' said William. 'Not without Father delivering something and I have never seen such a show before my food. We have curtains at home to stop outsiders watching our shadows at night time, but what a shadow her chest would cast, my friends.'

The lads bit their lips, trying to hold the laughter inwards.

'Have you ever drunk to excess before, William?' asked Simon seriously, trying to keep his face still.

'Oh yes,' he said. 'At home with some of Father's wine and a little ale.'

'We have things to show you, then.' Simon smiled and raised his eyebrows.

'No, not with drink,' said William firmly. 'I have seen the results of drink.' But he then added lightly and glanced with slight hesitation,

'But since my childhood, I declare that I have never seen so much of a woman before.'

William seemed to have deflected the conversation, which seemed to hold back further talk of drink, and Will changed the subject back to childhood. 'What was your most stupid thought as a child, William? You know – something a parent would never know, a foolish act or a secret thought.'

William shrugged, looking at Will to put his suggestion forward first.

'I have one,' Simon said brightly. 'Listen to this. I once tried to kill a chicken with a blunt axe. I hit it, but it ran away clucking. I told Mother that I had trodden on it by mistake.'

'What happened?' asked William.

'Well,' he said, 'my father always made me watch him drown puppies or kittens and so forth, so I tried it myself. The poor chicken must have suffered, because it made quite a splash. I have to look away from them now. I cannot bear to see them being killed.'

'How terrible,' said Will with his lip twisted.

'I know one,' said William, 'but it's not gruesome like your tale. It was more the result of my own ignorance.'

'Go on then, tell,' said Will.

'It was at meal time,' said William smiling. 'But the thought still embarrasses me. I was at an age of being interested in learning what fitted where and so forth and in front of me was a board full of food.'

At this point a chesty barmaid came over to ask if they wanted to eat, so the conversation stopped for a time. 'Oh, beef, beef and ale all round,' said Will, passing his money to her without asking for change. 'And?' he encouraged, not about to let William get out of it that easily. Simon and Will then turned to hear the conclusion, but each of them kept glancing at the "feast" passing before their very eyes.

'The board, yes, the board,' William continued. 'As I said, I had a great pile of food in front of me. I looked at it then felt the size of my head. Then I tried to put the whole lot in my mouth. I thought that my head was just made up entirely of a mouth. I could not understand why I had to put a small amount in at a time.' William finished with a stare at the table, waiting for a reaction. Silent laughter crept out from the other two, followed by William, who still thought his experience was funny to this day.

Just as the laughter had died down, the maid brought them a board of meat and three jugs of ale to share. However, as they started to eat, both Simon and William looked at Will with an inquisitive smile. Then they looked at each other as Will stopped eating to enquire of their shared, surreptitious glances.

'Have I dribbled?' asked Will.

'No, no,' Simon replied with a further smile at William. 'We are just waiting for your story. We have to compare your story to ours, long before the wax begins to block our ears!'

'Oh, er, well, I may have something,' said Will, looking down in an attempt to direct their eyes away from his face to the food.

'Well, what is it?' asked Simon.

'Have you kissed a bull like the one you are eating before you?' asked William, causing Will to squirm with the disgusting thought.

'No, I have not.' Will lifted his eyes. 'But you will laugh all the same. I once crept into my mother's room and …'

'And?' William and Simon asked together.

'I just looked under my mother's ruffled dress as she was sleeping, just to see what lay beneath, that is all,' said Will, looking back at his food.

'And did you find anything?' Simon kicked William under the table to encourage him add more to the debate.

'What is it that lies beyond ruffled dresses?' asked William.

Will had thoughts of a tale with a twist, so by stretching out his humour he would have the other two following the chase. 'I think I had better not tell you both,' he said, shaking his head. 'I think I may have said too much already.'

'If you have then we certainly have,' Simon said seriously.

'Are you sure you want me to continue?' Will asked William.

'Yes,' he said. 'It is only fair that you must.'

Will took in a deep breath, followed closely by William and Simon, who leaned forward to encourage him to continue. Staring straight ahead of them in an attempt to avoid eye contact lest he laugh, he said, 'My eyes crept slowly up my mother's dress, then further, then right where it ended – it was the cat!' he cried, before laughing out loud. 'It had been there all morning under her chin.'

'Oh, you had me then. You fooled me good and proper,' said Simon.

'And me,' William laughed.' You had me with your story. I was once fooled by an old tale I once heard of a boy-eating dragon living down a well in the same manner.'

'I have been listening to you both for long enough.' Simon shook his head. 'I knew you would be of the same mind.'

William paused for a moment to eat further, but after another bite, he laid down more bait. 'I am confused now, Will.'

'Why is that?' Will asked, still with victory on his face.

'Is this the reason you are without a woman of your own?' William raised his hands as claws. 'For fear a cat might spring from the folds of material with its claws and hiss and spit should you walk near them?'

'Ah-ha, not quite,' said Will, now a little flustered. 'I ... I see your point, though. How about you, William? Has your family decided upon a woman for you yet? Or do you have your own lustful quarry hidden away deep in your mind?'

'My parents have hinted, but I have ignored their guidance,' William said quickly. 'I dream like most lads of our age, but I have many things to discover and entertain me to pass by my life before I think of this. I have to think of a roof over my head first. I think of myself being like a gentle rowing boat, just drifting by, looking for a tempting mooring place. I am not yet tempted by the rapids of lust and hidden rocks!'

After they had eaten, the boys went for a walk around the town to speak further of their future plans and to allow their meal to settle. They stopped to rest outside the church and sat under an ancient yew tree to watch people pass by. The seeming barrel of ale William had drunk made him wish he hadn't tasted it, but he managed to keep his head still. Simon and Will were used to this bending of the college rules, for they could afford the luxury and they had money to spare.

'Look, William, see that rounded man over there?' said Simon, pointing. 'He's had more than his fill and he looks so jolly.'

'Yes, I see him,' slurred William, looking across at him. 'But look at his hand on his pocket. He is patting the gold he carries. That is why he is so jolly and why he cares not for our slim looks. He has what he values most.'

'The owl from Stratford, we should call him,' said Will with surprise. 'Did you notice the hair growing from his ears?'

'No,' said William, now with the gauntlet of challenge picked up. 'But I did see his cheap wig and copper-buckled shoes pretending to be gold.'

'How do you know this?' asked Simon.

'His wig has washed a little straight from the rain and his buckles look too thick to be gold. It would make more sense to buy dark boots and a good wig. You seldom look down at the feet of those you meet, do you?'

'Oh, you are like my desk partner,' said Simon, looking at William. 'Every answer has to have a winning swing.'

'No, not really,' said William, patting Simon on his back and hiccuping. 'It helps to experiment with your answers with friends first, before the person you meet next makes a mockery of you in front of strangers or family. But I could be wrong. Would either of you like to chase him and ask of his riches?'

'William has a point, Simon,' said Will, joining in. 'I had never thought of it like that before.'

'Neither had I.' Simon nodded to agree.

'Nor me,' said William. 'It has only just come to my mind. With every day that passes, more comes to mind. Like the clouds passing silently up there, we learn quietly each day, without the trumpets or drums heralding a new finding. Thoughts pass into our mind so gently, much better than the drum beat of a schoolmaster's cane or his trumpeting shriek!'

'Steady as she goes, Erasmus,' said Will with open hands towards William to stop him from tottering. 'We are away from school but the desk is still here with you.' Will held his position for only a short time and William nodded gratefully at him.

'What are you going to do in your life, William?' Simon asked, looking across to a pair of sparrows fighting in the dust.

William took in a deep breath of the churchyard breeze, paused and answered quietly. He was trying to steady the alcohol to serious thought. 'London.'

'London is filthy with narrow streets and black slime running down them,' said Will with his nose up as if smelling the streets for real.

'London it is,' he said again, 'and I will not be moved. Inside my heart it is as if cupid has aimed to this place, but I have told no one how deep the pull is before. I have something to find there. My twisted belly tells me that this is the way I should go. Somehow, I want to open my arms and shout out to the crowds that London is my love. But I do not know what to say. I feel it inside me, the pain from my voice and my outstretched arms. I feel it. Sometimes travelling players come to town, with their bright clothes and wheels, and faces and hair to match – they are all from London. I look at the players from time to time and see how happy they look when they act, but behind it they are acting only for bread, in the same way as we all have to work. It should be for love. How can you portray love with rhyming verse? My father and mother do not speak so, with up and down tones to their voice and jolly hoorays pretending it's for real!'

'Is that it, William?' asked Will. 'A player? You cannot be serious with this. This is not an ambition – it is a step up from a hedger and a ditcher. You may even end up being thrown in a ditch for your efforts.'

William retreated from speaking. His secret was now in the open and he had shocked both Simon and Will, because they were both frowning with surprise, making a mockery of his aim in life.

'I admire your strength of mind and, I must say, your quick mind, William,' said Simon. 'Are you sure you want this? But I suppose we only judge by what we have seen. If it is in your heart and you have judged it yourself to be right, then let it be your way.'

'I am not a glover,' he replied. 'You would not believe what I have in my mind. The words flow through me like a river of letters. All I have to do is put my hand in to cup what may be passing by. They twist and lift up like snakes, then change to seek other ways, sad or happy. They just need glue to be read. Oh, my head is this way, I confess.'

'I do not think badly of your thoughts, William,' said Will, followed by a sigh. 'You are still my friend, but take careful steps in the waters you are thinking of. If you see a way, you must take it. Do not fear wet ankles. If you feel it in your gut, wade through the deepest parts and you will make it to the other side, I am sure.'

'Thank you both,' said William with a growing smile. 'I still have to give it some further thought, I know, but support from just a few friends will push me onward. The London streets are, indeed, filthy, I believe, but what does muck on the fields do? It helps the next crop push through to swell up, ripen, fill our bellies and brighten our lives.'

'I am convinced,' exclaimed Simon, standing up. 'You are indeed a relative of Erasmus.'

The three young men stood up and shook hands firmly, as if they had just met for the first time. They were all smiling, but doubts still pervaded their minds and leapt about from one thing to another as chirruping robins hop between bare branches in winter time. The three friends then went for a long walk around Banbury, before meeting up with Eldman's barley cart in the town centre.

William was a changed man when he returned home late that evening. He was surer than he ever was that he was on the right path and although it was a long journey from Stratford to London, it was nearer in his heart than anyone around him would know. William continued to write to Will and Simon with a joint letter, but only when he could afford the paper. His friends were the only ones to know of the deepness of his pull to London, unlike his family who thought it was just a passing phase.

Rotten Wood

Occasionally, his work in the family business took him away from home and on one such day William had to go with John to fetch a cartload of barley. John bought and sold whatever he could to make ends meet. If there was profit in it, he would grasp the chance of it with both hands. The family were eating together one morning, but hard times were still with them and they had little money to go round.

'Are we all going to Charlecote today, Father?' asked Joan.

'No, we have work to do here,' Mary said in his place. 'Only William is going with Father. There are heavy sacks to carry.'

'I had better get my boots on, then,' Gilbert said with a laugh.

'I can lift the sacks with ease,' William said, defending his weakness. 'You chase the chickens. You are good at that.'

'Enough of your brotherly spite,' John said. 'Eat your crusts, William, or put it with the rest for Mother's pudding.'

'Where is Charlecoot, Father?' asked Richard, looking longingly at William's crust.

'Charlecote, not coot.' William handed his crust to him. 'You can have my crust. My teeth ache this morning.'

'Aren't there even any crumbs for the chickens, Richard,' John said, looking at Richard's trencher board. 'They won't be able to reward us with eggs if we don't feed them,' he teased.

'I meant to leave them some. I will have to find them some worms, instead,' said Richard, taking him seriously.

'Jest, my son, jest.' John rubbed Richard's head and looked straight at Mary. 'We will be going now, my love, but before we do will you find me the strong twine for William's tooth?'

William heard this, so he stopped pulling silly faces at Joan and stared at John with his mouth open.

'Is it so bad, then?' John asked, smiling.

'No, just a little pain,' William said. 'I mistakenly chewed on a buckle Mother may have dropped in the cake.'

With this, the tables were turned as the finger of wit was now pointed in Mary's direction, but she carried it well. 'Yes, Father,' she said sharply, 'I will find the twine. No, make that a rope!'

William made a pretend dash for the door, but Gilbert and Richard pulled him down before he got there.

'Two against one is not fair,' William cried from his hopeless position.

'We will need more still to hold him down.' Mary tilted her head for Joan to follow.

But Joan's idea of helping was to save William by pulling Gilbert's arm away enough to allow William to escape the trap.

Gilbert scowled. 'You were supposed to help us, Joan.'

'You are to be split evenly now.' John laughed and banged the floor with his stick. 'Two pulling either way, but let us not spend the day fighting. We all have jobs to do. Help Mother clear up now.'

It was a signal to end the game, indicating that they should all stop quietly and straighten their clothes; the serious matter of work was now at hand. Gilbert and Richard had the task of helping John's friend with the leaking shop roof and Joan had some milking duties to attend to. Then she would help Mary bake while looking after baby Edmund.

John and William were soon on the cart trotting up Henley Street towards Charlecote, but they had a few bumpy miles ahead of them.

'What is wrong with your teeth, William?' John shouted, lashing the reins. 'Should I bring the tools with us?'

'Oh, it was just a chestnut. I mistakenly chewed on the hard skin yesterday,' he shouted back, rubbing his mouth. 'I poked it out this morning with a needle.'

'A boot needle?' John exclaimed, knowing how thick and sharp it was.

'No, I used a fine one, but the pain will pass quickly if I try to ignore it.'

John whipped the horses harshly to gain more time. The journey would be a hard one; recent heavy rain had cut away parts of the narrow roads in places. This in turn left hollows with puddles, but they didn't worry John – it was the previous two days' rain that did. It had been a bright start to both days, but it was followed by torrential rain and new streams running down the streets. Although the barley would be bagged up already, it had to be kept dry to stop it from rotting.

The uneven ride to Charlecote was a near silent one. The clatter from the cart wheels made conversation possible only by shouting. Labourers in the fields had an even chance of hearing the conversation on some roads, they were so rough. As they sped towards their destination, they passed a large house that was set back beyond some tall trees. It was the largest William had ever seen.

'Who lives there?' William shouted, pointing.

'Sir Thomas Lucy,' John shouted back. 'If we shout even louder, he may be able to hear us.'

William stared at the house, but then sat forward again as the trees obscured his line of sight.

Within half an hour they had found the farm they had been looking for, so John steered the cart down the badly repaired side road. The farmer had died recently, so John had bought a wagonload of barley from the estate. As they pulled up outside the farmhouse, they were waved by to load their wagon first. This was not normal practice, because this would normally end up with the buyer fleeing without payment. John was a well-known figure, so his trustworthiness was never questioned. He would always pay up, eventually. They proceeded to load up the wagon and then walked over towards the waiting farmer's widow. John wanted William to watch the dealings, so he was at his side when the money was counted and handed over. The formalities were soon completed, but as John walked away he suddenly had a thought which made him stop and look at William.

'Do you know what I have just done?'

'No, Father,' William said with surprise. 'We have paid for the barley, have we not?'

'Oh, we have paid for it alright,' he paused before stepping onto the wagon. 'But I have used the last of our money – the last. We must be getting back.'

John jumped up with speed and William followed, noticing the darkening sky.

'We must hurry. Watch the sideboards, we have to go with speed,' John said.

He gave the horses a mighty crack of the whip, so much so that they jumped up a little before obeying. When the horses had settled into pulling the load, John whipped them to gradually go faster until they were cantering for a mile or so.

They would easily have beat the rain that day, but it seemed that good fortune wasn't to be theirs today, for not only had they used up the last of the family's wealth but a rotten wheel collapsed as they slowed down to join a new road and the cart dropped to the clattering cobbles. They were both fine, but the wheel was just a rim and a load of sticks suitable for kindling only. The cart came to rest in an upright position on the edge of a bank, much to John's surprise. All the weight must have been placed near the front axle, so it wobbled to and fro as it teetered. John jumped off inspect the damage. There wasn't much left of the rear wheel, which was now scattered over a wide area and none of the pieces was bigger than his arm.

Tears came to John's eyes – something that William had never seen before. John held his cap tightly and wept as he stood looking between the hub and the sky.

'We are done for, my son,' he said softly. 'I have failed us all by rushing instead of taking my time. The wheel has been stood in a stream for over a year,' he said before shouting, 'but it may as well have been a damn well. The cursed wood is so soft that it is like pig fat!'

John let his head rest on the cart to think further, so with this William stepped down and stood by his side.

'Father, you have said before that whatever dirt splashes our feet, we should have faith and wait. The rain will always come and wash it away in good time.'

'Yes, that is so,' John said tearfully, pointing around them. 'But I do not see tools at the ready and a pile of seasoned timber at hand. There are only bushes, as you can see, and the rain lies in wait above, ready to ruin us.'

'Then I will find help. There is the large house over the fields,' William said, pointing.

'Yes, I know,' John said with an empty sigh. 'I know, but we are the wrong sort. They will laugh at us if we ask for help.'

'I will ask,' said William with determination. 'So what if I am laughed at and turned away from their land. A scolding maybe, but it will hardly be an invitation for an arrow.'

John turned around and looked at William, shielding his reddened eyes. 'You can try,' he said sadly. 'That is where your strength lies and your resolve is much stronger than arms, but I fear we will have to wait for the bush to grow a wheel before we can get ourselves out of this one.'

William put his hand on his father's arm but didn't speak. Then he turned and ran for over a quarter of a mile to the house as if a crossbow was aimed at his rump. All the way he rehearsed his introduction to the owner. He didn't see anyone else on the way and just leapt over each rain-filled hollow, glancing up to the sky in hope.

William's thoughts of an innocent meeting with the owner of the property were soon dashed. As he stopped at the end of the driveway near the imposing house, he looked up with surprise, pausing to catch his breath. The head gardener had seen him running towards the house, so he had called his men from their lunch to block his path. Soon, there were six men and the head gardener, all with folded arms lying in wait for William.

'Stop there, lad,' the head gardener said with his grubby hand up towards William's face. 'What does town muck want with this house?'

William was shocked by the insult, but he kept his cutting words at bay; for the moment, anyway. 'Sir,' he puffed with his hands on hips, 'I would like to ask the owner of the house to help my father and me to get home.'

'You think you can run here and address Sir Thomas directly?' the head gardener laughed, encouraged by his men. 'He speaks to me only once a month, so why should you be any different; or have you gold to give him?'

'Not gold, sir, but payment in kind for his help,' William replied firmly.

'This is not the town's inn stable,' said the head gardener, pointing. 'You have an hour at best to run in that direction!'

'I have done you no harm,' William said with a frown. 'I have only come to ask for help.'

'Go on then, lad, tell me what you require,' the head gardener asked with his head bowed, as if he were speaking to royalty. 'What do you require from your subjects, with pockets flowing over with coppers?'

'Only a wheel, sir,' said William bluntly, knowing he was in for further ridicule. 'But, sir, not just an ordinary wheel,' he said in poetic verse, thinking he would soon have to run, 'but a jewelled one for my golden chariot outside your walls. This wheel has been borrowed for a time by an angel on an errand to help other poor souls.' He knelt on one knee before raising his voice. 'Souls who think they are superior to God as they paint his garden with poisoned fingers, not knowing where or when the fruit will spring, failing to notice weeds in the spring.'

'You piece of town filth with fancy words. I think the compost heap is the best place for him, eh, lads?' said the head gardener, looking toward his open-mouthed men.

William turned to run, but he was stopped by a voice from above him. 'I do not think so,' said a voice from an upstairs window.

It was Sir Thomas Lucy himself; he had been listening to the flow of the conversation from the start. The head gardener took off his cap, as did his six men, while William stood up from his kneeling position.

'Boy,' called Sir Thomas, 'your verse and temper astound me, but can you read as fast?'

William straightened himself up, dusted himself down and walked towards the house. 'Yes, sir, I can. And I can write quite well.'

'Hmm. Show him the front door, Smith.' Sir Thomas scowled at the head gardener. 'And on the way, look down for weeds.' He smiled and turned away from the window.

Smith shooed his six men away with the only authority he had left and pointed for William to follow him.

'If I get the chance, I'll pitchfork you,' he muttered.

'Be sure you don't prick your lip while you eat with it, Smith!' William said rudely, to rub salt in the wound.

He followed Smith towards the front door, but he could sense by the glowing fume from his ruddy neck that he was seething with anger.

Sir Thomas was already standing outside the front door when Smith and William walked up to it, so Smith bowed his head before retreating. Sir Thomas was dressed in black, from his boots right up to his moleskin hat; even his eyebrows were deep black.

Ah, a silver-topped black cane, William thought as Sir Thomas twirled it around. Costly, though. The silver top has been crafted with sweat and pain to earn it, but I see that the birch below, like the one used in school, can deliver pain from its blows. Each has a price to bear. Like his cane, the man is hard and yet I feel he is soft within.

'You have imagination with your words, young man,' Sir Thomas said, looking at William from his muddy boots to his tangled hair.

'Thank you, sir,' he replied, looking towards where Sir Thomas was pointing his cane. He indicated that William should accompany him in the garden. 'I must apologise for my rudeness to your men.'

'He had it coming. What payment in kind had you in mind, then?' Sir Thomas nodded to accept his apology as they continued to walk.

'Whatever work you have available for me, sir,' he said, now with his hands behind his back. 'We have just used the last of our money to buy a wagonload of barley and we need to replace the wheel of the cart before it rains and spoils our purchase. I will do anything you wish, for we have nothing but ourselves to give.'

'I admire your honesty, boy.' Sir Thomas turned back to look William in the eye. 'To tell a stranger of your family's financial strain is out of desperation, I am sure. But I wonder what you are willing to do in return for a wheel. Scythe the weeds down, perhaps ...'

'Yes, if that is what you wish, sir,' William said with eyes wide. A cheap repayment, indeed, he thought.

'No, that is not enough for a wheel. They are costly,' Sir Thomas said, trying to think of further way of teasing him. 'Cut and prune 12 yards of bush – twelve spokes for 12 yards – to begin with, of course. Now that is a fair exchange, do you not think?'

'Err, yes, sir. I will try,' William said, now fearing his offer of his services was beyond him.

'Perhaps you could build me a new barn, with help, of course,' Sir Thomas added with a further mocking smile, trying to look away to avoid eye contact lest he may smile. 'Not a large one, though – ten paces, no more.'

William looked up at Sir Thomas and stopped walking. 'Sir, I respect your position,' he said without removing his cap in hand to grovel, 'but a barn is too much that you ask of me. I fear I must ask elsewhere.'

'Wait. Don't be so hasty. I am only testing the length of your rope, my friend,' Sir Thomas said with the word "friend" sticking in William's mind. 'What would you say if I asked you, in exchange for a "golden wheel", as you put it, to teach my two adopted daughters to read and so forth?'

'I ... I am shocked, sir,' William said, his mood lightening with each breath. 'It is not work you ask; it is something I love doing and would find a pleasure. But paper is so costly. I ... I would gladly teach them in exchange for making a whole cart, let alone for repairing just our wheel!'

'It is done, then,' Sir Thomas said calmly. 'Except for two things.'

'Yes, sir, just ask,' William replied excitedly.

'Your name for one ... and the position of your wagon?' he asked.

'Shakespeare! I am William and my father is John.' He pointed towards the trees in the direction of the cart. 'The cart is over there. My father is waiting with it lest thieves should take an opportunity.'

'Ah, I have met him. He was a bailiff.' Sir Thomas shook his head and turned away to think. 'I fear that we had stiff words when we last met.

Neither of us would back down, so I just walked away from his temper.'

This brought sadness to William's face, but he could not have known his charge towards the house might have been in haste. His father had said nothing of his previous acquaintance with Sir Thomas. But worse – a conflict.

'He was right though, William,' he said with forgiving words. 'He was right, but I made him pay for his insult.'

'Insult?' asked William, now not knowing how to continue, fearing the assistance might be withdrawn.

'No, William, I will not go back on my word, even though we did not shake on it, it was a promise all the same.' William's heart sank like lead, seeming to push his feet into the grass. 'I made your father suffer for my ignorance of his wisdom. I was to blame for the trampled crop he suffered from my escaping herd. But we are here now and so are your hopes. It is a chance to redeem myself. The wheel is yours in exchange for the lost crop. You will still receive payment to teach my daughters, so go now before I change my mind. Be back on Sunday after church. I will be waiting.'

'Thank you, Sir Thomas.' William shook his head with disbelief and nodded several times. 'Thank you. I will be there.'

Within a short time William was back at his father's side, jumping with excitement. John hadn't time to ask of the pot of gold he thought William had found; he could see it galloping down the road. Sir Thomas had turned out his own wheelwright and several helpers ran alongside his wagon. They changed the wheel quickly, John shaking his head in disbelief as he stood back to watch the men. When they had finished, they thanked the men for their help and were on their way once more in just a few minutes.

'Faith, eh, William? Have faith.' John tapped the horses to head for home. He was still in a state of shock, so he leaned over and patted William's knee in thanks.

'Words help,' said William with a victorious smile, 'when they are used wisely.'

'You are right,' John said. 'And they work a good deal faster than my praying to a bush, I see.'

'Faith won the day for us, Father,' he said, now smiling at the thought of his new job with Sir Thomas. 'The wheel did come from the bush in a way. It came from the place directly behind it.'

'Yes, William,' John shouted across. 'I would like to know how you did it. We have crossed paths before, did you know that? We nearly came to blows.'

'I will tell you later,' he shouted as the cart rattled away once more. 'I have plenty to tell you.'

They didn't get home in time to stop the rain wetting a little of the top layer of barley, but the majority of the load was saved by the heat of the home fire and with constant turning.

After they had sorted the barley out, the family had a late supper together, but William had a story to tell that would shock everyone more than the rotten wheel had.

'I will tell you all quite bluntly,' announced William, standing up to address the family. 'Today has not been about using the last of our money to buy the barley here, or even about having the wheel fixed by Sir Thomas Lucy's men. There is much more and it is something I could not have imagined before Father and I set out this morning.'

William paused to help calm his excitement, but everyone knew by his expression that it was not just good news but great news that he bore.

'Sir Thomas overheard me debating our plight with his head gardener. Then, after ordering his men away and inviting me to walk with him in the garden, he offered me a job teaching his two daughters to read and write.'

There was little reaction to what William had said. The family was stunned by the revelation. Even the youngest realised that he had done something far above their expectations and they knew it would lead to greater things.

'William, you have made us proud. It must be the work of the Lord. How can a rotten wheel and my ensuing despair turn our day around and bring us fortune out of misfortune? I am happy but stunned, my son. Only you could fall from a tree and land on a passing hay cart, only you, William, only you. You always seem to step into a shallow puddle, while others end up wet up to their knees.'

New Beginnings

The week passed quickly for William and all around him could sense his happiness. His attendance at the morning service at church that day was one of special thanks for the Lord's hand at their change in fortune. His prayers that day were more willingly recited and his reward had been greater than he had ever expected. William's promotion of sorts had been reflected down the ranks to everyone, for William would now bring new wealth to the family. But it was important that he should not rise too far above his home duties. He was still their son and the eldest and with it he had duties and responsibilities that would still be expected of him.

Mary laid out fresh, clean clothes for William, wanting him to look his best. With a kiss and a bag of suitable books, William stepped out of the house to mount his father's horse.

'Do not go in haste, William,' Mary cautioned. It was a phrase she often used.

'Bring us a rabbit to share from the park,' said Gilbert.

'Let him go now,' John said, raising his arm to stop them holding him back with their demands so he could be on his way. 'He is going to work, you know. An eager man should be on his way.'

William kicked the horse into action and with a struggle and a reddened face, he eventually aimed it in the right direction.

William arrived at Charlecote Park with time to spare and was able to admire the vast, well-kept gardens, despite having ridiculed the gardeners the last time. Oh! this place it is so beautiful, William thought as he trotted down the drive. How did I miss this pleasant garden? And the house is real brick, just like New Place in town, built for all time. This is not a place of work. It will be like a down bed to sleep on working here. I will bring a pin the next time to keep me awake. So this is what well-kept grass looks like when cut short; for some time as well I should think. My head was so fixed last time that I saw nothing of this. Could Eden be like this? I wonder.

The stable lad soon roused him from his daydream and offered to take his horse and tether it up, leaving William wondering which way he should enter the house. William looked in vain for the servant's entrance and eventually a cook tapped on a milk pail to attract his attention. 'The front,' she whispered, pointing to the side.

William tipped his cap at her then walked around to find the front door. The knocker was just like the one at church, so it reminded him of his past fear of the dark church doors. A maidservant answered the door. She was obviously busy as she had a cloth of some kind in her hand and she tilted her head to indicate that he should follow her but she never spoke.

Once inside, William followed her along wide passages, passing several thick doors also resembling those from church. They stopped outside a door that looked just like the rest, with panels each side of it and whitewash on the walls and ceiling above. The servant knocked on the door before entering and then peeped around to see if it was alright to show William in. She turned back and waved him through and he squeezed past her to get into the room. The maid wore a cold expression, almost as if she had done something wrong, or maybe she thought him to be out of place, but it made William shiver as he passed by her.

Perhaps she sees hate in me? William thought. Oh, there again I think she must be the gardener's daughter. Of course, she has to be, she has his nose!

Sir Thomas was sitting between his two straight-faced daughters, but William had to wrench his eyes away and think of his new task ahead of him – to teach his daughters. The room was panelled from top to bottom and there was furniture with thick carvings and rugs between each piece. Sir Thomas' daughters were both quite attractive, but William hadn't come to judge their looks, for it was he who would be the one to be judged.

'This is William,' said Sir Thomas.

His two daughters tipped their heads slightly, but neither of them stood up. William felt like he was on display on the humble mat.

'This is Agatha, sixteen, and this is Jane, seventeen.' Sir Thomas pointed at each daughter in turn before looking back to William.

Agatha had fair hair and wore a scarlet dress and Jane had red hair with a fair dress. William wondered if these comparisons were designed to be this way. On first sight, they could easily make me laugh out loud, but I am here on a serious matter. Stop drifting off, William! They are waiting for me to speak.

'I am pleased to meet you both – and you again, sir,' William replied politely with a bow and one hand behind his back.

'Will you give me an example of your work, William? I take it you have books with you?' Sir Thomas asked.

'Yes, I have, sir,' he replied. 'But these books are to help your daughters to read. I can give you something from in my head, though, if I may?'

Sir Thomas nodded his head and William composed himself before speaking. He then held his arm out to speak directly to Sir Thomas and his two daughters, just as if he were dictating a letter.

'Sir Thomas, thank you for your letter and kind invitation, but sadly I cannot attend. I have been cast into a dungeon, wrongly accused of writing slander. I wish so much that I could be with you and teach your daughters by the lakeside. If only my accusers would listen to my gentle verse, instead of prejudging my face, then they would surely let me free. I have no wit for women, only serious compliment in mind.' All eyes followed him as he turned around and spoke to the corners of the room. 'From my confinement here, Agatha and Jane are a great distance away from me, like the Avon is from the Thames. A strong arm or two could, in turn, splash the waters of the Avon from here, but only imagination could make the waters of the Thames ripple so. However, in my mind they are sat just a pace in front of me, arm in arm with you and reading my truthful letter. The accusers say that I mocked your daughters' dress and hair of red and yellow to match. But truly now I must confess, I compared your daughters to flowers in their appearance, their gentle petals soft as a kiss, with fragrance all but you should miss.'

William finished speaking and knelt on the rug in the centre of the room, then lowered his head to wait for a reaction. Time passed as his audience digested the compliment which lay beneath his words and applause followed, much to William's relief. He raised his head to accept the praise where it was due and received further smiles.

'I had my doubts, as well you know, William,' Sir Thomas said with a satisfied nod. 'I could have given a wheel to a beggar for all I knew, rather than just a quick-witted young man like yourself.'

William had got off to a fine start with his introduction to Sir Thomas and his daughters and from this a steady friendship grew.

William kept his place and taught as he knew best from the heart, but they were never to follow his skill. Instead, they were more interested in catching his eye. More good fortune from the outcome of their relationship came later for William, as Sir Thomas had a library full of books, of deeper wealth than even his old grammar school, and he was given the privilege of being able to use it.

After William's first day at work, he trotted home feeling like a returning knight, but with little sweat and without bruising or blood. He had earned his first day's proper wages for the family. I have been paid for this, he thought, feeling his swollen pouch, and yet it was real money for easy graft. Oh, what a place the whole world would be if it was like this for everyone. What an easy life we would all lead.

When William opened the door on his return that day, all the family was lined up to greet him. It was one of his best days ever and one without sweat or toil. But he still had his other duties to perform and the first one was giving his wages to his mother.

'Sir Thomas said he would pay me weekly from now on,' he said. 'But for my first day he said he would pay me that day, to encourage my return.'

Not a word was spoken, but seeing the pride on all faces present was payment enough for William. They were all speechless with pride.

Escape to France

As William was walking down by the riverside one Sunday afternoon, he was not alone. He was the envy of all the young men from the town, because four young ladies accompanied him, all eager to listen to his imaginative prose and wisdom. The ladies were all from local families and William had two on each side, linking arms. They each held their heads high with pride, as if they were sharing a great prize. With William that day were Agatha, Elizabeth, Jane and Judith, who all had designs on him and held on to every word he spoke. Agatha and Jane had been receiving the benefit of William's teaching whilst Elizabeth and Judith, both sixteen, were friends of William's parents, so he knew them all quite well. John wanted Joan to join the group that day, as a chaperone of sorts, but her mother wanted her to bake and work at her embroidery. William had a stern lecture from his father when he took him to one side before he set off with the ladies, but he had other things on his mind than his father's advice. The family was keen not let their son rise too far above his status, so he wore clothes to suit his position, not too colourful and not too fancy. John and Mary had great plans for their eldest, so they tried to keep his youthful reins as tight as possible, lest he may make a mistake.

'William,' said Agatha, steadying herself with William's arm, 'I remember a verse you told Jane several months ago. It was sharp and to the whole point and was about schooling. Do you remember it?'

'Yes, I do,' he answered. 'The servants were cleaning at the time if I remember rightly, but they were scratching heads with confusion or lice. However, what I do know is that it was not such a beautiful day as this and nor was I in such beautiful company.' William directed his compliment towards all the ladies as he smiled at each in turn.

The ladies tilted their heads down a little with slight blushes, each one wondering which one of them William would favour the most.

'Ah yes, it was this,' he said, suddenly recalling the words. 'Do not force children into schooling like a wagging finger directed at poison. Let them taste a little of its sugary tip, then they will run for more!' He bowed to the gloved applause from his four ladies and then they went on their way towards the river's edge.

'What do you see today, William?' asked Judith, with her hands clenched and nostrils flared, breathing in the scented air. 'What do you see looking around us? You always see so much from comparatively little.'

'Please, William. For all of us,' said Elizabeth, tugging his arm. 'For Jane, Judith, Agatha and myself, please tell us from your gentle mind what you see around us.'

All four ladies surrounded William with a submissive ring of hands. He was trapped and in great danger of being squeezed – he hoped!

'Sit down, then, and I will think,' he said softly.

The women collapsed to sitting positions, as if he had blown them all an uninvited kiss and they had swooned at his feet.

'But my mind may not be on the sun, the trees or the children laughing behind us. It may not even be on the river.' He looked up to the trees, then back to the ground and finally out towards the river for inspiration.

William was soon in a trance-like state. It was as if the women were not with him as his eyes just stared into the stillness the river.

'I think only of the river and how still it appears,' he spoke suddenly. 'Even though we are gathered here on one of the hottest of days of summer, my mind is elsewhere. Its journey through all the villages and towns will lead directly out to the cold sea, where an aged galleon is making its shady escape across to France, hiding beneath low dark clouds with its sails hoping to catch the slightest draught left unwanted by the birds. The ship has two passengers, a woman and her son. Think of her as The Dark Lady of my imagination. They are looking out to where our river joins their sea.'

' "Look, son," said the woman, pointing, "I wonder where the river has been? There may be people miles away thinking of where their river might lead to. And as we think of them, they may be thinking of us as our thoughts meet halfway near some innocent halfway bridge. We are afloat and tossed around by the will of the sea, but they could be watching weak waters at their feet. Our escape to France is to live, for there are so many murderers in our village and the soldiers too far away to help. It is the open sea we look to now, my love. Thoughts of the stern's estuary will be replaced by those of new rivers beyond the bow. You will soon take to the new language. Better that than have you turn to pick up a bloody dagger or worse, feel it in your side.

' "The man I loved so much, indeed your father, he is gone, I fear. For he was accused of a murder two nights ago and was then hunted on foot by the murderers themselves. He may have escaped their knives, but on their return, we would have been next. We often visited his family at Stratford. We used to meet on the riverbank and bask in the drifting scents skipping over its still waters. Oh, how I wish he were there now, thinking of us and our plight. I wish he could smell the same sweet scent and think of our return.

' "If he did escape to this paradise, I am sure he would write to France and ask us to return with greater speed than these sails are capable of. But alas, my son, he has no ink, paper or mind for writing, or even knowledge of the foreign town we are escaping to.

' "As we speak he could be moments away from death, but still with us in his mind, pushing him onwards through the thorns. Our love goes out to him over both waters to his Stratford paradise. Just before he closes his eyes I would like him to spare a thought for us. With luck, these thoughts could be our saviour; indeed, there could be others from this town, feeling our anguish from this tale and yet powerless to help our plight.

' "Try yourself, son. Breathe in the sea air and think of the river. Then think of your father and gain strength from the good you wish to happen and the evil you wish to end. Whatever our hearts desire and our minds turn to, I am sure one day it will come to be. To console ourselves, we must take courage from the fact that the rudder is turned well away from the bawdy murders of our village. Let its wake settle to nothing in the same way that their arguments settle nothing. We will return to our country soon, but for now we must smile at the people upriver who, I hope, may be thinking of us. Smile and wave at them. Do not feel out of place waving towards the estuary, for they may also feel out of place waving at their own reflection in the river waving back at them. Or perhaps it is we who wave back at them.

' "There is one thing for sure: we can all look up to the sun without clouds or birds between and hope. We can all think of each other. Their breeze is ours. Our water is connected to theirs and the sun warms all of our faces. You see, son, we are not alone in our escape. There are others who have us in mind. Think of them and hope they, in turn, will pray for our safe passage." '

The four ladies were close to tears and quite unable to speak. William stared out at the river without expression, his thoughts lost. Jane stood up and was soon followed by the other three as they waved silently downriver in response to William's words. Their sadness could be seen in their reflections as they became involved in the story. Who were they waving at, themselves or the fictional couple who were fleeing for their lives? A silence descended between them but for the wind, which brushed gently past their ears, taking the story with it into the trees and the bridge beyond.

'Oh! William,' said Jane on the verge of tears. 'Is there anything we could do to help these two victims on this cheerless vessel out at sea? Could we send them money or a prayer, perhaps?'

'Yes, we must,' said Agatha, fighting back her tears. 'We all feel for their plight.'

The women were now looking downriver to where it turned out of sight, being drawn with its gentle flow.

'No! Don't be had by my story,' he said, snapping out of his dreamlike state with a smile. 'It is only from the mind. I used it to demonstrate that there are other thoughts than birds and trees in my head.'

He jumped up and pulled at the women's clothes to encourage them to dance with him, but they seemed almost hurt by his sudden change of mood. He had taken their minds with so much power and ease that they were speechless for some time. The women forgave William's unromantic ending to the story, but each walked away from the bank with mixed emotions from the story. He had touched each and every one of them with the power of words and it preyed upon their minds with each step.

As they walked, each lady stole a glance at William, each with a hope of catching his eye. William loved an occasional Sunday afternoon with the ladies, but he knew he could only choose one for a wife. Or perhaps he would end up choosing some other unpicked fruit lying in some as yet undiscovered orchard.

His thoughts were like his words, only deeper and more direct, but he had the sense to keep them in mind. Oh! How tempting it is to pick one of these. When picked, though, they soften and bruise. But if left alone, they may swell better, only falling on a windy day, to be picked up by passers-by, who were otherwise unable to reach the fruits or to turn heads with some sonnet or sad story at hand. Do I wait until the day before the wind to choose my fruit or do I pick the highest I can climb to now, the best on the day? What thoughts I have – four fair maidens fighting to hold my arm and gain my attention. I wonder if they would fight to lie with me in the same barn. Yes, if my unchecked arms and wandering hands were allowed freedom of will, I dream of plundering deep. Such a wicked man I am, but my feeling is to collect an armful today and another tomorrow.

Oh! my greed is like a fat man's stomach that will never be full and satiated. But what I really want is to pick them all and never be full! My polite smiles and wicked thoughts will not be joined as a quill joins words to make sentences. They will never read my thoughts as boldly as they hear my neatly placed words. But if they knew, I wonder – would they run away or fight the others away? They must think the same, but dare not say. I dare not, either. We are all drifting upon the same course. Like yonder boat, an oar apiece, we have the same conflicting directions to choose from. The scent of women nearby makes me feel like a year-round fruit picker, surrounded by ever-ripening fruit. The harvest is mine for the moment, till a taller or more handsome man should pass them by with gifts in hand. Then I would be left with the fallen fruit, shooing the birds away as I kneel to the ground in search of the best left whole.'

As he had suspected, William was not alone with his thoughts, though he would never know of them. Only the smiles radiating out from each face would betray the fact that they had eyes for him.

Oh! he takes me away, thought Judith, closing her eyes. I wish I were on a vessel with him, escaping to sea. It would rock so gently, from side to side, but we would not sleep.

I wonder if William has plans for one of us, thought Agatha. The happy nest we have here will one day be blown away, but my hopes are that I will be flying alongside him, not falling by the wayside with the others.

He did look then, he did, Jane convinced herself. Men like women with voluptuous shapes like mine. He looked below my locket. Oh! it is yours, just ask. Oh ask, William. I have the best looks and shape to tease you with and to hold your attention. Why does he smile at her? Look at me, I am yours. Your smile is just a key. Smile and my lock will fall to pieces at your feet. Oh, please smile at me. If only I could catch his eye ...

I wonder: could this be a game to William? thought Elizabeth – four women trying to catch his eye. But he acts casually and speaks with the care of a spider's feet. His words trip across us from mind to mind as if it were a fine thread but never missing a foothold. Will we all have a portion of disappointment pudding to share one day? I am sure at least three of us will, but will it be four if he chooses another? I will look ahead to the future and enjoy the pleasant company today while it lasts. Whoever he chooses will delight in his company.

'Ladies,' William announced. 'Can I offer to walk with you past Marston's orchard? I will pick the best and freshest apples for each of you. Your looks of roses in full bloom remind me of the blushing fruit.'

With this bold compliment, all the ladies blushed as they accepted William's offer. Not the offering in his mind, though, for the picker would have to mature first.

William kept his word and later plucked them all an apple each. They then found a quiet area to sit down and enjoy the feast, but as they did, Agatha suggested they should all take part in a game.

'A thought has come to mind!' said Agatha excitedly. 'What if we all spoke about our thoughts and wishes for the future. Without exception, we must all join in.'

The ladies looked at each other and then finally at William's face, so he smiled and tilted his head with approval. Agatha straightened her head and made known her intention of speaking first, so the others sat back on the grass to listen. Agatha was all smiles, but mischief was clearly growing judging by her guilty face.

'Marriage for me,' she said, with a teasing look to the side. 'It will be a marriage of love and we shall have children, but I would not allow them to steal apples. The great house we would live in will have its own orchard and fields aplenty for them to play in. My husband would have to be able to read and write. I would want a pile of prose to stack to the roof, but once read, they would never be seen by others.'

'Oh, that sounds so grand, Agatha,' said Jane, who was next in line. 'I would want similar, but I wish for an heir to great lands. A man with more wealth than he could cope with. I would tease him, of course, and he would have to chase me with gifts for my chastity. And more, I would only allow him two children. Oh, the thought of all the mess – but that is for the servants to contend with.'

'It is your turn now, Judith,' said William, smiling.

'Oh yes,' she said, thinking that great wealth was a long way from her grasp. 'I think more of the simple things in life. To eat plenty and to have children to share my life with and to look after me in my dotage. I wish for only the basic needs as I think of my own mother's wishes, also. She always wanted piles of sheets in the box, ready to warm all should the weather turn. So I, too, wish for the same and for a strong husband to love and provide for us all.'

'Now you, Elizabeth,' said William. 'Although we have no well nearby, what is your wish?'

'I want to prosper like the rest,' she said, but knowing her means were much less than the Lucy's two. 'I will not rush for the first man to speak softly to me. I will take my time to think. The future is not just the word marriage, it is living with someone and providing for one another through many unwanted storms. So I have patient thoughts for the future and men will have to wait to touch me.'

All the women then turned to William, eagerly hoping that he would lower his guard and release some clue as to his romantic ambitions.

However, William knew that some of what had been said reflected their true thoughts and some merely bait, so he veered away from the net and into the deeper waters of his mind. He put his head down to think. The game had turned his way, so he would deflect the attention on him just as quickly.

'I fear I have the advantage, for you have all spoken before me, so I must first comment upon what you have said, because you have all spoken about many different things. The pile of prose for only Agatha to read, an untouched heir for Jane, a stack of new sheets for Judith and the distance put between Elizabeth and a man while she chooses the right one. You all want to marry, as I do, but the timing of such a sentence for me will be sudden, I fear, and not planned with great detail. I have a head full of prose, but it is in my head only and only a few friends like you hear my words. But I can look at the hardened buds beyond and compare my future with them.'

With this William stood up to look at some unopened flower buds and he walked forward a pace to point them out. 'All buds will open in time, but after waiting for the rain to finish, their patience is well rewarded. They know the sun will warm them all equally, but it is rain that will nourish them. And so it would be wise to wait for the rains to come in the same way and not to rush too quickly into grasping the first thing that comes along. The breath of nature is always at hand and as the petals spring open to invite the bees, by the same token the buds know that above the dark rain clouds lies a blue sky. If it be rain, snow, wind, sun, dusk or dawn they know and they hold back, blossoming only when it is the right time to do so. But do we? I see my future as being like the bud. It will open a great door to me, but the clouds must pass first. They will give rain and bring colder climes, but they will pass all the same.'

'None of our thoughts were for a man with wisdom, William,' said Agatha. 'They were all for our own pleasures and gains. You must be meant for another bud of your own kind.'

'That may not be so,' he swiftly replied. 'All buds are different and they flower side by side with the rest. Look at the flowers in the meadow ahead,' he pointed. 'People are the same, all different and yet all living together side by side. Will you all join me to walk further?' he asked, changing the subject, once again distracted.

William had outmanoeuvred the prying of his mind again. Even though he knew he could only end up with one, the thought of teasing himself that he could have more was tantalising. But in truth, he feared the reality of his lustful thoughts coming true. Beyond his bold imagination he had doubts about the idea of his first love. The temptation to ask more from one of them would shatter the other ladies' fantasies and may even commit him to the hook before he was ready to lose his youthful freedom. The women had hoped to glean more from his thoughts by asking a direct question of him on his thoughts for the future, but all William did was set them wondering again.

When William left the four ladies after a peaceful afternoon spent in pleasant company, he found himself smiling to himself all the way home. On arriving back, his father's stare brought him back to the present and to the reality of life away from prose.

'William,' John said deeply, pointing towards the kitchen. 'We must talk now.'

'Oh? What of, Father?' he asked with raised eyebrows.

John didn't answer; he just waved his hand for William to sit by the fireside. William sighed to himself and did as he was asked but with little eagerness. Expecting trouble, William sat with his legs and arms open to indicate openness, but his father knew the old trick.

'Sit any way you want, William,' said John, with his hands on his hips, 'but it will make no difference to what I am about to say.'

William then knew exactly what John was referring to: his afternoon without Joan as chaperone. His day spent in the charming company of four admirers had ended with swords crossed with his father.

'Do you really care what becomes of us?' John asked.

'Of course I care!' exclaimed William. 'Why should my afternoon away mean that I do not?'

'Do you care what we do while you play?' John was looking straight at William, his teeth clenched in anger.

'Father, it is Sunday,' he replied quickly.

'Yes,' he continued in his familiar deep tone, 'but walking around the town with your lustful desires stamped on your face is a day I would prefer not to see, and especially not on the Lord's day.'

'But we have only walked and shared conversations on this day of rest,' he replied defensively. 'No sin has taken place.'

'Talk indeed!' snapped John. 'But on this day of rest you speak of, tell me that your mind hasn't sunk towards deeper thoughts of these shapely maidens and their teasing allure?'

'Are we not allowed to walk and talk on a Sunday, then?' he added cheekily. 'Others do, I see.'

'What?' shouted John, turning to point his finger at William. 'Others ... these others you speak of have to work in the home or in the fields. Joan has been baking for hours, just to feed you when you return from gallivanting around the town, like ... like ... like a mother goose showing a trail of goslings the way. Just because it is a Sunday it doesn't mean there isn't work to be done.'

'Right then, Father,' William said sharply. 'I will do the baking next Sunday. I ... I will bake us a feast.'

'That is women's work and you know it,' John said, his temper now simmering down. 'You know what you should be doing. You should be working towards putting food on the table rather than just taking from it.'

'Yes, Father,' William said quickly. 'But how am I to acquaint myself with women if I am to be cooped up inside? I will marry one day, I hope, and so I need to be aware of the best pickings to be had.'

'Yes, when you have a trade and not before. You will walk no more with these ladies of your fancy. You should have declined to go with them when you knew our Joan had to stay here. Your escape was like a fleeing hare. Your future ties have to be planned carefully. You cannot act as if you had the freedom of the queen. Know your status.'

William had lost the exchange. He just sat with his arms folded, waiting for a further onslaught. John had said enough and Mary had heard the exchange from outside and she came in to make it known that she agreed with him and to let William know that this was a serious matter. This ended the loosening of the reins for William and his freedom was curtailed. He would have to content himself with the lessons he gave Agatha and Jane. William accepted having his movements restricted but he still had his mind set on adventure. At just over 17 years of age, William had plenty more days ahead of him to learn. He would let things simmer for a time, whilst underneath he was yearning for more. William had had a taste of freedom and nothing would keep him from stoking the pot to a blaze.

Anne Hathaway

William danced in his mind as he tripped back across a field towards Clopton Bridge. His head was alive from the travelling show he had just seen and his thoughts were on bettering the performance.

I have seen Richard Tarlton perform many times, he thought, but his like fail to impress me. If they had only half my mind, the laughter and taunts would be doubled in worth. Most players seem happy to take the bow and drink in the applause, but do they know what the cheers are for? Is it for the excitement they display, unlike the dull lives of the watchers? Or is it for the mockery of such like the river dweller? It is easy to imitate a duck, but they should use its feathers with a better stroke of the quill. An educated thought, or even a feeling from the heart, would show better use of the quill than this. Or is it just made up off the sleeve? I wonder. They have such an envious life, food and shelter wherever they travel, flocks of townsfolk following their hurriedly painted dreams. Of limited words though, for some sentences could be shortened to give the same impact with two words whereas others need more to assist their ill-constructed aim. Ah, let them be. They find food and give most a happy cheer. There are black and white sheep and all have wool to give, so what does it matter? But if the townsfolk did not laugh at them, who would they laugh at? Their own faults, perhaps. Or maybe they would fight each other from boredom. Laughter and happiness is good, I think. Better to throw laughter than aim arrows.

When William had finished his critical analysis, he took his attention away from the distant applause and imitated a player kicking a stuffed duck as a stone tempted him to kick it in the dusty road. With his last kick, it rolled in front of a young lady's hurrying feet. William looked up and saw a woman a few years older than himself and he watched her for a moment struggling to drag a sack of flour towards the town. He had seen her before, but it was many years past. The woman didn't look up, though, and she had a look of determination on her face as she pulled at the heavy sack. After tilting his head both ways in thought,

William could see nothing else but the woman; the road and town beyond were just a blur.

The green light, thought William. Yes, it is her. The woman in the green light from the woods of long ago. Both Joan and I were witness to it!

'Would you like some help, lady?' he asked politely, twirling around in front of her. 'You look to be in need of strong hands and I have a vacant pair.'

The woman glanced at William and shook her head to say no. But then she stopped as her eyes met William's. 'I know your young face. Have you been to see the show? Is that where I know you from?' the woman asked, pausing to sweep the hair from her face and think back. 'Your dancing about seems familiar.'

'Yes, I have. My name is William,' he replied, adding further steps to his dance for the benefit of his new-found audience. 'But I last saw you singing in the woods some years ago, do you remember?'

William shyly caught the woman's eyes, so she could see a glimpse of his mischievous face. Then he looked down for his stone once more to hide his nervousness.

'Yes, it's you! The boy with the little girl.' The woman straightened her back. 'So quiet you were. Do you know how much you frightened us that day? Oh, sorry, my name is Anne and yes, I would like a helping hand with this sack. I have over a mile to walk to Shottery.'

Anne stole another glance at William's shy face. He didn't have an insolent look to him but it was more an inquisitive tilt. She seemed to be looking for something, almost trying to lift his head with an imaginary finger. Lift your head, young man. Look up so I can see your face, she thought.

William's mind was in turmoil and his nervousness turned into great fear lest he may slip up or make a wrong move. The expression on his face changed like a passing cloud takes the sun for a spare moment to whisper a secret to it. This was not normal behaviour for William. He was used to spilling out his charms and relishing the attentions of women, not hiding his face like a young child expecting a scolding tongue.

Her name is Anne, he thought. Our Anne has not long since passed and now a new one stands before me to remind me of her. My bruised mind feels like an apple healed, new and fresh with barely a scar. A new rosebud and yet the same name and oh! what beauty lies within my reach. My luck now poised like a scythe, just a gentle swing and all could fall before me, waiting for me to reap without first having sowed!

'Before we make our way to Shottery, Anne,' William turned to pull two heads of corn from a joint in the bridge, 'let us throw a head of corn apiece into the river. I bet mine will beat yours to the other side.'

Anne was surprised at the suggestion. What a bold young man he was to approach her thus. He talked with his hands, aiding his speech, and his confidence was like that of an older man.

Like a hovering hawk, he wanted to make sure he would secure his prey when he made his plunge. He wanted to play the game, to see which way she might run. William thought that it would help his nervousness. His mind was all over the place and he needed time to think.

'Have it your way, William, but mine is sure to be the faster of the two because I am the eldest.'

Anne held William's gaze as he pressed a head of corn into her hand. They spoke in a way, but with their eyes. Slowly, they released both heads of corn. The heads of corn fell unnoticed, but their eyes were fixed in a stare – a long and meaningful stare; they were both transfixed by the other's gaze.

Suddenly Anne turned away and William followed her gaze in the direction she was now walking. William had a clear view of the road and her next step would have been fatal for sure if he hadn't intervened. A speeding farm wagon was passing at the same instant that she was taking a step forward. Anne heard nothing of its approach, but William saw the wild horses and careering wheels, so without further thought, he grabbed Anne to prevent her from taking another step. The wagon bounced carelessly past, the hay brushing past Anne's face as its wheels just missed her toes. Even though it happened so fast, it felt frighteningly chilling but comforting all the same.

Everything seemed to happen more slowly than normal. Sounds, vision, his sense of touch and the breeze seemed to numb William's senses.

'My Lord! that was close,' William said, blinking hard to awaken his senses. 'Closer than a bailiff's paper fingers sticking through the gap in a closed door. That was close if ever I saw it.'

'A bailiff?' she said with a deep frown, her eyes and mouth open in shock.

'It is a picture I have, Anne. His rolls of paper being handed to a debtor, the door slammed tight shut and missing his fingers by a thread.'

'Oh!' she cried, leaning towards William for support. 'Danger only a wheel away and you analyse it like it was a mere butterfly floating past us to seek another flower. But what a grip you have ...'

William held Anne firmly and he could feel her heart thumping against his chest. With Anne taking the lead she had turned away to run, but William's hand was firmly pressed against her breast as he drew her to him. Anne seemed to instinctively put her hands around his neck.

Oh, her breast! he thought.

Why did I turn in haste? Anne wondered, turning to look up to William's equally shocked face. Had I not done so then I would not be here now, with his grip, oh ... his strong arms and wild hair ... my mind was lost with the corn.

Had we not stopped on the bridge to play, William thought, we would not be here now in each other's arms. How fortunate that we find ourselves in this position. And yet I could have chosen a different game to play ... But why did I pick a game such as this? My hand rests where my daydreams look to. Should I move? What will she say? Surely this could be considered impolite, with my hand resting on her breast.

'I did not mean to hold you in this way. Forgive my careless hand,' he said nervously, pulling it away.

Anne was shaken by her ordeal but she clasped William's hand firmly, reluctant to let go. 'No, William,' she said, breathing deeply while pressing his hand back into her breast. 'You may have saved my life. My body has no fence or boundary to you now. Your action has saved me from certain fate. I was only thinking of the game and playing it out to the full.'

'The blame is mine – it was my game. I am a young man, yes, and with it I have strong desires. But in the street my face reddens quickly with such conduct.' When William had finished speaking he looked around for any witnesses to their embrace, but they were alone. The moment was theirs to explore.

'Look at me, William. Fix your eyes on mine. Feel my body; it is yours. Help me with the sack now and think for a moment.' Anne pointed down to the sack with her eyes. 'Does the spider question the direction the fly has blown from that it may benefit its day?'

'No, that is true,' said William, now warming to the suggestion. His mind was closed to the parental words of caution about going "straight there and back" and having "duties to fulfil". This time, William's heart took first place and lust took little time to drown out thoughts of any consequences. He'd been given a second chance at meeting this woman and he was prepared to incur the wrath of his parents and ignore church teachings.

'William,' she said, pressing his hand further to her. 'My heart beats, but not of fear, for this has now passed. It beats for something else. Feel its gentle blows ...'

William slowly let his hand drop to his side having felt it, too, and he then took one side of the sack without speaking. His face had coloured at the warmth resonating from her breast as she had drawn his hand to it. A warmth which had spread up his arm and through his body lower down. William had a young man's eager, impure thoughts, but with them came an equal fear with each stride. As they set off walking, Anne had her head up with a pleasing smile, but William glanced around furtively, looking for any would-be witnesses. With each step along the path towards Anne's farm, William felt drawn to her. Anne kept glancing and smiling at William as she led the way home. It was a look as if she was returning with a great prize. William's initial embarrassment gradually lessened, but anxiety increased as he noticed the farm gate ahead of them.

'Hewland Farm,' said Anne. 'This is my home where I live with my brother, Bartholomew, my mother and two sisters. My father died, leaving it to my brother, but we manage well enough.'

William didn't pass comment; he just nodded to acknowledge that she had spoken, gripping the sack whilst wishing it to be her hand. They entered the kitchen and William's anxiety returned and could be seen in his grip as he held on to the sack tightly. Ann closed the thick door behind them and William's throat felt dry, seeming to close with it. As she pushed it into its frame it made a clunk and then she turned and started to walk towards him, making him gulp. The kitchen was large and it had a hard stone floor with plastered walls, making every sound seem louder.

'Come, follow me,' said Anne, taking William's hand and leading him past the table.

William was powerless to resist. He still held on to the sack of flour and he now manoeuvred it between the chairs as they made their way towards the dairy. The sack knocked against his knees and made a trail through the herbs that had been laid out on the kitchen floor to dry. Anne stopped suddenly outside the buttery before turning to give William his first kiss. A strange sensation ran through him as cooling as the room they were next to before a warmth spread to his loins. Her lips were a soft, buttery cool but with warm, inviting sensation as he melted to her touch.

What have I done? thought William, glancing back towards the stove and hearth. From a sack of corn to the touch of a breast and now to here – oh, I will fear bridges in the future and should steer well clear.

Uncut logs and a dim fire were far from Anne's mind. Indeed, a raging fire was alight in her mind.

'Leave the flour for now, William,' she said, leading him upstairs. 'Come with me. I have wood and lace to show you in my room.'

'Your family, your brother, your ...' he muttered, with hesitant looks as his sweating hand let the sack drop.

'The market, the fields and the door is bolted,' she replied with eyebrows raised and a firmer tug on William's hand.

William's mind was muddled and his fear increased with each creaking step. His heart said yes but his mind said no. Anne's hand was like a fish on a hook. Its warm touch had him following her like it was the signal to the end of a great fast.

The bedroom was as lightly furnished as the kitchen. It had floorboards beneath, a high window above, and to the side was a coffer, with a thick-posted bed in the centre and white linen and lace like William had never seen before. They were a sharp white, not dark and rough like he was used to at home.

Anne began to remove her clothes and he averted his eyes and stood admiring the room. The confident elder disrobed at ease, but the younger, as expected, needed a jolt to make him jump years. Anne stepped over to William with her arms outstretched, her top half exposed, and then she drew him to her.

'William, fear me not,' she said, taking his hand in hers. 'Think as if you were a man that had been saving all his life. You have just saved me. My heart is yours and it lusts for you. Let your hands feel and touch what they have saved. You can spend all you want – my purse is open to you.' She guided William's hands toward her willing body.

His first touch of a naked woman began with a tender stroke, then slowly and softly, he explored her face more sensually. Soon, he let his fingers slip near to more sensitive areas. Then he took in a deep breath of her scent and his blood began to surge, his fear now dissipated.

With the warmth from another's body and a gentle caress as neither had felt before, William felt like a man and Anne seemed complete. She had captured her dream and, of course, William had surrendered willingly, casting his shield of caution aside.

Their passion spent, the lovers looked up from their cosy warmth to watch a bird sunning itself on the window sill with a worm in its beak, poised to take flight to its nearby nest. Smile they did, but smile they might not have done had they known of their implanted egg. The bird had only worms to find and a humble nest to tend, not explanations and money to find, or parents to fight. The shared need for warmth and a loving embrace had put thoughts of consequences to the back of their minds. Their meeting had been like a changing wind to their lives. Both would now have to follow it, whatever the storm or direction it took.

'We never watched to see who won with the heads of corn,' said Anne in an attempt to take William's stare from the window.

'Yes,' he said, 'but if we had, would we be here now? I wonder. Had we not stopped to play the game and watch the corn, you would not have been nearly run over by a wagon's wheel and so we would not have found ourselves where we are now.'

'You are right, William,' she said, smiling.

'Anne,' he said softly, 'this feeling I have inside me from our first touch, I could never have imagined how settling and peaceful it could be once spent. What a wonder it is that our imagination cannot give us a taste of this before, leaving us wanting to seek out the mystery for ourselves.'

'Yes,' she sighed. 'I also never thought it would be like this. This feeling of connection we have between us has thrust upon me something greater than the highest of my past thrills! I feel as if I have won without knowing what I had been trying to win, only now I have a sense of contentment.'

'I agree. It is the most strang of feelings. But as I lie here, I notice my heart is pounding less and the heat within me cooling by the minute. I fear that work and family commitments will now put a strain on the scales of our lives. It leaves me wondering which way they will tilt, now we have done as our lust intended. But as for all things there must be balance. But I do not regret a single moment of what has passed between us. I do not feel I have won a great prize, which is mine to cherish and to hold, savouring in its warmth. I feel I have won a step on a pathway, leading to a feast or a famine, who can tell?'

'Our minds will be distracted after what we have shared here today.' She turned to stare into his eyes. 'I have prayed for this day for oh, so long and I will savour it forever more now I have what I asked for. I will never complain or challenge what I have to face from this day forward. I have what I have desired – I am now complete.'

The News

Following their chance meeting on the bridge, Anne and William decided to meet every week in secret. Their first meeting had been one of a lustful encounter, but after that day, a deeper love took over and began to steer their lives forward. Anne's mother was widowed and with the farm being left to her brother and with two other daughters living at Hewland Farm, she had a busy job keeping home so her mind was preoccupied. Whilst they had several farmhands at the time, they all had work to do most days, making it difficult for Anne and William to share time together. But it was the same for most other courting couples. The Shakespeares had been going through a hard time for several years and so William had work pressures on him as well. On the other hand, Richard Hathaway, Anne's father, had been a successful yeoman farmer, so his family was a little more at ease with their finances.

Some days Anne and William would meet halfway between Shottery and Stratford, and lose themselves for a time in the long meadow grasses. As well as finding time to explore the outbuildings at Hewland Farm, they often talked of their future together. The only thing in the way of their plans was William, who was still too young to marry. It was normal in those days for couples to marry in their mid twenties, which was the age when most men would finish their guild training, depending on what trade they had chosen. Anne, however, was already twenty-six, eight years his senior, but to wait for another eight years or so would have put her in her thirties.

When Anne discovered that she was pregnant, it was a testing day for all. Anne dared not tell her mother first about her condition for fear of her dragging her by the ear all the way to Henley Street to confront William's family. William had to be told first, and then she would know if his intentions were honourable or whether he would run after his youth like an escaping fugitive. After this, they could discuss plans for any future they might have together.

The day Anne chose to break her news was one quiet Sunday morning; a day they could meet relatively easily without raising suspicions. Anne chose one of the dilapidated out buildings on the farm in which to confront him. It turned out to be a good choice because it had been raining all night, so at least they would have shelter, but William was soaked through by the time he arrived.

The two sat down facing each other on two old boxes and then just held hands, gazing into each other's smiling faces. Not a word was spoken to spoil the morning farmyard quiet. It was as if they had been stealing apples, for all they could hear was their guilty hearts beating fast. They faced each other knee to knee. William thought she was teasing, but Anne was using all her strength to keep him steady as she sought for words. Eventually, the silent stand-off reached its climax: Anne could not resist another twist of her hand and neither could she resist speaking any longer. William thought she was teasing him to test his strength, but in truth she was searching for how best to tell him

'William, I have a child within.' She patted her stomach, looking for his reaction. 'It is confirmed. I have waited weeks now.'

A look of shock crossed his face, eventually settling in his gut as the reality of what she had imparted sank in. Without a further word, both loosened grip of each other's hands so they could think for a moment.

William opened his mouth to speak and Anne leaned forward to catch his words, but shock held them back; only thoughts came out. With each passing second Anne willed the nearby cart to turn over and bury her in loveless shame.

Then William spoke out, but not as the poet, or the man of verse to turn all heads. Instead, just a single word escaped his mouth.

'A ... Anne ...' Then he spoke once more, but this time with more conviction. 'Anne!' he said gulping deeply. 'I have not thought of the consequences of our actions. Should I bang my head upon a tree, or plunge my bare chest into thistles, it would not wake me from this disbelief I have in mind. But now I can only speak from my heart when I tell you that I love you.'

Anne seemed not to hear his words or acknowledge his gesture. She had expected an eruption of, 'Oh no,' and to see expressions of terror. Even betrayals of a false love and a meaningful tale as he retreated in denial, running for the hills. But he said "love", she finally realised. He said love! He truly loves me ...

'Anne,' William said softly, pressing his hand upon his chest. 'I love you. Wake from your stare.'

Anne moved towards him, quickly slipping her knees past his to hold him close. In her haste to hold him, Anne's head knocked William's teeth against his lip. William blinked then frowned with pain.

'Anne, oh my Anne,' William said tenderly, stroking her hair with one hand and his bloody lip with the other. 'It is daylight and we cannot see the stars right now through the morning's blue sky. But they are there and as long as they are, I will be here with you. I sit here a man, no longer a boy. I have tasted as men do. But now I will push back the wooden steps meant for a boy and stand upon the ground by my own feet. I will support you both as a man should.'

'Oh, William,' she snivelled. 'If the stars could hear you now. Your words and love lift me up towards them, but I am grateful for the hay I sit amongst by your side and my feet thankful of the earth for its support. As I hold you I realise this is no dream. It is real muck around us here, real as the cold rain outside, just as it is real love inside of us.'

Anne rested her head on William's chest like a mighty elm. As they held each other the damp from William's clothes seeped through to Anne's dry ones and soon they were both as one. After a short time they pulled away from each other, smiled and returned to the warmth of each other's arms. Their first meeting had bonded them together, but love hereafter would prove to be the greatest test.

Testing Love

Early the next morning, William walked down to the riverbank to share his thoughts with the moorhens. He was in a mixed state of mind, for the pleasure he had been partaking in had culminated in its most common side effect, so he wanted time alone to think and plan his next move. With this came further thoughts of what a child would mean for him, knowing how much Edmund had screamed for two years since his birth.

My mind, it sees far into the future, yet here I am talking to the moorhens and ducks. I speak here and I am confused. I think here and I am confused. I walk here and I am still confused. But when I close my eyes, a whole playhouse of people wants to shake my hand. So as easy and as sure as the pebbles skip towards deeper waters, I am a father to be. I cannot cry, but should I try? The worry is of my own making. Regrets, though, I have none. When the two heads of corn dropped from each hand, downstream they would go and not up. That is the way. To go against the flow would bring a great strain on my weakened oars and I would have to paddle hard upstream as the ducks do. I have reached the point in my life where I am a man and yet my fingers shake with the blade with which I now I shave. They might be soft hairs but they are whiskers all the same. Either the blade is blunt or my aim was bad, but whatever the cause, my face belies the trying. William rubbed his chin and face, checking his shaving skills and to see if his spots had stopped weeping.

When I first saw Anne in the woods, my finger was sore and bleeding and my sister clung to my neck. Now, Joan has matured to the age where she bleeds as women do, but another woman clings to my neck now and soon a child. I can no longer tell Anne stories meant for a child's ears, for her age will see through them and they will have less impact. I must save them for my own on the way. I can compare life with the pebbles here on this bank. No one knows how far across or for how long each one will skip across the water before it sinks. Oh, it cannot be so; the sun has fragmented behind the looming clouds! Is there no future? No, I am wrong. It is just me looking at the rippling water, creating a shadow. The sun is still whole above. But as it looks down at my future, will it break the light like my shadow or be whole, as one. I wonder, my lord. I wonder, will the waters be calm or will they rage like a torrent for me? A woman and child will soon be resting upon my shoulder, so I must prepare to take the strain. The ox in yonder field has an easy pull, I think.

A few days after William's encounter with the moorhens, a young woman came into the Shakespeare's shop to enquire of a handyman. The lady was Anne Hathaway herself and the visit was for a comparatively small purchase, but with a view to expanding her acquaintance with the family before they met on a more sensitive occasion. A few days before her visit, William had told Anne of his dislike for working in the shop when it wasn't busy. This had given Anne the mind of a chivalrous knight, one to give a helping hand in a time of need. So with a warm smile and a deep breath drawn to garner confidence, Anne entered the shop in what one would consider haste. Both John and Mary were in the shop that day and both smiled pleasantly at Anne as she approached the counter.

They have a smile for me. Pity they know nothing of what I carry that is part theirs, though, thought Anne, returning their smile. They look to be good people, my new family, but I will test the ground further.

'Good morning,' said John. 'I recognise your face. Are you from the town?' He bowed his head and waited for a reply.

Anne coughed politely before speaking, 'Oh, I'm from Shottery, but it's not quite the town, Mr Shakespeare. I am Anne, Anne Hathaway.' She smiled pleasantly, trying to hide her belly with her cape, even though there was little showing.

'I thought I'd seen you before. I knew your father, Richard. He was a good man.' John lifted his arm to introduce Mary. 'And this is my wife, Mary.'

'Hello, Mrs Hathaway,' said Mary. 'Have the paths been cleared of overgrowth to Shottery yet? I always seem to cut my legs when I take the children berry picking.'

'Oh yes, last week. But I am Miss Hathaway, not Mrs,' Anne added with a slight blush.

'Oh, I am sorry. What can we do for you? You look as if you might be looking for something in particular,' Mary stated with a polite smile.

Anne seemed a little flustered as she began to speak, hoping William wouldn't wander in from the house; her visit was without his knowledge. 'There are three things, really. First, I would like a pair of gloves for my sister. I would also like you to repair my bag, but the final request is not of your craft. I have a floorboard that has crumbled away. I wondered if you knew of a young man who could take on this easy task.' Anne was quite relieved her words had been delivered as she had intended, but she avoided eye contact nonetheless, expecting her plot to be exposed at any moment.

John looked at Mary, brushed his hair back a little and then turned around, nodding his head, intending to leave the two women to it while he examined the bag.

Anne thought he was going to say that he didn't know of anyone, so she spoke further before he answered. 'Oh, it doesn't matter, Mr Shakespeare,' she said, fidgeting with her clothes and hair in an attempt to release the tension she now felt. 'I will find the carpenter if you are unable to help.'

'No, no, William will be able to help you. Won't he, my dear?' John turned to Mary.

'Oh yes,' she replied. 'William is not a skilled craftsman as John is, but he will be able to fix the board for you easily.'

'And your bag, Miss Hathaway, how bad is the damage?' John looked down to it before speaking to Mary. 'Would you bring through the new gloves, dear, so that the young woman might select some while I attend to this repair?'

'Oh, it's just a tear.' Anne lifted the bag up to John, glancing at the door again lest William should walk in. 'It must be the result of a hurried journey, I fear. I must have caught it on something along the way. How long will it take, please?'

'While you are inspecting our wares and selecting a pair of gloves, I will repair the bag,' said John, pausing to inspect the tear. 'Should you buy the gloves, the repair will free of charge.' John continued to frown and nodded, looking at the relatively easy repair.

'Well thank you, Mr Shakespeare, that is very generous of you,' Anne said. 'If your service now is anything to go by then I will be in good hands when it comes to the floorboard. At this rate I fear it will take longer to walk to Shottery than it will to replace it. But where can I get such a board?'

'William will bring one with him.' He turned to walk into the workshop. 'He will carry a few tools and new nails with him. I am glad to be of service, Miss Hathaway.'

Mary showed Anne a range of gloves with the innocence of a clear mind, walking back and forth from the shelving selecting different-sized gloves. Anne's face was reddening by the second. But the attention was drawn from her as they both looked up to the ceiling towards the sleepy cries from young Edmund which now filtered down through the floor.

'They want you there all the time,' said Mary. 'Every moment of your life is no longer yours when they are so young.'

'Yes, but is it not a pleasure to watch them grow and learn?' said Anne, looking up from the box of gloves to reply. 'And to love them as your own, as they are indeed a part of you, does that not feel special?'

'Yes, you are quite right,' Mary answered. 'William was the first to survive after losing my first two. Now, we have five children whom we love more each day. They have you in awe of their accomplishments in just a single day, that is until the demands grow and with it the cost and the wanting for more. Not to mention the worry each day for their safety when they return home late.'

'I am sorry for your loss.' Anne caressed a pair of gloves, lovingly turning them over in her hands to inspect the expert needlework. 'My time will come soon enough, I suspect.'

'Yes, Miss Hathaway,' said Mary, smiling. 'And hopefully you will not have to go through the loss that we did.'

When John returned with the repaired bag, Anne suddenly put aside thoughts of choosing a pair of gloves carefully and took the nearest to her, paying quickly in her haste to leave. The sound of William's voice had filtered to the shop from outside. He was talking to a passer-by about the season's gentle changes.

Anne paid John and Mary a complimentary smile and then turned to give Mary hasty directions to the farm for young William to come and fix her floorboards. Seconds after Anne had closed the door latch, it clicked once more and William entered.

'Hello, have we had many customers this morning?' William asked as he entered the shop. 'You look like you have both seen the town ghost?'

'We have a job for you, son. I cannot believe you have just missed the lady. Did you not see her on your way in?' John looked past William into the street to look for Anne.

'What lady?' asked William with a confused frown. 'Have I a sack of peas to deliver later?'

'No, son,' John turned back to look William in the eye. 'You need to replace an oak board for a Miss Hathaway. And she looks to be capable of paying us well for the job.'

Unusually for William he was without reply. He just nodded his head as he thought how he might make further enquiries. He was struck with fear at what may have passed between them lest she had told them of the impending new addition to the family.

'She was a miss, you know, William,' Mary said before retreating into the house to attend to baby Edmund's cries. 'But of course there are younger eyes which have designs on you, aren't there?'

A look of guilt crossed William's face as he watched his mother leave the room. Then he turned back and looked at his father before enquiring after Miss Hathaway's oak board. He then turned his head to look out into the street in the direction his father was looking.

'I am quite good with an adze, but to cut a board ...' he said, inventing his concern for the job.

'I will come with you if you feel unable to do this simple task,' said John before turning away from William's side. 'But you may have to do jobs like this on your own later in life. It will be good practice for you.'

'I am sure I will manage, Father,' William said, hoping his father wouldn't persist. 'I have seen Jack the carpenter fit one before. It seems like an easy enough task.'

'That is the right attitude: take the job on if it pays.' John turned back to his stitching table. 'If it pays, the answer is always yes.' John had a pleasant smile when he picked his needle up once more, but William wanted to stab himself with it to test the reality of what had happened. The relief on his face was palpable.

The following morning, as arranged, William set out on his first carpentry job, with nails in pockets, tools in hand and a long board under his arm. *Anne is so daring*, he thought with a mischievous smile. *But what a bold step. We share a great secret but not for long, I fear, after her actions today. Mother would have me married to the richest she could find if she had her way. She seemed to like the fact that Anne was older. It will be a good day today. Instead of having to make an excuse for my absence, an invitation now awaits me. Oh it is a treat. I can feel it now. The grass might be wetting my legs as I walk to Shottery,* but Anne's warm fire will dry them off, with the promise of further warmth to come, I hope.

Passers-by who William met on the way were all greeted with a heartening smile and a nod to bid them good morning. Most knew William, but not of his new trade, or how it had brought a smile to his young face, which normally wore a still expression as he studied his surroundings.

William's arms were aching when he set his things down to knock on Anne's front door. I will tell her to let me know of her visits in the future. I will tell her firmly lest she thinks she can play with me again.

When Anne opened her front door, all William could do was smile and embrace her, his anger now forgotten. Anne held her hand over his mouth so she could speak first.

'William!' she said brightly, pulling him to her chest eagerly. 'I could not bear waiting until Saturday next to meet you. Forgive me. Hold me. Squeeze me.'

Anne had been preparing bread in the kitchen and in her haste to open the door, she still had a part loaf in her hand. William saw the remains of the bread, so he stepped back half a pace to comment, pulling Anne's fingers from his mouth so he could speak.

'Is that all I am worth?' he said, looking down at the blackened bottom edge of the half loaf. 'The lower part has burned and you think you can offer me that in payment for my coming here today to work on your floor.'

'Oh, I was just preparing food for later,' she replied before giving William a further embrace. 'You are worth the upper crust and more besides, my love.'

'Mind the baby,' he said. 'I don't want my son to have a flattened nose. Be easy on him ... and my lungs.'

'Your son?' she said, stepping back in an instant with a coy smile. 'The child will be a girl. I can feel her fingers making lace,' she said, laughingly guiding his hand to her stomach.

'Will you have her make lace for our family shop?' he asked, turning away, pretending to be hurt. 'But no, you will teach her without my knowledge, like you visited my parents without my knowledge. The matter is in your hands – as usual I am not to be consulted.'

'I make no apology, my love,' she replied before emphasising deeply, 'As you are well aware, I have a need for you right now.'

This invitation lightened William's mood and a lecherous smile came to his face, thinking he was about to get his just desires.

'My foot dropped right through the board last night. It is a matter of urgency now, my love. After all, it would be terrible if I should fall, especially in my condition.' She smiled at her victory and William's sinking expression as she ran her hands over her belly.

'So, my wooden love,' he said before raising his voice, 'show me this floorboard of yours which you seem to place of higher importance than myself. Let me save your feet from falling down a hole again!' But then in a whisper, as he pushed past her in the doorway, he added, 'You can also show me your neck while you're at it and let me nibble your ear.'

But William was to be disappointed, for Anne had in mind sharing his company fully clothed that day. To her, talking and being in the same air as the love of her life was just as important as sharing the same bed. After William had tested his carpentry skills out, he joined her to help pack the bread and fruit for lunch. Anne's two sisters were at home that day, but they went about their duties with just occasional glances towards William and Anne, who were talking on the settle. Anne's mother was attending to her sister as she had been ill for some time and she wasn't expected back for a while and Bartholomew was at a nearby market.

'Whisper, William,' she hissed quietly. 'I have decided to tell Mother and my brother all tomorrow.'

'How do you think they will react, Anne?'

'They will have questions, no doubt, but I'm sure they will give me plenty to think about.'

'Let us both think for a moment. Yes, we shall think only and give our tongues a rest while we work this out together,' he replied with a serious expression and his teeth biting his cheek in thought. 'Will that be silence enough?' he questioned after just a few moments.

Anne smiled at his impatience and then glanced furtively in her sisters' direction before touching William's knee. 'What do you think of me apart from between the sheets, when we share kisses and love? We have had many weeks to compare our early lust with what we have now.'

William bent nearer to Anne's ear before whispering further, 'I think more of beds, kisses and love,' he said, smiling.

'Oh, William, be serious. Tell me and stop fooling around. You see so much from observing nature and from others' thoughts. But what of the real me?' she asked, looking up.

'Hmm, yes, I think I will tell you a little something of wood to explain my feelings for you.' He nodded with serious evaluation.

'Wood? Such a romantic you are. What about flowers and birds instead?' She frowned and crossed her arms, expecting further ridicule.

'Wood and love it will be, my Anne,' he said with smiling eyes as he took her hand. 'If I be the first love in your life, wood must be the second. As you walk around this house of yours, your fingers tell me so. Each time we speak or lie between the linen, your fingers caress the wood nearby and in doing so you make it appear both smooth and loved. Your nails and fingertips touch the beams and doors each time we stop to speak. Wood is your affinity and is as equal to me in this house. This house and its wood are your second loves. You know every twist and split about this house. Every knot and hole tells a story. Each time we speak of things when there is wood nearby, your mind wanders deep beyond your fingertips. Sometimes your lip quivers as if sensuality has kissed you back from your love's roots. My worries, though, are mixed. I fear you will make me the second love in your life one day or even rub my scalp bare to make it as shiny as your wood.'

'William, my fears are stripped of the worst!' she replied with surprise. 'You watch every move and breath I take down to the last detail. It is true, I do have an affiliation with wood and when I touch it I feel its power. It is the tree's past beauty that I touch, though, for my wood once supported fruit and blossom, yet now in death it feeds my mind. I feel the strength it once had, gripping the rock and earth, and reaching to the skies. And yes, I do love its feel, my love, but you are my true love, William. You have no trade or great wealth as you sit here, but as for your second love of words, I hope that before death it will feed plenty who wish to learn and hear you speak and write. I see a great future from your mind, my love, just as you see my hands caress the majestic properties of wood and find yourself coming a close second in our relationship. Your awareness is a wonder to my eyes. Your words kiss my ears and yet stab my heart to its knotted core at the same time. You are a great seed, but not as yet of a known tree. I feel your future may stretch to higher confines than the tallest of Scots pines.'

'Anne, your compliments smother my mind with surprise,' he said, pressing her hand on his rough chin. 'I say this more true than honesty ever could. I love you more than a poor man's belly might seek out a king's feast! I did not think you had woven such scrutiny into your mind, as indeed you must have thought the same of me. But speaking of my words, think of this. I so much want to replace my words with good food and prosperous earnings in the future so that I may rest on the pillows of my mind's paradise. My destiny will not be spoiled and as sure as a tree will not stop growing, nor will a stone ever jump or a cow learn to fly. Even if an axeman aims for my head, I will still go my own way. Instead, I will curse him so that if the handle is infested with woodworm, the head will fall off and cut his laces clean off. If he then poured oil and fire on my head, my tears and clothes would muffle it and make it merely smoke and smoulder to nothing. And more, if he then cast me into a winter's day without clothes or food, my warm heart would melt the ground and I would then walk on the earth's bare pelt. My food then will be of thoughts for my destiny, filling my belly like a sack of corn, of which there is too much to eat. But from sharing my seeded words, I would only need a grain. From this, farmers and hungry fields will queue up for more, all wanting that which they had cast aside in the hedgerows with the weed. Thoughts of my destiny make me happier than a child on their birthday or perhaps a swallow returning to its springtime nest, knowing all was still intact.'

'Oh, William, if only I could write this now or remember some of the verse,' she said, moved by his words.

'My mind is full of more verses such as these and you hold the key to unlock it. But one question intrigues me deeply,' he said, sitting back to think. 'I will not dwell on thoughts of yesterday, events which I cannot change, but how come I did not see you pass by me into the shop when you went to visit my parents? You must have passed straight through me like a fog.'

'Green, William, you have never seen me dressed in green before,' she said, pointing towards a cloak hung up on a beam. 'In the same way that you saw me that day under the green canopy of light, you must have been enchanted by it.

'Yes, I did see you then, but you looked much older from the side. I thought you were even older than Mother at the time,' he said cheekily, bracing himself for a blow from Anne's hand.

'Older, yes,' she handed William a basket of food, 'but much wiser. I heard you talking of the seasons when I visited the shop, I believe.' Anne stood up with her nose in the air. 'I know much more than you think.'

'Oh, we were so close,' he said, eyes wide open with shock. 'And yet I never saw you. And Father's eyes, he looked at me as if I were a simple horn book a child could read when I told him I wasn't sure I could do the job on my own.'

Anne and William walked outside into the garden. They turned and faced each other to kiss, but with eyes on the lookout for her sisters first.

'Shall we eat by the river near the old elm?' she asked, looking up to the courting swallows above the trees and then tilting her head as she waited for his reply. 'You can whisper a string of loving words to me. That should be longer than the longest of loving verses ever told.'

'Between the sticky crumbs of our lunch?' he said, to wreck the pleasing thoughts from her mind and images of the bird's happy flight to paradise above them.

'You can be so cold,' she said, running to stop William from escaping into the roses. 'Be soft once in a while. Your humour may slap you in the face one day – not as hard as I shall, though.'

Eventually they made it to the old elm holding hands. A playful truce had been reached just in time for lunch. They both sat down and leaned back on the old tree holding hands, one eating with the left and one the right. They were deeply in love, which could be seen by the way they held themselves.

'Look, stepping stones.' He pointed. 'The men who put them here are all but forgotten in the annals of history. The toil they sweated was a great sacrifice so others could tread upon their work. They must have known as they laid the stones that others would pass over them. I feel God spoke to these folk, not for reward but surety that they would rest in heaven one day for helping others keep their feet dry.'

Anne pulled William to her side and kissed his lips. 'Let us step across to our own future and let no one tread on us and use us as stones. Oh, you have a new spot on your face which has just appeared from nothing! It sticks out like a stepping stone from the still waters here.'

'You are right, it is a spot!' he replied with a hurtful frown. 'But at least it is not a tor! You make out that it is enlarged to the size of a reddened nose on a frosty day.' He turned to look away from her.

'William, your words seem to express hurt amongst them,' she observed with a smile to worsen his wound. 'I did not mean to tease, but if you hint at such in verse, do not complain when I reply in the same manner. When I talk of the great peak on your face, the sun is highlighting your chin. I wonder how you can see over it to shave.' Anne stopped speaking with a playful smile and turned to gaze out on the river.

'Oh, so you continue to tempt my anger now.' He turned to challenge her, 'Perhaps I will have to throw you in the river to dampen your tongue. With your heavy belly and old bones, why! surely you would only sink into the mud,' he said cynically, 'my love!'

'Oh no, my love,' she replied, calmly gazing into his eyes, 'that is not exactly a true stone one should fling. My belly is of your making. The old bones are of your choosing and that spot is also yours. Your taunt is poorly aimed, for it merely puffs like a failed cannon.'

'Ah, your tempting allure caused my arousal in the same way that your salty bread caused my spot.' He ducked as she lashed out to slap his arm.

'Your cheek and words always win,' she said with narrowed eyes. 'Let me at least half win just once.' She took a further swing at William, but only managed to slap his leg.

'Yes, my love,' he said with a nod and a teasing smile, 'but if I let you win, then I would still be victorious by the very nature that I allowed myself to lose.'

'Oh, William,' she sighed, holding on to the tree to help her stand, 'you twist words around like a thatcher weaves his tight thatch on a roof. You will not let a single drop of light or rain through, such that there is not even space for a flea, you are so defensive.'

'But Anne,' he said, 'I have just had a terrible thought about our baby. With your wit and tidy mind, she is sure to complain about my curly, unruly hair as soon as she sees my face.'

'Ah, so you are admitting that it is to be a she, so I win! I hope she is without your spots, though,' she said with a victorious smile in William's direction.

'Perhaps we shall agree on at least one thing then, my love,' he said, embracing her. 'Your victory is won. By your own tongue, my love, you have me beat. Like the swallows catch flies, you caught me swiftly, but I wish my spot would go at the same speed,' he said, once more fingering his chin.

The Parents

While William was helping his father in the shop one day, he had been thinking deeply of how he would tell him about his unborn child. The conversation had skipped between the heat of summer and the quality of the leather goods in the shop. John was becoming suspicious because William was showing more interest in the passing issues of insignificance than he would otherwise have been.

After testing the air with many prying questions and with William's eagerness to agree, John stopped working to enquire more of his son's apparent frustration.

'William, are you planning to steal a horse and make haste to London? Your mind seems not to be here but in the distance. We both know where your dreams take you but this seems different.'

'You are quite right, Father,' he replied, quite relieved to be able to get things off his chest. This is the time, he thought. 'There is something I need to tell you,' he explained, lifting his head high. 'I am to be a father like you, but not as you and Mother planned and wanted of me.' When William had finished speaking he looked down to his shoes, waiting for the certain reply. There, I have said it. What great relief, he sighed inwardly, but he was quite sure his father's frown would take days to lift.

'What riddle do you taunt my ears with this time?' John asked sharply, carefully placing his tools to the bench. 'Like me, a father? You look frightened, son.'

'Well, Father,' William's hands began to shake as he spoke, 'you would have Mother bear your children because you are wedded. So in that respect I am not as you are.' He paused to take a breath, but his father appeared to turn white. 'Her name is Anne Hathaway,' he said, still looking down at his shoes.

'Is she sat at your feet, William?' John asked quite calmly, trying to attract William's attention as he walked toward him. 'Look at me when you are speaking to me, son.' Then reality dawned as he realised who he was talking about and he raised his voice accordingly, his eyes widening. 'Not the woman with the rotten floor! Not the same one with the oak floor and stitching work to her bag and the gloves for her sister?'

William nodded and swallowed, expecting a further hail of questions as his father also looked down to the floor.

John began thinking about what William had said, with the occasional raised eyebrow, deep frown and shake of his head. After fumbling with several tools pretending to be doing something useful, he looked across to William more brightly.

'William, it was only Friday last that you did some work for her. The nails will still need a final tap they are so fresh. Children take longer to grow than it takes to repair a board or two. Do not worry. Wait and see what time has to tell. Did you, then? Have you taken advantage of this woman through our own foolish need for money or is it the other way around and she has taken advantage of you?'

William started to compose further words, but John's thoughts caught up with him again.

'But even so!' he shouted. 'That would have meant that you must have fixed more than the floor if your fears are directed such that they are. Were you paid by this woman to fix everything, and by that I mean more than just the floor!?' John turned away with his eyes nearly as large as his gaping mouth. He turned away from William to rest his outstretched arms on the shelving and lowered his head as if he were praying.

'No, Father. I fear I have another tale I must tell you of,' William lifted his head to speak.

John was now fixed in shock, staring up and down at the stock on the shelves, looking for answers within them.

'The work the lady gave us was to help us out with our lack of available funds – a kindly thought, I think you will find.' William finished speaking and waited patiently for the inevitable outburst. John didn't reply straight away, so the pressure and worry built up in William's mind as he thought about his impending doom.

'You told her of our affairs?' John shouted, gasping for air and turning back. 'A stranger!' Then speaking quietly, 'But then I guess she was not a stranger to you, my son, for you had been meeting with her all along, putting her in her current predicament.' He turned away once more, shaking his head with a worried stare. 'Tell me this is not a story with one of your dreamy plays in mind, testing the onlookers to the full. Oh please, let that be so.'

'It is the truth, Father. Inside she is already part of me and our family,' he said, just as Mary entered the shop to see what all the raised voices were about.

'Oh, are my ears true to me? Did I hear a worrying sentence from our son?' she said in alarm before raising her voice further. 'The woman who employed our son for some repairs to her floorboards; she had already had the sight of his stitches from both sides of his clothes!' Mary stopped with both hands on hips. Her lips were pressed together and she glared between John and William.

'Mother, did you overhear us? Have you been standing there all this time?'

'But, William,' she said in disappointment, 'you are promised to a woman of your same tender years. We had plans. We all had thoughts of a timely marriage.' Mary took in a deep breath and walked to the shop door to take in some air to calm her nerves.

Silence settled on the room a while as they collected their thoughts before they spoke further. Eventually, after John had arranged a dozen bags several times and Mary had preened her dress as many times, John spoke after clearing his throat.

'You must wed elsewhere now, William,' he said with a reassuring look at Mary. 'It will have to be. There is no other way for it. It is for God to say if the crop shall rot or ripen. If men fail to restrain their seed and cast it wildly amongst weeds, we must do our best to harvest it wherever it lies.'

'But, Father,' implored William with his hands out before him, 'had you ever thought that it may be God's will, this seed. Although it was the produce of a lustful lapse of mind, I love her dearly and it is more than just that.'

'Do not talk of your careless ways near your mother's ears,' John snarled. 'A quiet corner, William, a quiet corner.' He muttered to himself. 'What other of our plights did you speak of to this Anne? Does she know what property I have to sell or to whom we owe what to?'

'None, Father,' William replied. 'That is family business and of no one else's concern. My loyalty lies with the family. My passing comment to Anne was of my reluctance to sweep and clean while we were not busy. I did not think anything other than that. Anne came here to help and paid for my work.'

'Yes, she did,' said John solemnly. 'But what price will we all have to pay now? We have another one of our own already to feed.' John pointed upstairs, hinting at young Edmund. 'Did the board take first place Friday last or did it take second to your lust?'

'No, but –'

'Does she think us to be fools?' John looked straight at Mary. 'Chirruping false tales to your mother and me, making polite conversation. But all along she had thoughts of bedding our eldest!'

'The board took first place, Father. I did not know her intentions that day and nor had I knowledge of her visit,' said William nearly in tears. 'Her concern was genuine as was her needing her floorboard fixed.'

Mary held her hand up to call a cease to the conflict – she had heard enough. 'Come here, William,' she said, her arms open. 'You also, John, both come to me. What is done is done. We just have to make the best of it.'

John and William fixed each other with testing glares. It was too late to fight, the damage had been done, so after a brief pause they did as she wished.

'What has been done has been done,' she said, softly. 'Once the corn is cut we cannot wish we had waited for it to swell another week. It is done, so we have to plan what to do with the harvest now.'

'I regret my careless lusting,' William whispered tearfully. 'I regret not taking heed of your past wisdom, but I am still the same. Whether I make a mistake or achieve success, I am still the same son. I am still good in my heart. I didn't plan it like this but we love each other.'

Mary embraced him tenderly and with welling tears, William spoke softly once more.

'We are a family and I love you all. I can do no other than tell my closest of my fears and of the blade I feel in my gut which is now wrenched. My shame is great, but to lead a life of shame after one mistake I fear is wrong. I will take my future steps as a man and follow my heart and mind. If God took my sister away without reason or cause, then I accept my actions without blame or throwing stones. I have done what I have done. It cannot be unsewn.'

Mary lifted her head to speak. She also had smarting eyes and was nearly in tears. 'Your quill arranges words like a comb straightens knotted hair. Both hair and words flow as neat as none can equal, both through teeth and well guided as they pass. Compared to grass with the wind's new direction, the rest must bend and listen or be flattened with the rain, for it is not their decision to make. Tell me about this text from your school book. Will all follow your words as the wind commands the grass to bend? Will you make others take heed?' she asked as if hoping for an easing of the pain she now felt.

'My words will not dig holes or cut wood, Mother,' he said calmly now the shock of the situation had been accepted. 'But when folk work they can think of my words. Many have toiled to dig a dry well or have mistaken pebbles for seeds and have reaped not that which they have sewn. My being here is from you wanting a child, but as day passes to night I must think now of tomorrow's new life. The sluice gate is now open and the land flooded; repair is needed and we need to learn from our mistakes, not harbour thoughts of an ill-fitting bridle Father sold last week or a pheasant you left to stand too long in the barn. My mind is not corn but words will grow from me. I can feel it. It is part of our family.' William lifted his head at last and looked his parents in the eye. The burden was gone and they could now move forwards, having come to terms with the situation.

'My William,' said John seriously, 'we have love in our hearts for your child to be and for Anne, but your words must be straight to us. Do not talk to us with such powerful words that we fail to understand, for a change in the breeze and they will be altered to suit. Be like the flagpole and be straight and still. Spill your sins in straight answers and thought. Your words can be as the wind or whatever to others, but do not use their power to make us take shelter from them.'

William nodded to agree. They had reached a mutual understanding on all sides so that they could now look to the future.

'Go and see your Anne now,' John said, stepping back. 'Tell her we will not have our grandchild brought up in any wilderness. Tell her ... no, give her our love.' John gripped Mary's arms as they both straightened their backs with pride. More strong words would have to be said, but they would have to wait, because for now they had cause to be proud that their son could stand by his own convictions. For the first time John felt William was now a man. No longer would he have to find an excuse to walk by the river, for he could make his own decisions and his own judgements. The strict family order had taken a dent to its armour, but it was still there and William would be reminded of it constantly as he had respect for his parents.

As William stepped out of the shop to walk down Henley Street, his thoughts were of letting the weight of a horse down from his back. The strain he had carried and the thoughts of how the news would be taken had put a great weight on his mind. But before William could think further, Mary called him back into the shop. William turned and ran back to his mother's side, thinking he had forgotten something.

'Answer me this,' she said with her arms folded. 'The thought has me twisting and writhing in my mind as I try to think of a possible answer.'

'Yes, Mother, what intrigues you so?' he asked, expecting a further kiss as Mary held his shoulders.

'Tell me,' she said, 'how did you first acquaint yourself with Anne? Was it your words? Did you tempt a gentle cloud with a quill to whisper into her ears?'

'No, it was not so,' he said with a smile. 'I will not lie to you, although by the look on your face you were expecting a string of my loving prose. It was a game with two heads of corn that we engaged in. A race from one side of the bridge to the other when we dropped them from the bridge into the water below. Love's first glance presided over the corn and the river took the corn away, leaving us entranced with each other's gaze. We never knew who won, for if we had, as I said before to Anne, then we may not have been here discussing just this and she may not now be in her present condition.'

'Thank you. Go and see your lucky Anne now, for I feel sure she will be waiting for you.'

William turned and walked on a few paces before turning to look back. He could see the outline of his parents embracing through the dull windows. They had been shocked by his revelation but they still loved him and would support him. I did not expect arrows to be embedded in my back, he thought, as his face lightened with a smile. Or a sword to be thrust into my side, but I certainly didn't expect the tips to now be embedded in the ground and sword in its sheath. I feel the spring of the bow in my feet as I walk on without fear. And even though the danger is past, their minds are still at war. My time away will help them boil down to a simmer once more. A retreat is best under the circumstances, I think, but not from loss or defeat, for strength will be built on from this.

William had arranged to meet Anne at the far side of Clopton Bridge later that day. It was to be a neutral meeting so they could discuss their future. Anne had told her family about the baby and their plans to marry and they were happy with the match. With Anne being eight years older than William, her mother must have feared that her daughter would end up a servant. But this was not to be. Anne and William had fallen in love, so the child would be accepted by both families. Most eligible ladies of Anne's age had been snapped up years before, but she had been waiting for someone special to turn her head and her find was most precious. Her family had already celebrated the news, quietly expecting William to have his parents' blessing to follow soon after the news had spilled out.

Although William had set off towards Shottery as his parents had thought, he still had a little time to spare before meeting Anne later, so he took a short walk and sat down by the river. 'Look how the gentle waters pass by,' whispered William to himself. I feel like a dam that has burst and my injured waters are relishing the escape. My mind is full of excitement; I will think of this moment in future years. My mind is now free from challenging thoughts, not grasping for a sharp reply, or thinking for others' sakes rather than pleasing myself. I can now drift along and get on with my life like the still waters here. The moment is without any burden to my mind; its stillness, like the river, patiently laps up pleasures unseen. Oh, what heaven life is. It is fate that I am here and there must be many others with far greater burdens than the one I now have to bear.

Anne had set off early to meet William, but her head was full of opposing arguments. She could picture the Shakespeares damning her name and presence and William cowering to his parents scorn. With their next planned meeting on Clopton Bridge in mind, Anne had decided to sit on the opposite bank, to look back towards its splendid setting.

Our first meeting took place just here, she thought. William must have stood over there laughing while I was on the road below, struggling with my sack. I wonder if he doubted his moves when he approached me. I wonder if he thought of me long after seeing me bathed in the green light of the forest as I did he. I will ask him some day, but my belly has bound us together now – by love, though, for I do love him. He is young but his spirit of mind is much older than his years. My father was a boy compared to his wisdom; he is sadly gone now. I have so many questions, but none I could ask before today. I think he will be beaten and thrown onto the street. Bartholomew says he could stop at the farm for a time. But then what? Without his family he is nothing. He loves them as much as I love my own, but we would both be split apart and forced to lead separate lives. I will be left bringing up a baby on my own, I am sure. Oh, why do I have these thoughts? They may even be so happy for us that they could send a messenger for me to join them in their good house. That I doubt. I think it more likely they would throw us onto the streets. I have soiled their precious eldest, trapped him into submission. Temptation has drawn him into my bed without courting first. Oh, put your thoughts away, Anne. Our strength lies in our love for each other, not fear of its lacking from his family. It was love, not lust that brought us together and the baby is a product of our love – not something to be scorned and ridiculed. I will think only good things from now on until he arrives. Besides, I can't change the outcome. What will be I will accept with my head held high. With her thoughts still fighting against each other to justify their love, Anne decided to walk towards the bridge, but some local women had begun to watch her and point. Anne had occasionally been seen in William's close company, so the locals had been adding things together and whispering about them.

Oh, you can point, Anne thought angrily. You certainly will when the news comes of our child. But I hope you tread in dung while you do, for you could never hope to understand the special love we have between us. No, I will not turn away from their fingers. They are not crown judges. I will hold my head high and look them straight in the eye.

As Anne walked towards the group of gossiping women, the women dispersed with haste, falling over themselves into bull dung as they did. She smiled to herself. Her wishes for them to step in dung had been answered as she watched all three scrape the grass with their feet before scurrying away. With this silent victory, Anne went to sit on the bridge and wait for William, now feeling more relaxed.

William said he would try to meet her on the bridge at midday, which was the exact time the post rider normally rode by. He soon passed with a clatter and then the dust settled. Then a wagon passed by, again disturbing more dust, and with it Anne's heart began to stir with worry for William had still not shown.

Eventually she saw him walking over the bridge towards her, but she could not guess by the expression on his face what the outcome was. She had by now convinced herself that he had failed badly to appease his parents. But then he ran towards her, over the bridge, unable to contain his excitement any longer as he took her in his arms and swung her around.

William was unaware of the depth of Anne's worries as her feelings were usually kept to herself. If they could get through this awkward meeting between the two families then they could survive anything, for surely had neither party been in agreement over what should be done then it could have turned out to be a bitter feud between the two families.

At last! Anne thought. 'I see your limbs are still intact, William,' she said as they embraced carefully so as not to jostle the baby. Anne stuck her behind out to take away the fear of pushing her belly in his eagerness to hug her.

'Our child will be loved by all,' he said more relieved than a burst barrel. 'The foolish doubts I had of my family were blown away like old cobwebs. They are more than accepting towards you, my love, and they look forward to meeting you and their grandchild properly.'

'Oh, William, we are to be unopposed? We are free to hold our heads high,' she said, overcome with tears of relief. 'I can breathe out in the street and tell all of our intentions. They need never know that we had a baby out of wedlock, for I am not yet showing. It is a dream. Perhaps it is a dream and you lie to me.' She stood waiting for confirmation that her fears were wrong.

'No, Anne, it is not so,' he said with a reassuring embrace. 'I have not lied to you. The words that make you happy are from my naked honesty, just happy, truthful words.'

His account now accepted, the two of them sat on the low sides of the bridge to discuss further plans together.

'We can now talk of our future together,' he said. 'We are not thieves or murdering looters. We have done as countless others must have done before. I have no regret to curse this bridge with, only praise for our introduction and the strength I feel beneath my feet. We must work together now and build a future for the new baby. It is all good news, Anne. I can feel it within my bones.'

'I will work hard with you,' she replied, looking up. 'I feel great strength from our bond, as strong as the joints we sit upon.'

'We will hold our heads up high and thank the Lord for our gift of a child. And in time we might repay this reward with our own gifts of happiness and kind prayers sent back to him. I doubted His intentions many times in the past, so I hope I can be forgiven for having thought this way.' He then said quietly, 'Some may look at our marriage without thought of their own leaking roofs, for there are plenty who look towards the faults of others without seeing themselves. Those who pass judgement upon others' clothes, whilst their own coats have patch upon patch. When their lives are so perfect, then they can be the judge of ours. We will be surrounded by our family and friends. I had few friends in school, enough to count on one hand, but I have all I need now right here in front of me.'

'Where will we live, William? Will I have to leave Hewlands?' she asked tentatively.

'A decision like this is best talked over with my parents,' he answered, glancing towards the river. 'I am not yet a man with means to help run a farm such as yours and my home chores are plenty. Father increasingly relies on his eldest two for fine stitching and I fear he may still need our help.'

'I do not doubt your capacity to work either on the farm or with leather. I love you more than any building, but I have my family to think of now my father has passed on and you must do your parents' bidding. We must pull together and make this work for all our benefits. You have faced plenty of hardship and battles to date and now you can face even more with my support. Whatever decision you make, if you should become a cobbler, a preacher or a player, I am yours and support you in whatever decisions you make.'

William turned back from the river, nodding his head. With his arms wide and hands open, he answered. 'Yes, it is good that you remind me of my strengths, for when I wander in thought I weaken. Keep me dusted down after work and thirst less for love. From this I will give you real substance from my mind and I will change all dull words into laughter. All this I will share with you.'

The couple stood and linked arms as they made their way across the bridge towards the town. Anne lifted her head with pride and William lowered his to think. Oh, this great bridge has given life to the town for generations before and for my family in the future. Thank you, Sir Hugh, for the past and future, but more for myself and Anne. Our chance encounter here all those months ago brought me a crossing far greater than its span and I thank you for this, for without this bridge we would not be where we are today, both in love and trade.

'What are you thinking, William?' Anne looked up to William's wandering eyes, staring into the Avon again.

'I give thanks for the knighted gent who built this bridge,' he said, 'and for all the people who have seen the benefit from it. But more so for our introduction. This bridge has awakened me to another great crossing in my life.'

'But, William,' she said, 'say your modest words to my face, not the water below. Do not keep them in your mind. You must share them with me. Your words, likened to hands taking water from a stream, should be cupped now we are to be wedded, then offered to my lips to taste.'

Anne and William kissed, giving the town further cause to gossip, for it was a long kiss and far more than just a fond goodbye.

Supper

The weekend after William broke the news to his parents, Anne was invited back to the house to acquaint herself further with the Shakespeares. The four planned to have supper and then talk together about the imminent wedding and what they would be expected to do afterwards. William escorted Anne there that afternoon, but John and he would walk her back home to Shottery later in the evening. Anne had a knotted stomach as they walked towards the house, but William kept squeezing her tense arm with reassurance.

'Oh, I hope they do not mention the oak floorboard, William,' she said despairingly. 'I feel my stupid lust for your company will be revealed if they do.'

'No, it is finished,' he said. 'They assured me there would be no further mention of it.'

'But your father,' she added with a worried stare. 'He has a high position in the town.'

'He has, but he is also my father,' he said, drawing her close. 'Sometimes he shouts and cracks his belt, and grumbles like a creaking door, but he will treat you in the same way as he does me – besides, Mother will be there.'

She paused in her tracks to make known her dislike of his comment. 'What will you do, check his buckle is still fastened each time your mother leaves the room?'

'I am sorry,' he said, regretting his words. 'I am only trying to make light of your fears. They will like you, you will see.'

'I hope so,' she said sharply. 'At least it will be better than your untimely wit!'

William chose not to take the argument further, which could only bring about more tension, as they approached the house. Anne followed closely behind, clutching his hand as William stepped inside. They walked into the living room where John and Mary were waiting by the fireside. John stood to greet Anne and nodded when William introduced her and she and Mary shook hands as they exchanged smiles. They sat down in the middle of the settle, which could easily have seated six.

John was the first to speak. 'Your mother and I have decided that you should have the lads' room when you are married, William. You should both be comfortable with its size and view. But you will have to help me make a new wall elsewhere to give the lads somewhere else to sleep. Our apprentice has served his time now, so Gilbert will have his space. It will have to be tidied up and made better, of course, but we shall manage.'

Mary smiled pleasantly as she sat with both hands neatly on her lap. She was proud of her tidy room and newly arranged furniture. John paused, either waiting for William to speak or listening to the children who were supposed to be sleeping upstairs. William chose not to speak at this time. He wanted the direction to come from his father first.

'I understand your father has left you a sum of money?' John stated as he looked straight at Anne.

'Yes, Mr Shakespeare,' she answered with a glance at William. 'That is right. He has put aside some marks for my wedding day, some of which I will gift to your family. My love is not for money, it is for William.'

'Well thank you, Anne.' John shuffled about in his chair. 'You are most welcome here. We have young Edmund, as you know, and Joan. The lads can look after themselves, for Gilbert and Richard are older now. Anne, you must call me John and we should dispose of the formalities if we are to be living under the same roof.'

'Thank you, I will,' she said with an accepting smile.

'What duties will we have, Father?' William asked, joining the conversation. 'Have you plans for us with the chores and the like?'

'We will look at this once you are married, William,' said John, not wanting an unmarried couple to be sharing a bed in the same house. 'After this we will do our best to work together. Whatever the task or job in hand, we shall all continue as before.'

'The wedding,' said Mary as John nodded for her to continue. 'We have a date in mind but we cannot afford a costly, grand affair. It has been suggested that it should take place on a quiet Monday morning.'

'Where?' asked Anne with a slight hint of shame to her face.

William sensed this, so he gently reassured her of his tenderness with a stroke to her hand. Not too friendly, though, for they were in open view. Sometimes a young man would be seen to be carving a spoon as they sat opposite a chaperone, but they were beyond customs and traditions in their present position.

'John will escort us there,' Mary answered as her stiffness started to relax. 'A friend of his has arranged it all. It is not far from here but you must trust our judgement, my love. We have decided to go out of town to confirm your marriage, for as you both know, we cannot have one here as we would have wished. There will be many frowns and plenty of fuel for gossip, but we are unable to prevent this now.'

'What will happen after that, Father?' asked William, hinting at details for house rules.

'We will speak later, William, but let us toast the wedding. Mary and I wish you both well. And Anne,' said John, pausing briefly, 'I must say that you are, indeed, a beauty!'

William was pleased that their introduction had gone well and the evening could be hailed a great success. He had thought his parents would think Anne was too old for him and that they might take a dislike to her for "encouraging" their son into an easy conception. But none was more relived than Anne. Her fears of being accused of taking their young man of words had also now abated. Anne blushed slightly at her future father-in-law's compliments, but it was little competition for William's constant supply. Mary filled four small goblets with a home-brewed drink favoured by John, but it always caused newcomers' throats to burn a little. Having partaken of a small tipple, they ate bread and goose together. This was the warming point of the evening.

Anne spoke first after they had finished eating, but it was not a subject William or his parents would have thought possible from her.

'Do any of you here believe in witches? Some say they may be about around the villages, and even ghosts.'

'What brings you to mention such as this, Anne?' asked John with surprise.

William and Mary had also stopped eating with shock at her chosen subject.

'My thoughts were of me leaving Hewlands,' she said in all innocence. 'My father was told a witch lived there before we moved in. That was why he bought it so cheaply. I just wondered if there might have been witches in your street or other things in this part of town.'

'I wish my broom would fly about the house,' Mary said with a look in William's direction with his avoidance of it. 'It is a tool not many have mastered, though it is simple to use.'

William smiled, but once more he felt it better not to reply to any criticism, especially as they had to act quite humbly.

'I think we have enough trouble in life without inviting more tales of hearsay, Anne,' John said. 'There are many questions unanswered from the unknown and, of course, from God. I look and taste what is under my nose. I cannot decide an ale is bad on opinion alone until I have tasted it for myself.'

Everyone smiled politely as the warming of the conversation continued and the tension gradually burned away like the light from the flickering flames passing silently over their faces.

'I have heard of no rumours or recent tales,' added John, shaking his head. 'But there is always gossip about if you follow it. There are no ghosts in this house. Besides, the lads would have seen them away with hands raised after a first sighting, I am sure.'

With this they all laughed, as the witch debate had been exhausted, but William had other ideas.

'What about the tale of the falling-spoon omens, Father?'

William discreetly threw his spoon behind the settle unnoticed and the rattle brought everyone except William to a state of readiness as it clattered in the corner, but then they saw his smile which was met with great relief by all present.

'You and your pranks, William.' Mary shook her head as if he were still a young boy. 'You may end up on the receiving end of a bigger spoon one day.' When Mary finished speaking her head was pointing to the kitchen, with reference to the large wooden cream spoon they had hung up.

This light-hearted banter made way for more discussion about what would happen after the wedding and blankets and babies were next on the agenda.

'If the child is a boy,' Mary said, hopefully, 'Edmund has several clothes he's outgrown that he could have. I could easily alter them.'

'Thank you, but if we have a girl,' said Anne, looking shyly at William, 'I will just have to make fresh. I can sew and embroider.'

'William did not mention that you were good with your hands,' Mary said with raised eyebrows. 'He tells me little of what he knows.'

'Sorry, Mother. Anne has made a pile of fancy sheets from hours just thinking of my looks, but it will be a boy,' he said, trying to contain a smile. 'Think of the cost of clothes for a girl.'

'That's right, I have made some,' Anne confirmed. 'But my thoughts were for a baby and not William's untidy locks.

This brought further conflicting smiles. Mary wished only for a healthy baby, whilst William wanted a boy and Anne had dreams of a girl.

'Oh, not another boy,' said John with his hands clasped in prayer looking up. 'Please, Lord, let it be another rose as our Joan is.'

Whilst the family was equally divided in what they wanted the baby to be, the child would be loved by all unconditionally, whatever sex it was.

'Before we retire for the night,' John turned to William and Anne more seriously, 'is there anything you want to ask us? Marriage is a long road and often there will be unexpected fords to cross.'

'Well, I certainly have fears for the future,' said Anne. 'But my Mother gave me some sound advice earlier today. She said I should treat marriage like a tree that you are both about to cut down. Once down, it is done and yours to keep. The tree will last a lifetime of winters, but check each further cut in turn. Over time you will find soft areas and some solid parts, for it will not be the same right through.'

Mary smiled. 'She has wisdom with her advice.'

'Yes, but I think it is time we should walk you home now, Anne.' John looked towards the window. 'The drunkards' shadows have started to pass by. Your family may be worried for your safety.'

'Yes, well thank you both for a lovely evening,' she said sincerely, with growing warmth for her new family. 'I have enjoyed both your food and company and I look forward to living here under your roof. I was initially fearful that you might question my age and our love.'

'Our son has made mistakes before,' replied John, quickly inviting a frown or two. 'But we do not see this as a mistake. We see a man learning from his own steps. Some may say it is better that he take his own steps than follow in the easy path of others. You should not worry about age or love. This is for others to gossip of, my dear, and it is their problem, not ours.'

Anne nodded and they all stood up to wait for John to open the door and William to fetch their cloaks.

'Come again next week, Anne,' Mary said with a broad smile. 'You will meet the rest of the family next time.'

'Yes, I will, thank you,' she replied, turning to kiss Mary before allowing William to help her on with her cloak.

'And one for me, too, Anne,' John invited, pointing to a space at the side of his beard.

Anne tilted her head shyly before accepting the offer while William eagerly stood behind waiting for his turn. John saw what William was trying to do, so he righted his head and offered William his chin.

'It is still as rough as ever, you will see.'

William retreated instantly towards Anne's side.

'Oh, let us hurry along now lest he have other ideas,' said William.

John smiled at Mary and led the way to the front door onto the street. William followed last, pausing to give his mother a kiss on the cheek.

'Thank you, Mother,' he said. 'Thank you for your help and understanding.'

Mary acknowledged his kind words with a smile before closing the door behind him. Her expression was one of sadness, for her plans for her first-born to have a huge wedding in the church would now never happen. But perhaps she would get her chance again with one of the others. Her thoughts soon turned towards the future at least he would be staying at home for now. My plans were only mine, thought Mary. And their plans can now be as they wish, God bless them.

John remained silent all the way to Shottery as though he was studying something high in the treetops. William and Anne couldn't believe their luck. Here they were with John holding the lantern to light their way and they now had their parents' blessing. It was a crescent moon that night – not enough to light a path but just enough for them to be able to watch it silently stalk them through the treetops. Their peace was awakened by a yelp and dash as a fox scurried away after its mate. None spoke.

Another fox, William thought, dashing past so close again. The light of the moon shows its fleeing tail. I will mention it later; I do not want father thinking too deeply. It was just foxes and there are plenty more where they came from. Father's thoughts follow its hurried escape and yet mine go beyond. Ah! not everyone witnesses the same thing in the same light. Things are not always how they appear.'

For the last few steps towards Hewland Farm, William squeezed Anne's hand to reassure her. Then, bravely, William kissed her on the cheek in front of his father and then stood aside to watch her walk through the farmyard to the door. John was unperturbed by this gesture, for the child was growing up fast and a few stolen kisses could do no further harm. John's soon gave light to what he had been hiding on the way there, now breaking the silence between them. As they set off towards home, John asked William to hold the lantern as he slowly pulled out a leather bag of wine from inside his coat.

'We will celebrate this momentous day as we walk back, son.' John offered the first swig to William. 'This night, you know, it will never happen again. You have moved forwards in life and have become a fully grown man. Your childhood is in the past now. The same as your wedding day, it will pass and then you will wake up to another day and another and another. Then,' he lowered his voice, 'you will want to take hold of your life at that point and you will wonder if you should have gone left before right, or stopped when you should have carried on. So without regret, we must gorge on the moment's peace and drink a little wine together. You have responsibilities now, son, with a new wife to welcome into the family and a baby on the way.'

'You are right, Father,' William said, wiping his mouth. 'We should enjoy and savour the moment. It may be some time before we share another moment like this.'

As they continued their journey home, John had a few more points to put to William and he had obviously planned to impart some fatherly advice. However as they walked, two fighting badgers spun around in front of them a few feet away and this in turn made them both jump with shock.

'A fleeing fox on the way here and now badgers aptly fight before us,' said John. 'Marriage is like them in a way. It is not just about a warm touching shared beneath the sheets. There is more to life than this small act together. Marriage is a sudden change! It is all about compromise. Things fail and tempers rise. Money is short and the rain leaves us with a soggy crop.'

'We can manage a while with Anne's dowry.' William took another swig.

'Only for a time, William,' John replied, slurring his speech. 'It will eventually run out. Wealth has to be replaced. Think of it as a loan. Something that will not last forever – just a temporary windfall.'

'Father,' said William seriously. 'Can I tell you my thoughts of future work?'

'Yes, but we can only offer you work in the shop with shared coppers.'

'My thoughts are this ...' William said 'I plan to go to London. But I hasten to add that I won't be leaving Anne before our marriage.'

'You do not surprise me,' John said. 'Your head is not here in Stratford. But how and when to do you plan to leave?'

'I think I would like to see my child settled first,' William answered. 'But Anne knows where I am looking for work and that it is far away. She knows my thoughts and even encourages them. I feel she is so right for me, Father. Any other woman would want to see me chained up in this town with little chance of my dreams ever bearing fruit.'

'For different reasons, I fear,' John said. 'Madness, jealousy and fearing your loss might be reasons they would give.'

'Anne does not fear it. She merely wants to encourage me to achieve my dreams,' said William with his hand resting on his stomach. 'And it is what drives me. Indeed, the lure of the city is just as strong as my love for Anne and my family.'

'Mother has told you many times before, William,' John stopped to face him in the lantern light. 'Think before you act. Remember the pheasant?'

William nodded. He remembered the comparison with the chicken and pheasant from years past when his mother was advising him how to think before writing and speaking.

'In Stratford you can grow at ease. A planted seed will grow strong enough in the soft, familiar soil around us. London is different, with rough ground and strangers. Your roots will have to take to this, then force their way through to find the sun. It is a hard ground you want to plough, but if you master it well the field will be yours, year after year.'

William nodded again. He hadn't expected his father to have been so accepting of his plans, so he listened further to his lecture.

'Think deeply, William, but do not spend all your time thinking only of the next year. Think of your marriage and other problems in hand before moving on to London. To play and dance to suit the merry mind is not going to pay any rents or set you on your future path. Working leather is for now, so rein in your thoughts a little. The future is like waiting for good news. Don't just wait for it to come to you. Go forward and try to meet it head on! Let the future add to your former thoughts, not just be the centre of them.'

'Father, I will always take your advice in the humour it was intended,' said William. 'Although we find ourselves in this predicament because of me not taking it, I would like you to help me to get to London. Passing through villages without permission is a thought. I know there are many tolls and boundaries to cross and folk eager to pick fights with strangers passing by.'

'Yes, but as I have said, think for a time first,' he affirmed, pointing the way forward.

'I am and I will,' William said, sighing audibly. 'I was hoping Sir Thomas would help, but I have already upset him with my marriage plans.'

'He will just have to be upset and your impulsive behaviour must learn how to wait and be patient,' said John firmly, indicating that he should walk further. 'I have made money easily in the past, but you have to do the same in your own way. We have lived through many hard times, failed crops and many a flood after a long winter.'

'I understand. I think I have had enough wine.' William replaced the stopper. 'But I will think more about your advice.'

'Ha, ha, there is more to come, William, more to come,' he answered calmly. 'It doesn't stop just there. Your bed habits; try not to let the whole household know what you are up to. Keep your love-making to yourselves. And not during the day, either, when the rest of the family is about. Keep your lusting to your own time.'

'I had thought no other,' he said with a note of embarrassment in his voice. 'The novelty of marriage concerns me more. I do fear it, not the sleeping arrangements but the life and bonding together that comes with it.'

'I thought it would,' John said with his chest puffed out, trying to shake the wine's effect from his head. 'You must remember this and despite the fact that my speech is slurred, it is meant seriously. Be true to her. No matter what temptation or loose breast is put before your eyes, think of the love it alone cannot provide. Temptation as one lusts after the female form is the same. They all look the same, feel the same and taste the same, but the choice, aside from shape or good looks, should always be faith. The connection above all is to God, and lesser to yourself. This faith for the one you love gives you love no other can match. It cannot be seen, but it is there. You have to believe in love from your heart. This is the strength of your armour that none but Anne should penetrate. But if you do wander and the temptation is easy, the reprisals will dissolve you to a twisted heap. The damage done by wandering cannot be smoothed over by words; it can only be covered up by them as if they were a cloth. Damage is final and cannot be undone. Let what I say sink into your mind a little now. My advice will keep you strong. You must fight with the same armour for money, children's ills, debts, floods or fires, for they are best fought together, as one.'

'Thank you again,' William said, his head swimming with the revelations of father's speech. 'I will keep my word to Anne and your words will stay in mind when temptation passes my eyes.'

'Good, William,' he added, with a nudge to wake William from his sleepy stare before whispering more loudly, 'that is the right way to go about it. But there is no harm in looking up from your quill to browse, it's just tasting the wares that becomes a problem.'

It took a moment for William to realise his father's change of heart from a serious lecture to playful banter, but he soon followed his wit and laughed quietly to himself. Their laughter had to be kept quiet because they had just reached the house door, but what a note to end the evening with, and what a night William would have with his thoughts for company.

Settling Down

The December after William and Anne were married, winter bit hard upon Stratford. They had just moved into the lads' old room on Henley Street at the time and William had left Anne to go fishing with Richard and Gilbert on the riverbank. Anne had settled into the house and she had found her own niche, helping in both the shop and with the chores. It was a bitterly cold day and thoughts of a fish supper kept it beyond the boys' cloaks as they amused themselves trying to fasten the hooks to the twine in the cold while laughing loudly. They had all been fishing before, but not in such a cold month and never to try to fill so many mouths.

'Will we catch anything today, William?' asked Richard, dropping a little mud into the water as he slipped on the bank.

'Not if you splash,' William replied awkwardly with a hook in his mouth. 'Fish need quiet. Wave your arms if you are cold.'

'No, I am warm enough,' he replied. 'It will be the fish who are cold.'

'Not when they are on the fire,' said Gilbert, gently lowering his hook into the water.

'What I mean is that there are so many others fishing.' Richard pointed. 'Will they not take all the fish for themselves?'

'Here, hold this.' William handed him his twine. 'It is by chance we catch the fish and we all have the same chance of catching one.'

'But there are so many others.' Richard frowned, looking at the others who were fishing along the bank.

'It is like this,' said William, tutting slightly to himself. 'If a spider spins a web, it cannot demand a fly, but if spiders spin webs, flies will get caught in some of them by chance.'

'Oh! I see now,' said Gilbert brightly. 'So some here will catch fish but not all?'

'Yes, it is all a matter of luck,' he answered. 'And we all have a fair chance, but first we must dangle the bait.'

'But, William,' Richard asked with a deeper frown, 'if the others catch fish, will there be less chance of us catching one?'

'He has you now,' Gilbert said, smiling.

'No, not quite,' said William. 'The river flows down to the sea and with it the fish, but the fish also swim up it. It is not like a barrel of toads, you know.'

Richard let the debate settle in his mind for a moment and then he looked up to William again with further questions in mind. 'William?' Richard asked, smirking to himself.

'Yes, my brother with empty look and hook,' William answered.

'If all toads are both a mixture of male and female, why do they call each other Edip?'

William and Gilbert exchanged frowns. Then they both laughed out loud, finally seeing what he was getting at, but in doing so they disturbed other people who were fishing alongside them.

'Edip, edip, edip,' said Richard again and again.

Obviously the cheeky wit was shared amongst all the family members. The brothers caught four large eels and a perch that morning. The latter's sharp spines had to be wrapped in cloth before they dared touch it. The splashes from the fishing had frozen on the floor and their hands were now frozen in pockets, signifying that it was time to call it a day. After gathering up all their twines and wrapping up the catch, the boys left the freezing riverside to walk home. However, as they walked through the streets Richard began to study the women walking past. He didn't volunteer what he was thinking about, so eventually William asked him what he was looking at.

'What are you studying, Richard?' he asked. 'They are much too old for you.'

'I dare not say,' he answered shyly. 'Father would shout and Mother more so.'

'If you do not say, you will never know the answer,' William said in a higher tone. 'Better to say now than let Father or Mother see you looking and question your motives.'

Richard paused for a moment, but then plucked up courage to ask. He looked around him tentatively to see if Gilbert was within hearing distance.

'Oh, it is simply this,' Richard sighed, a little embarrassed. 'I have seen a painting of the queen, women on the street, Mother and our Joan at home. They all wear different dresses and high hair. Some have fair and tender faces to look at on the outside, but what are they beneath the facade? There must be something else, as well as the obvious things we notice when we undress.'

William didn't laugh at Richard. He knew his question wasn't meant in a distasteful manner. He was referring to expressions from their gender. Gilbert was out of hearing range, gawking at a farmer striking a limping ox to walk faster, otherwise he would have laughed for sure.

'Think of them as simply this, Richard,' he said seriously. 'Women are covered in bright feathers, with fancy hair and eyes so narrow, yet underneath they are but a sparrow. Try not to look at their outside appearance, with their freshly combed hair, fancy clothes or flickering eyes. Try to look beneath at the real person behind them all. They are all the same despite what covers them. Women must look at lads in the same way and yet see different things. I will ask Anne some day how she assesses the motives of men and see what her thoughts are on the matter.'

'Her thoughts, what about them?' asked Gilbert, running to catch up.

'All minds think differently,' answered William, looking down at a frozen puddle. 'You look towards the farmer and yet I look where I am walking. Different things catch our eyes.'

Gilbert slipped on the ice a little but soon righted himself on William's arm as they continued on their way home.

Supper that day was late but it had been worth waiting for. Both tables had been placed together to seat the whole family around. Fish made a change from the usual meat, so the mealtime chatter encompassed the tales from great fishermen.

'So you missed a sea serpent then, William?' asked John, looking down at the fish.

'Yes, Father,' he answered. 'Sadly, we could only carry the tail, but the beast had great strength.'

'Yes,' Gilbert added, 'it took thirty or more arrows before we managed to blind it. It even scraped the underside of the bridge.'

'And, Joan,' Richard joined in, widening his arms to exaggerate, 'its teeth were as big as a chair and its mouth was big enough to swallow this house whole.'

'Sea serpents cannot be so big.' She looked up with surprise.

'Oh, enough of this wild talk,' said John. 'I started the tale, so I will end it. The fish is good, lads. You have our thanks.'

'Will you catch fish more often, William?' asked Joan.

'It is hard to say,' he answered. 'But if I were to look into a sorcerer's beryl, I could tell you then.'

'Who is Beryl, William?' she asked.

All the family turned to William to hear more of the mystery beryl.

'It is a crystal globe belonging to John Dee, the queen's astrologer,' he answered seriously. 'I have heard he can see the future, assisted by the inflection.'

'Who has told you that or did you have the thought after a wish down a well?' Mary asked, doubting his answer. 'We have had plenty of fishermen's tales about size.'

'A friend from London,' he answered, with his nose up slightly.

'Let us talk of the moment now,' said John, to curb the thoughts away from the globe. 'Have you attended to your new feather stuffing and lace in your room, Anne?'

'Yes, I have, thank you,' she said. 'It is warm and much larger than I had first thought.'

'Have you put the crib in the corner?' asked Mary.

'It is full of blankets at the moment,' replied Anne. 'But I think we will put it there.'

'A little early yet,' John said. 'But preparation is good. Empty hands are not weapons for an army. Think ahead, I say.'

'Talking of weapons,' Anne said, 'I have an old shield of my father's. Could you sell it in the shop?'

'Do you not want it for a keepsake?' John asked. 'Richard must have kept it for a reason.'

'No,' she replied, shaking her head. 'The shield is an ornament, not a jewel to be hung around my neck. I have other keepsakes and the tangible ones are the most valuable to me.'

'Yes, that will be fine, then. But let us drink to fish for now and sort that out another time,' John said with his tankard raised.

The family ate the fish and with chunks of bread, they mopped up all the juice, leaving only bones on the side of their plates. It was still a growing family and soon they would have to squeeze another mouth around the table when it arrived the following year.

William got up one early morning to sit and look through the bedroom window, his favourite vantage point. The view from the window was still tempting as it always had been and his thoughts wandered outside to follow the season's wintry shapes. He didn't wander far. He just let the cool air bite his face while he gazed at the stillness of the street.

Anne soon felt the cold from William's absence and awoke with a shiver to look for him.

'William, has fear of having to look after a child given you thoughts of jumping?' she asked, rubbing her sleepy eyes.

'No, my love. I am simply enjoying the season's views.' He stretched out his arms. 'The snow is like mud in that it shows where people, birds and animals have been, but never where they are going. The path they choose and whoever follows them have the choice to either tread the same path or make fresh marks and follow their own mind's needs.'

'Come back to warm me,' she asked, with her arms out. 'Then whisper what you said again, pillow to pillow.'

William returned to bed with a smile. They were newly married and he was enjoying the moment. The pillow talk continued for a short time, but mostly of Anne's fears of settling in and being accepted by her new family.

'This is our first place together, William. We are fortunate enough to be able to share a room together. Then one day, I hope, we will share our first house, then −'

He interrupted her with a kiss, silencing her. 'Perhaps we can make this our first kiss ...'

'We have had the first,' she said, teasingly retreating under the sheets.

'Yes, but there will be a first every day and every morning for as long as we both shall live,' he said as she stopped his advance again, turning to look up and think.

'What do you think of the presents your mother gave us above the fire?' she asked, pointing to a yellow and brown potted jar.

'I have seen it before. I liked it then and I do now,' he answered, nodding his head whilst trying to claim a further kiss. 'It is still yellow and brown and it will be the same tomorrow.'

'Well, yesterday it was nearly broken,' she said, her lips firmly sealed.

'Why was that?' he asked, frowning at the rejection. She seemed to favour the jar to his lips.

'I knocked it and it fell on the hearth. Fortunately, it landed on a pile of washing!' she said with surprise.

'But it was not damaged!' he exclaimed falsely. 'So it seems to me that not all that falls will break. Some things will land softly like a cat, but whatever it is, its fate is never sealed. It is the same with people. You and I really, when we fall we shouldn't be dismissive of our tumble, for we may even learn from it.'

'You have an answer for all problems,' she sighed lovingly.

'Not all, my love.' He shook his head sadly.

'What answers do you not have, my love?' she asked with a slight frown.

'Tempting a further kiss from you – it has me beat if nothing else!'

Anne pulled a sheet around her head, showing only her face, temping William to uncover her. But as he leaned towards her, he turned his head to pause and stare at her changed appearance. He then pulled back and leaned away from her.

'What is it, my love?' she asked. 'What great thought takes you away from my invitation? Have you noticed a new spot?'

'A play, my love, yes, you have just given me an idea for a play,' he said, staring up and down at the blanket. Even a playful tug from Anne would not shake him from his transfixed state. 'The idea for a play has come from the most surprising place. It is your face, my love, but nothing to do with a spot.'

William sat upright in bed, staring more intently, then he twisted his head from side to side. He smiled to himself, raising his eyebrows as if he could see the play unfolding before him. Anne knew it was something she should be patient about, so she draped a sheet around his shoulders to keep him warm and then she waited until he snapped out of his faraway look, the plot complete!

'Tell me, William, tell me now, let me be the first,' she said, gripping his arm and rubbing her swollen stomach. 'This is as exciting as what lies in here.'

'Oh, apples, my love, only apples,' William sighed. 'A Barrel of Apple's may be the title, or I might have it represent one of our own past monarchs, or even something from history. Greece and Rome, perhaps. I have often thought of apples in the past, using them to compare my thoughts and actions. I will tell you part of it now, but the idea came from your face, your changing face with white sheets for hair. To begin with there was a king who lived many years ago. He had wealth, land and a family. However, he became bored and sad and no matter how his family tried, they could not make him happy. One day a suggestion was made by his daughter Eravive that a competition should be held. Anyone who could make the king laugh would be given a great prize for helping to take the great cloud from the king's mind. Eravive had befriended one of the young kitchen assistants and she had told him about the competition so he could watch for himself. The stage was set for the many jesters and merry folk; however, the plan went badly wrong when one of them took a liking to Eravive after making the king laugh. This lead to a marriage, several identity changes, lies, deceit, laughter and eventual humiliation when the plot became exposed. The entire king's family were involved. I have no paper to write with now, but I will remember it, and one day I will write it down or one with a similar plot, but I think it will be a comedy.

'And it came from the sheets pulled tightly around your face. The idea came from you, and ... and I could see the whole plot before me as if I were reading the Bible. What luck it is how we met. How could it have been foretold that the seed of this play would spring from your face. Your hiding behind a sheet, my love, made you look like a stranger. So simple are ideas such as this – so simple but oh! so strong.

William traced his finger around the outline of her face, then tenderly moved the sheet to expose her cheek and caressed it with a swirl before taking her in his arms.

'Oh, William,' she sighed lovingly. 'What will become of you? I wonder.'